Yellowstone Survival

The Yellowstone Series

Book Four

by

Bobby Akart

Other Works by Amazon Top 100 Author Bobby Akart

The Yellowstone Series
Hellfire
Inferno
Fallout
Survival

The Lone Star Series
Axis of Evil
Beyond Borders
Lines in the Sand
Texas Strong
Fifth Column
Suicide Six

The Pandemic Series
Beginnings
The Innocents
Level 6
Quietus

DEDICATIONS

To my darling Dani, and the girls.

There is nothing more precious to me than the time I get to spend with you. I love our life together.

To a courageous young lass in the United Kingdom named Ella.

Your life is just beginning, with a disadvantage, to be sure. I hope one day, you can read the story of the fictional Ella in this novel and realize no matter how difficult life may seem at times, you can overcome it because you are blessed with the power to persevere. Our love is with you as you tackle life and we have no doubt you'll accomplish great things!

DEDICATIONS

To Dusty Holder, In Memoriam.

You took a young, pudgy boy under your wing and turned him into a golfer who came within one bad shot of qualifying for the U.S. Open at age sixteen. More importantly, you taught me that life is full of mishits, and only a true failure *wallers in his anger or sorrow.* I heard many times – *get your head on straight and keep playing.* I've lived my life accordingly. I've been up and down more times than I can count. But I always keep playing. Thank you, old friend.

To Wild Bill Cherry, In Memoriam.

Professor Bill Cherry taught Geography and Geology at the University of Tennessee, Knoxville when I was an undergraduate there. Known for his unusual approach in lecturing, he earned the nickname Wild Bill. Readers of the Blackout series might recall a character by that name. Anyway, Wild Bill Cherry taught me to love science, and rocks. He also taught me that the landscape around us didn't happen through the assistance of unicorns and rainbows. Most of our planet's appearance came about as a result of violent conflicts underground, which changed the surface above. Wild Bill, I'll never forget sharing a Budweiser with you at The Last Lap on The Strip. This one's for you, Professor.

ACKNOWLEDGEMENTS

Writing a book that is both informative and entertaining requires a tremendous team effort. Writing is the easy part. For their efforts in making *Yellowstone: Fallout*, book three in the Yellowstone series, a reality, I would like to thank Hristo Argirov Kovatliev for his incredible cover art, Pauline Nolet for her editorial prowess, Stef Mcdaid for making this manuscript decipherable in so many formats, Chris Abernathy for his memorable performance in narrating this novel, and the Team—Denise, Joe, Jim, Shirley, and Kelly—whose advice, friendship and attention to detail is priceless.

For the Yellowstone series, I had to make use of a wealth of source material and studied the research of every form of scientist imaginable in my attempt to get it right. There are so many to thank, so let me get started, in no particular order.

University of Utah, Professor Emeritus Bob Smith, the world's leading expert on the geophysics of Yellowstone National Park. Professor Smith's research at Yellowstone began in 1956. He has conducted pioneering geophysics investigations of the Yellowstone hotspot that have become a model for evaluations of volcanic hazards worldwide. My single biggest takeaway from Professor Smith is this: When the earthquakes stop, that is the time to start worrying. Earthquakes relieve pressure. Without them, the planet would burst. If you'd like to learn more about his perspective on Earth's creative forces, purchase his book, *Windows into the Earth*, on Amazon.

Dr. Brian H. Wilcox, an aerospace engineer at the Jet Propulsion Laboratory in Pasadena, California, co-authored a research paper titled *Defending Human Civilization Supervolcanic Eruptions*. Wilcox boldly raised the proposition that the greatest threat to humankind may not come from above, in the form of a near-Earth object, but rather, from below, as an eruption from the Yellowstone supervolcano. Dr. Wilcox made headlines in 2017 when he posited the idea of pumping water into Yellowstone to cool the magma chamber with the ancillary benefit of extracting steam to drive electricity-generating turbines. To his credit, he warned that such an expensive, risky proposition would have to be undertaken with care and done correctly.

Dr. Michael R. Rampino, Professor of Biology at NYU, conducts research in the area of earth sciences and in the causes of mass extinctions in particular. He has focused ongoing research on large supervolcanic explosive events that result in catastrophic climate change. The episodes of volcanic winters in our history may have caused the near extinction of humans. Dr. Rampino believes a reoccurrence would most likely threaten our civilization and existence. For more on Dr. Rampino's work, purchase *Cataclysms, A New Geology for the Twenty-First Century*, available on Amazon.

Finally, to my new friends at GeoScienceWorld in McLean, Virginia, who helped guide me during my initial research into the subjects of earthquakes, volcanoes, and anything else going on under our feet. You folks are way smarter than I am!

Thank you all!

ABOUT THE AUTHOR

Bobby Akart

Author Bobby Akart has been ranked by Amazon as #71 in its Top 100 list of most popular, bestselling authors. He achieved #3 bestselling Horror Author, the #3 bestselling Religion & Spirituality Author, the #5 bestselling Science Fiction Author, the #7 bestselling Historical Author and the #10 bestselling Action & Adventure Author.

He has written over twenty international bestsellers, in forty-plus fiction and nonfiction genres, including the reader-favorite Lone Star series, the critically acclaimed Boston Brahmin series, the bestselling Blackout series, the frighteningly realistic Pandemic Series, his highly cited nonfiction Prepping for Tomorrow series and his latest project—the Yellowstone series, hailed by scientists as frighteningly realistic.

His novel, Yellowstone: Inferno reached #64 on the Amazon bestsellers list and earned him two Kindle All-Star awards for most pages read in a month, and most pages read as an author.

Bobby has provided his readers a diverse range of topics that are both informative and entertaining. His attention to detail and impeccable research have allowed him to capture the imaginations of his readers through his fictional works and bring them valuable knowledge through his nonfiction books.

SIGN UP for Bobby Akart's mailing list to receive special offers, bonus content, and you'll be the first to receive news about new releases in the Doomsday series.

VISIT Amazon.com/BobbyAkart for more information on the Doomsday series, the Yellowstone series, the Lone Star series, the Pandemic series, the Blackout series, the Boston Brahmin series and the Prepping for Tomorrow series totaling more than novels including over twenty Amazon #1 Bestsellers in forty-plus fiction and nonfiction genres. Visit Bobby Akart's website for informative blog entries on preparedness, writing, and a behind-the-scenes look into his novels.

BobbyAkart.com

Author's Introduction to the Yellowstone Series

June 15, 2018
Anniversary of the Mount Pinatubo eruption

Let me get right to the point. While most people look at volcanic eruptions as natural disasters, the fact of the matter is, without them, the Earth would explode.

When I began outlining the Yellowstone series earlier this year, I came across numerous articles about telltale signs of Yellowstone's imminent eruption. Many of them came from online news websites in the United Kingdom. Sometimes, alternative news sites in the United States would republish their content.

As I furthered my research, I noticed that news reports of this nature dated back for many, many years. In other words, Chicken Little was at it again—*The sky is falling! The sky is falling!*

Too often, we become desensitized to the threats we face because the media, desperate to draw attention to their publications, in whatever format, overstate the signs of collapse.

Rather than focus on the news, I delved into the science. I've come to accept that volcanic activity is absolutely necessary for our planet's survival but is also one of the biggest threats to mankind's survival.

Volcanoes are the Earth's way of letting off steam. Deep beneath the surface of the planet, excess heat builds up, and it finds a way to vent. Over many thousands of years, intense energy is created by the heat from the Earth's core. Natural radioactivity in the granite beneath the surface couples with leftover energy from the time our planet was created some four and a half billion years ago, to generate an unimaginable pressure.

Imagine an extremely overcrowded city bus in the dead heat of summer, stalled in traffic, with no air-conditioning. The anger built up by the passengers reaches a boiling point until they force their way into the street, spilling out of the bus. Like an overcrowded bus, the overheated magma under our Earth's surface stews in its own madness, allowing pent-up frustrations to boil over, until it releases its fury—its *hellfire*—upon the world above.

The energy released by volcanoes varies in degree depending upon the type. To put it in perspective, consider this. Throughout 2017, the International Energy Agency estimated that the entire world used eighteen terawatts of energy. By comparison, the amount of built-up energy seeking to escape the Earth's interior is almost fifty terawatts—nearly triple.

This graphic provides a basic look at what lies beneath us.

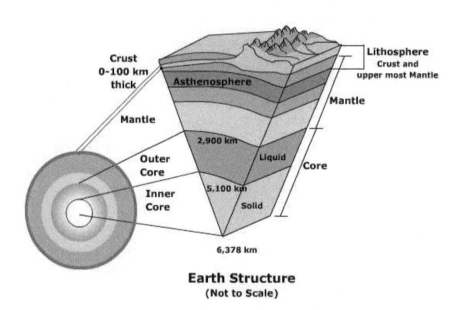

Earth Structure
(Not to Scale)

However, those who live near active volcanoes have something lurking below that most of us do not—magma. People who lived in Leilani Estates, Hawaii, and near Volcán de Fuego in Guatemala spent their days playing golf or walking to their villages. But beneath their feet, slowly, relentlessly, subterranean rivers of magma, the molten rock that constantly forces itself toward the surface, bullied their way through the mantle and crust. When it broke the surface, the eruptions in these two regions of the world faced devastating consequences.

Here's a graphic of the Kilauea volcanic activity.

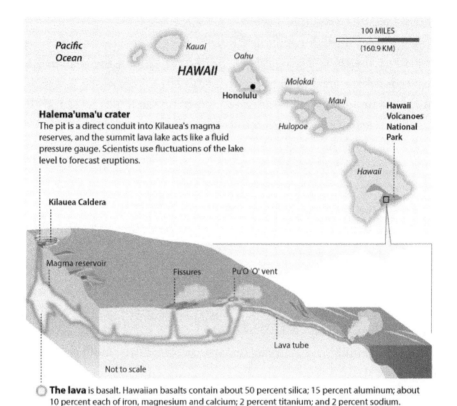

Pacific Ocean

100 MILES
(160.9 KM)

Kauai

Oahu

HAWAII

Honolulu

Molokai

Maui

Hulopoe

Hawaii Volcanoes National Park

Hawaii

Halema'uma'u crater
The pit is a direct conduit into Kilauea's magma reserves, and the summit lava lake acts like a fluid pressure gauge. Scientists use fluctuations of the lake level to forecast eruptions.

Kilauea Caldera

Magma reservoir

Fissures

Pu'O 'O' vent

Lava tube

Not to scale

The lava is basalt. Hawaiian basalts contain about 50 percent silica; 15 percent aluminum; about 10 percent each of iron, magnesium and calcium; 2 percent titanium; and 2 percent sodium.

While Volcán de Fuego, a conical stratovolcano, blasted an ash cloud that crushed surrounding villages, Kilauea was a perfect example of a slow eruption, featuring multiple fissures and vents oozing magma down its gentle slopes. To the casual observer, Kilauea appeared nonthreatening in terms of explosivity. Pictures began to surface of the aforementioned golfer, folks roasting marshmallows over the magma, and others taking selfies near the glowing flame.

With the attention given Kilauea, it's hard for many to fathom some of the more devastating volcanic eruptions such as Mount St. Helens in 1980 and Mount Pinatubo in 1991. Mount St. Helens registered as a VEI 5 on the Volcanic Explosivity Index. Mount Pinatubo was a VEI 6.

Using Mount Pinatubo as an example, which is located in the Philippines, the eruption ejected ten trillion tons of magma into the stratosphere. Another twenty million tons of sulfur dioxide combined with toxic metals and minerals to fill the air around the planet. For many months, a layer of sulfuric acid haze circled the globe. During a three-year period, global temperatures dropped half a degree, and the Earth's ozone layer was depleted temporarily.

Which brings us to our chart setting forth the relative levels of volcanic eruptions. Many factors go into determining the VEI, including the volume emitted during the eruption and the cloud height. Currently, the Kilauea eruption is scaled in the VEI 1 to VEI 2 range. The Volcán de Fuego eruption in Guatemala will approach a VEI 3.

The largest volcanic eruptions in history, known as *mega-colossal*, have reached a category of VEI 8. The smallest of the Yellowstone Caldera eruptions occurred six hundred thousand years ago and has been estimated to be a VEI 8. Scientific evidence shows an eruption of this magnitude to occur on our planet every fifty thousand years. The last VEI 8 supervolcanic eruption on a level similar to Yellowstone was on Sumatra in Indonesia.

The Toba super eruption, which occurred seventy-five thousand years ago, has long been considered one of the Earth's largest known eruptions. The Toba catastrophe resulted in a volcanic winter of six to ten years and a period of nearly a thousand years of global cooling.

Genetic research was conducted showing the number of modern humans dropped significantly about the same time the eruption occurred. Toba Catastrophe Theory posited that people today evolved from the few thousand survivors who managed to avoid the worldwide impact of the eruption.

The giant plume of ash stretched from Southeast Asia all the way to the Middle East. Since then, other researchers have found evidence that pockets of humanity continued their lives during this period. As a result, they cast doubt on the Toba Catastrophe Theory. The fact remains, however, that in the time period following the eruption of Toba, mankind almost became extinct, and no other plausible theory has been accepted by the scientific community as a whole.

The following graph depicts the various levels of volcanic eruptions. As you scroll down the graphic, note which volcanic system is associated with the highest level that doesn't appear on the chart—VEI 8.

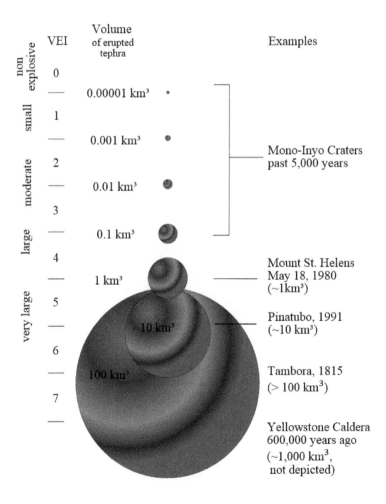

Yellowstone's three prior eruptions have been equal to, or greater than, Toba. Which takes us back to our VEI scale. A Yellowstone eruption will be at least a thousand times more powerful than Mount St. Helens and ten thousand times more powerful than Volcán de Fuego or Kilauea.

When seeing the death and destruction left behind by these smaller, more humbling eruptions, it's easy to see why the Yellowstone Caldera garners so much attention from scientists. It is easily the most monitored volcanic system in the world.

Yellowstone is quite simply the most potentially explosive, violent, deadly, active volcano on Earth, and scientists agree—a catastrophic eruption is inevitable.

Yellowstone erupted two-point-one million years ago and then again one-point-three million years ago. The last time it erupted was six hundred thirty thousand years ago. Scientists agree that Yellowstone, and our planet, is overdue for a massive, violent eruption. It will be an environmental disaster of global proportions. It might be, in fact, an extinction-level event. If so, it won't be the first time.

I can't resist repeating this often-overused phrase—*it's not a matter of if, but when.*

Yellowstone is not an ordinary volcano. It is an extraordinary killer that will show itself in due time. Will Yellowstone erupt during our lifetimes? Maybe, or maybe not.

But if it does …

EPIGRAPH

I am prepared for the worst, but hope for the best.
~ Benjamin Disraeli

*****

That which does not kill us, makes us stronger.
~ Friedrich Neitzke

*****

It is not the strongest of the species that survive, nor the most intelligent, but the one most responsive to change.
~ Charles Darwin

*****

Failure may be required in order to survive in life, because in order to rise up, you gotta know what rock bottom looks like.
~ Author Bobby Akart

*****

Survival is a state of mind that is innate in all of us, you just have to be willing to use it.
~ Author Bobby Akart

PART ONE

Sailing Away

CHAPTER 1

The Pacific Ocean
Off the coast of Big Sur, California

The ocean was a strange place after the sun dropped below the horizon and stars revealed themselves in the sky. As day gave way to night, the moonlight triggered phenomena in the water that can only be witnessed after dark. Bioluminescence caused the sea to shimmer in waves of electric bluish-white light.

Strange animals rose from the depths of the Pacific Ocean under the cover of darkness. Rarely seen creatures migrated to the surface to feed. By day, they lurk along the deep shelf that runs off the west coast of America, and each night, they are one of many animals that seek the surface to find their prey.

These creatures were not afraid of the dark, nor were most people. They were afraid of what's in it. It's the unknown we fear when we gaze into the darkness, nothing more.

The sixty-foot Grand Banks motor yacht easily broke the negligible waves on the calm seas of the Pacific that evening as it followed a generally south-southeast heading parallel to the coast of California. After the golden glow dissipated on the cliffs of Big Sur, the yacht's passengers turned their attention to what lay ahead for them.

Ashby Donovan planted a kiss on Jake Wheeler's cheek and stood to stretch. This spontaneous show of affection caused her to chuckle, piquing Jake's curiosity.

"What?" he questioned.

Her response was simple, yet profound. "Man plans, and God laughs."

"It's hard to argue with that," Jake replied with a smile that could barely be seen in the low light that emanated from the yacht's instrument panel.

Ashby explained, "My father used to say that phrase. Think about it. Our best-laid plans for our lives, sometimes meticulously charted and analyzed, can be upended in the blink of an eye by unexpected events."

Jake laughed. "You mean like the eruption of a supervolcano? Something small and insignificant like that?"

"Yeah, very funny," said Ashby as she administered a gentle poke to Jake's ribs with her elbow. "My father never used the adage in relation to something of that magnitude. He would talk about unforeseen roadblocks like an accident or a change in jobs. It doesn't necessarily mean that the plans are upended for the worse. Sometimes, it might be for the better and you don't realize it until much later."

Jake nodded and reached out for Ashby to join him on the bench seat next to the ship's wheel. "Fate can bring people together despite the violent upheavals in the world around us. Look at us."

Ashby snuggled closer to Jake as the night air grew cooler. Neither one of them were dressed for navigating the Pacific Ocean as temperatures dropped into the low fifties.

"This is what I mean. Weeks ago, when I was in that tense confrontation with Younger, I was oblivious to my surroundings. I was focused on directing my anger at him for being unreasonable and, moreover, insulting me in front of all those people. Looking back, it was all so petty and miniscule in the scheme of things."

Jake nodded and pulled her a little closer to him. He was also feeling the chill and wanted to resume their trip inside the cabin but wasn't sure whether he could let go of the ship's wheel and continue to control her from below.

"Luckily for you, I was standing between that toppling bookcase and your head."

"See, that's what I mean. I had big plans for my trip to Yellowstone. It all fell apart because of what I said in Los Angeles and the argument with Younger. God laughed at me, but in exchange, he gave me you."

"Fate."

"Yes, or destiny. Even in a moment of darkness, as my plans were tossed aside, new ones were laid out for me. And here we are."

Jake chuckled. "Did you ever imagine yourself sailing the Pacific Ocean with a handsome captain at the helm of a magnificent ship?"

Ashby pulled away and stood. "Every girl's dream, of course. One of these days I'll get to fulfill it. Meanwhile, I'm stuck with you."

"Hey!" Jake playfully protested, although he expected the feisty Ashby would have a quick comeback to his statement. They enjoyed teasing each other and playing off one another's remarks. In the face of great adversity, their friendship had grown to a deep love and respect for one another. One that would soon be tested.

*****

Mike Dorsey was a building contractor with a reputation for running his crews with an iron fist. Before the collapse, he had been on his building sites six days a week, cracking the whip over his guys, so to speak, to make sure his projects were brought in on time and under budget.

It was Mike's tenacity as a builder that had caught the eye of Kendall Kennedy years ago when he began to interview contractors to remodel the Kennedy home at Fruitvale West. The two men had quickly become friends, drinking buddies, and fellow womanizers.

Mike was in a loveless marriage, while Ken was simply a serial philanderer. The men frequently met up after a long workday. They typically found their way to local strip clubs, where they took pride in throwing their money around to the mostly naked women while downing the cocktails that provided liquid courage.

Ken had never disclosed to Mike the exact location where his girlfriend resided just outside the Fruitvale West gated entry. The night of his disappearance, Mike was simply told to handle things for the night while Ken let off some steam.

On day two after Ken's disappearance, the search moved outside the walls into the surrounding neighborhoods. Mike personally handled the door-to-door interviews. When a scantily clad woman opened her door to him that afternoon, he immediately knew he'd found Ken's mistress.

She recognized Mike as well, which was the reason she allowed him inside her home, the one bought and paid for by her lover. She was a dancer at the nearby club that had been most frequented by Mike and Ken during their happy-hour outings.

She quickly recalled the events of that evening when Ken went missing, prompting Mike to focus his search on the sidewalk and the surrounding homes. He found traces of blood in the grass, and then, like one of his best hunting dogs, he followed the trail of blood to the crawl space of a nearby house.

Using his best instincts, he began to analyze who'd fit the bill of an *old friend*, as Ken had put it to his mistress that night. Then he considered who might have the motive to kill Ken and dispose of his body. All fingers pointed to one suspect in Mike's eyes—the new guy, Jake Wheeler.

Mike raced to Ken's home and found Stephanie Kennedy in a near drunken stupor. After questioning her, Mike determined that Ashby was knee-deep in the conspiracy. He abruptly left and sped over to the Wheeler property, looking for Jake. In Stephanie's incoherent statement, she forgot to mention that Ken's Escalade had been taken by Ashby.

Mike quickly figured that out, and the chase was on. As he closed on Jake and Ashby on the road outside Fruitvale West, he considered the fact that he was alone. *No matter*, he'd said to himself as he stopped before returning to the neighborhood. He'd gather up a posse of his best men, grab their highest-powered weapons, and track down Wheeler and his girl.

He knew where they were going. The marina and the Kennedy motor yacht. An hour later, they were almost upon the *My Wet Dream* when Ashby opened fire on them. Obviously, Mike surmised, the two of them had firepower that he was unaware of.

He and his men watched Jake nearly stall the yacht as he made a hasty escape. Clearly, Jake wasn't well-versed in operating the vessel, and Mike immediately came up with a better plan.

He kept his boat parked at the marina at Monterey Bay as well. It wasn't a multimillion-dollar motor yacht like Ken's, but it was perfectly suited for another of his favorite pastimes, offshore fishing.

The thirty-foot, center-console Cobia cut through the water effortlessly as the six-hundred-horsepower twin engines pursued the much slower Grand Banks motor yacht.

Mike wasn't interested in overtaking the yacht in a hail of gunfire like pirates attacking a ship on the open seas. No, his mind had developed a more sinister plan—one that would get the yacht returned to the marina and exact revenge for Ken's death in a way he'd cheer on with enthusiasm from his grave.

CHAPTER 2

The Pacific Ocean
Off the coast of Morro Bay, California

Jake was relieved to find the instruments and controls within the salon of the Grand Banks to be nearly identical to those on the open sky bridge. With the passing of each nautical mile, he became more comfortable with the prospect of navigating the Pacific Ocean for a couple of thousand miles until they could reach a safer destination in South America.

"Help me find the other manuals for this thing," said Jake as he continued to watch the compass and glance toward the shoreline to follow the lights. The simple laminated start-up instructions provided him nothing on the complex electronics the yacht offered.

He had no idea how to use the yacht's global positioning instruments or its electronic charts. Using common sense and his recollection of the California coastline, he continued to travel south-southeast, keeping the lights of coastal homes in his sight.

"Come on, Jake," protested Ashby with a hint of a whine. "Can't we learn about how to drive it tomorrow? Let's get to know our new home and christen it properly, if you know what I mean." Ashby continued rummaging through the cabinets, looking for the manuals, alcohol, food, and anything of interest.

Jake hesitated before responding. He was pleased he'd managed to get away from Mike and his guys without destroying the yacht in the process. They could continue following the course along the coast, but he'd much prefer to travel during the daytime when he could see where he was going.

"Ashby, I know just enough about this thing to be dangerous.

There are electronics, radar, mapping …" Jake's voice trailed off before continuing. He looked in wonder at the complex system of instruments and gauges that made up the yacht's navigational panel.

Ashby stopped her quest for an adult beverage and approached Jake to hug him around the waist. "Listen, we're not necessarily in a hurry to get anywhere, are we? Frankly, the farther south we travel, the less likely we'll be exposed to the worst of the ash fallout that's hitting the Pacific Northwest and Canada. Once we reach the coffee belt and enter the lower latitudes, our air quality will begin to increase considerably."

"The coffee belt?" asked Jake.

Ashby chuckled, as she'd used a term that harkened back to her college days when she stayed up long nights to study. "Oh, sorry. I had a brief flashback. Coffee plants prefer rich soil, mild temps, with lots of rain and shaded sun."

"Like marijuana," added Jake with a smile.

"What do you know about growing weed?" asked Ashby.

"You had a brief flashback, so did I," he said with a laugh. "Tell me about the coffee belt."

Ashby's eyes squinted as she studied Jake before continuing. "The conditions for growing coffee are ideal in a band around the middle of the planet between the Tropics of Capricorn and Cancer. Some people call it the coffee belt, while others refer to it as the bean belt."

"Where is the Tropic of Cancer? Without this map thing turned on …" Jake was growing frustrated.

"No worries, Captain. Once we pass Cabo San Lucas at the tip of Baja California, we're going to cross over the Tropic of Cancer. It'll be smooth sailing from there."

Jake thought for a moment and studied the instrument panel. "I'm sure this thing has some kind of autopilot, but I have no idea how to turn it on."

"Maybe we shouldn't do that just yet," said Ashby with a chuckle. "My vote is that we shut her down. You know, just kind of park out here for the night. Let's see what tomorrow has to offer; then we'll figure out how all of this works."

Jake reluctantly nodded and then set about the process of turning the engines off. He'd left the instructions on the sky bridge, so he worked from memory. The thought of dropping anchor crossed his mind, but he assumed he was in deep water, most likely beyond the reach of the ocean floor. Besides, he didn't know what buttons to push to drop, much less retrieve, the anchor.

So *My Wet Dream* was set adrift, with the only sounds emanating from her being the music from the MP3 player discovered by Ashby and, of course, the laughter after the two found the liquor locker.

*****

Mike slowed the Cobia and reached for the Riptide Marine Binoculars he'd picked up at Cabela's years ago. Although they weren't night vision, the 7x magnification and large fifty-millimeter lenses provided him ample light transmission to brighten images at night. The Riptide model was ideal for marine use, as they were nitrogen filled to prevent fog and condensation.

An experienced boater, Mike immediately noticed when the yacht slowed and eventually stopped. He pulled back on the throttle and quickly cut the engines to avoid being detected by Jake.

He'd already taken a risk by tracking them at night without his running lights on. One of his guys continuously monitored the horizon for oncoming vessels or stalled ships that might impede their pursuit of the *My Wet Dream*. He didn't want to ruin his plans for Jake and Ashby by running up on them too quickly. Mike was a patient man, and he'd bide his time until he could make his move.

He cupped his hand to his right ear to focus his hearing on the yacht. He heard the music and occasionally heard voices coupled with laughter, which carried easily across the ocean's surface. Mike immediately determined they'd stopped for the night rather than stalling or some other unforeseen malfunction. He smiled, comforted in knowing that Jake and Ashby had a false sense of security. His job would be much easier as a result.

It was difficult to gauge the distance between the two vessels in the darkness that surrounded them, but Mike was ready to close the gap. With the sound of music blaring from the yacht, Mike wanted to take advantage of the opportunity by easing up on the yacht at idle speed. If he placed the Cobia properly, the waves would push them closer to the much larger motor yacht without the twin engines running. Then the three of them would quietly board the yacht and take care of business.

CHAPTER 3

The Pacific Ocean
Off the coast of Morro Bay, California

"Okay, I have to ask an obvious question," began Ashby as she poured another shot of Gran Patron Platinum tequila. Ken Kennedy had spared no expense in stocking his onboard liquor cabinet. The only thing the yacht didn't have was cold beer, but now that she was under power, the fridge was stocked with a variety, including their beloved Blue Moon Belgian White. "Would it be possible to live on board this boat, um, I mean motor yacht."

Jake walked around the spacious salon and then descended a few steps into the sleeping quarters. Both of the staterooms had full bathrooms and ample storage. The closets were filled with Ken's clothes and women's apparel in a size that would fit Ashby.

Jake replied, "Well, the floor plan is bigger than my cabin at Yellowstone. Space is not a problem, and the thought of spending the next several months, or even years, living aboard something like this is appealing."

"I feel a *but* coming," interrupted Ashby.

"It's the logistics. A big issue is keeping it fueled. Secondly, we can't live on seafood alone."

"Speak for yourself," said Ashby as she chased her tequila shot with a swig of lukewarm beer. "I can eat my weight in oysters. Straight up, too. No crackers or horsey or Tabasco required. I'm not a wuss."

Jake started laughing and led her back up the steps toward the salon. "I don't doubt that, but we're not gonna find many oysters out here. I wanna look in the compartments below the salon, but I'll bet there's deep-sea fishing gear. Ken spared no expense in purchasing this yacht, as well as outfitting it. We just need to explore a little and see what it has to offer."

"Are you gonna answer my question?" Ashby persisted. "Admit it, there's a certain allure to living on the open seas. Alone. Just the two of us. Right?"

Jake turned to hug her. They kissed for a moment and then he laughed. "The tequila is talking."

Ashby playfully slugged his chest. "Maybe, but a girl can dream, can't she? Come on, Jake, surely you've imagined living on a boat, or at least a deserted island, right? For heaven's sakes, you went on *Survivor* because you liked the thought of, you know, surviving."

Jake laughed and took the tequila bottle from Ashby's hand. He located the cap and closed it, much to Ashby's chagrin.

"Of course I did," he continued. "As a kid, I watched all of the versions of Robinson Crusoe. I studied and analyzed the *Cast Away* movie. Heck, my favorite television show was *Lost* on ABC."

"I liked it too," said Ashby. "I've always enjoyed survival thriller movies, I just never thought I'd be living in one."

"Well, I'm thinkin' it's not all it's cracked up to be. In the movies, the main character always prevails and survives. Usually, that's not the case."

Ashby crossed her arms in front of her and pouted. "You're a helluva buzzkill, Captain Wheeler. Can't we just leave reality behind us for a while and imagine a life full of adventure that involves just the two of us?"

"I'm a big believer in adventure," said Jake. "We've taken the first step already."

"What's that?"

"Every memorable adventure starts with running away from home."

*****

Mike carefully brought the Cobia near the motor yacht and set it on a course where its forward momentum would take the smaller vessel to the nineteen-foot-wide transom. Within a minute of Mike cutting the motors, the music was shut off on the motor yacht and the lights in the salon were extinguished.

Mike frantically motioned for his men to get ready, and both guys raised their AR-15s. They pointed their weapons at the yacht, constantly scanning the deck for any movement. Then lights were turned on, illuminating the single porthole toward the front of the yacht where the sleeping quarters were located.

"Stand down, boys," said Mike in a hushed tone. "It appears our lovebirds are turning in for the night. Grab those oars and guide us into place. We'll give them the opportunity to get settled in before we board."

The men shouldered their weapons as Mike walked onto the open bow. He recalled the layout of the yacht, as he'd been on board with Ken several times. As he considered the surprise he had in store for Jake and Ashby, he thought about how remarkably still the seas were tonight. He looked skyward to find the moon. It was still early in the evening, and he hadn't paid attention to the moon's cycle. In any event, they slowly drifted toward the transom, and his pulse began to race. He hadn't killed anyone before, and his gut told him tonight would be his first time.

As his men rowed, Mike laid out the simple plan. First and foremost, he wanted to take the two alive if possible. He hoped to catch them in a compromising position, in Ken's bed, without their weapons.

While Jake was held at gunpoint by his men, Mike would punish him by punishing her. Then to top the evening off, he would lead Jake to the bow of the ship and force him to admit what he'd done to Ken. He'd force Jake to beg for his life, pleading for mercy, before he was executed in front of his gal pal.

What happened next would be up to Mike and his mood. Either the party could continue, for several days if he had his way, or it would be brought to a quick close by throwing Ashby overboard to be with her boyfriend. Let one of the great white sharks have her,

Mike thought to himself as he reached for the side of the Grand Banks and tossed a line onto the transom.

"I might stick around to watch," he muttered to himself as the first of his men prepared to board *My Wet Dream*.

CHAPTER 4

The Pacific Ocean
Off the coast of Morro Bay, California

Jake had finally drifted off to sleep, entangled in sheets and Ashby's nakedness. Their pent-up emotions had poured out of them, fueled by the tequila, in a release of passionate energy that left him spent.

There was nothing better than sleeping on a boat. The gentle, rolling waves rocked you as if you were still in your mother's womb. The combination of a stressful day coupled with the serenity of lying in Ashby's arms put Jake into a deep sleep.

So it was difficult for Ashby to wake him when she heard something go bump in the night. She had not yet fallen asleep, opting instead to recollect the days since she'd met Jake and imagine their future together. She'd tried to broach the subject with him earlier as she discussed their options, but he was still too hyped up from the escape to consider their future.

Now, alone with her thoughts, Ashby was able to focus her senses on her strange new surroundings, which were comforting in a way, but unfamiliar nonetheless. She lay in the bed of the master stateroom, watching the play of moonlight through the small porthole dance across the foot of the bed.

Ashby had lost all concept of time. Not that it mattered. There were no schedules to follow. No deadlines to meet. There was only night and day and the need to travel to an unknown destination that was better than the one they left.

The first bump against the side of the yacht startled her somewhat, and her senses became keenly focused on the sound accompanying it. Her brain was unable to process the combination, as she'd never been in this position before.

What could bump a boat of this size at night? A dolphin? A whale? A piece of driftwood?

Her mind raced. None of the possibilities instilled fear into Ashby, only curiosity. She contemplated the fact that they were adrift in the ocean without anchoring. Her mind analyzed the probabilities that they could be swept toward shore on the gentle, rollicking waves, crashing into the rocky shore at the base of Big Sur.

She shook off the random thoughts, blaming it on the new surroundings and a long day. She hadn't slept, yet she wasn't to the point of exhaustion like Jake was. He'd had several frantic nights in a row and needed his rest.

Thump!

There it was again. *How long had it been?*

Ashby sat upright in bed, pulling the covers over her chest, and held her breath in order to focus on her hearing. It was quiet again. She looked around for her clothes, deciding it would be better to go topside dressed rather than naked.

She glanced over at Jake, who was gently snoring, but not loud enough to prevent her from hearing, and feeling, the two strange bumps.

Then the yacht shook slightly. It wasn't a continuous movement like a series of waves or the wake of a larger ship going by, which she was certain she would've heard. It was almost imperceptible, a brief drop at the back until it leveled itself again.

Her pulse raced as her anxiety levels rose. The tequila buzz disappeared as the soberness of fear overcame her.

"Jake, wake up." She shook his body gently at first.

"Huh," he mumbled sleepily.

"Jake, come on. I heard something."

"In the morning, Ashby. We'll talk about it."

"No, please." She shook him again and tried to roll him over. "I heard something and then the boat shook."

"Sounds carry strangely on the water. It's probably a—" Jake shot up in bed as he heard the sounds of footsteps.

"See, did you—?" started Ashby before he stopped her.

"Shhh. Quickly, get dressed and make your way into the bathroom. Lock the door. Where's your gun?"

She reached for her clothes and slipped them on as she responded, "It's still in the galley with the other weapons."

"There's no time," said Jake as he found his holster with his .45-caliber sidearm in it. He cocked the .45 and handed it to Ashby. Then he whispered in her ear, "Just like in the motor home. If anybody comes through that door, shoot them. Don't hesitate. Just don't shoot me."

She nodded and scurried quietly into the head. Ashby locked the door, which caused a slight click, but it was loud enough to be heard above. The slowly shuffling feet stopped.

Jake only had time to pull on his pants. Anxiety overcame him as he readied himself for battle. Standing barefoot, sweat poured down his chest and was illuminated by the moonlight as he grabbed his M16.

Here we go again, he thought to himself as he looked around the master stateroom to plan his defense. He eased into the hallway separating the guest head and shower from the guest stateroom.

For a brief moment, he felt a wave of fear. He was trapped with no exits and no cover from incoming gunfire. The interior walls of the boat were as thin as the fiberglass they were made from. Bullets could easily pierce them, leaving no ballistic protection for him or Ashby.

Jake took a deep, slow breath and tried to think through the impossible situation he was in. He heard the squeak of a sneaker on the deck above, coupled with the yacht listing to the port side. A brief thump was heard directly overhead. There was more than one person who'd boarded the yacht, and they were spreading out.

That complicated things for Jake. With the fully automatic M16 at his fingertips, he could take out a group of intruders, huddled together, with a rapid burst of gunfire. If they were spread out, he'd have to deal with return fire from multiple angles.

He backtracked from the entry hall into the master stateroom. He grabbed his knife and removed it from its sheath. He steadied his nerves and changed his mindset.

Jake Wheeler was nobody's trapped prey. He accepted the unknown in the darkness surrounding him, but instead of fearing it, he welcomed it. He became the assassin.

CHAPTER 5

The Pacific Ocean
Off the coast of Morro Bay, California

Jake swiftly moved to the first stateroom at the base of the steps leading down from the salon. He had the benefit of the darkness below and the more illuminated main cabin above. As one of the intruders made his way down the steps, Jake could see his shadow first and then his silhouette against the dim moonlight.

Jake set his weapon down as he pressed his back against the wall. He had no idea how many people had boarded the yacht, and he was gravely concerned for Ashby's safety if a gunfight broke out. Stray bullets could kill just as quickly as one that found its mark from a well-placed shot. He focused on his studies of knife-fighting techniques and the training he'd received for close-quarters combat as a law enforcement ranger.

There were two ways to fight defensively with a knife. Placing the knife in a forward grip, with the blade protruding toward the attacker, allowed the fighter to extend his reach. However, even an experienced fighter tended to lunge when attempting a forward-grip stab, causing him to lose his balance.

Jake decided to use his slashing techniques and, therefore, adopted a rear grip on his knife, with the knife edge out. He'd learned this was the preferred grip of a defensive, slash-style fighter. In the close confines of the ship's sleeping quarters, reach wasn't a problem. The key was to inflict maximum damage, and quickly.

A shadow crossed the top of the stairs, and Jake readied himself by taking a deep breath and exhaling. He studied the opposite wall of the hallway, waiting for the shadow of his attacker to reveal itself.

There it was, the barrel of a rifle. Thin, followed by the thicker barrel shroud. Not a shotgun. Short, like an AR platform. Jake expected the nerves of his attacker to be on edge, with his finger on the trigger, ready to pull at the first sign of trouble.

He waited, watching the gun's shadow systematically drop lower on the opposite wall, seven inches at a time, as the assailant hesitated as he descended each step.

Jake tightened his grip on the knife and waited patiently until the barrel of the gun appeared in the doorway.

Jake spun out of his concealed position and grabbed the barrel of the AR-15, sending it upwards toward the ceiling. As expected, the gunman pulled the trigger twice, sending two rounds into the ceiling before stumbling forward.

The heat of the rifle's barrel seared into the palm of Jake's left hand, but it didn't stop his counterattack. He punched at the man's arms, slicing into bare skin with the back of his Morakniv hunting knife. The serrated blade opened a deep gash in the man's arm, causing him to scream in pain.

"Arrgh," Jake growled as he pulled the knife back toward his body in a stabbing motion, plunging it into the meat of the man's right shoulder. He heard feet pounding the upper decks as at least two men raced to join the fracas.

His attacker was moaning in pain and still constituted a threat, which Jake quickly extinguished. The kill was not as personal as the one in which he looked into Ken Kennedy's eyes as he died, but it was close enough for Jake to feel the man's last breath of air leave his lungs as he punctured them with the knife.

Jake slid the knife into the back pocket of his pants and quickly reached for his rifle. He'd lost the element of surprise, and now he'd have to deal with his assailants by outsmarting them. He scrambled behind the bed in the forward stateroom and trained his rifle on the right side of the open doorway. He wasn't going to wait until he saw the proverbial *whites of their eyes*. He planned on using the thin interior walls of the yacht to pick off at least the first man in line.

He studied the hallway for shadows again. The first one emerged charging down the stairs quickly this time. Jake, however, didn't hesitate. He immediately opened fire, sending half a dozen rounds through the wall into the torso of the man at the top of the stairs.

The body tumbled down the steps in a heap, landing on top of his partner in a pool of blood. Now, despite two kills, Jake felt at his most vulnerable. The last gunman was still above him, and now Jake was trapped, just as he'd initially feared. The only way out of this situation was a barrage of bullets, hopefully finding their mark, or negotiation. His position was already compromised, so negotiation was an option.

"Are you ready to die, too?" Jake shouted as he scrambled across the bed to the aft side of the stateroom. The eight-foot change of location could make all the difference.

"Shut up, Wheeler! You and your gal pal are gonna die tonight, not me!"

Jake immediately recognized Mike's voice. He silently cursed himself for not standing watch on their first night on the ocean, or for stopping at all. He ignored his self-admonishment and began to consider Mike's words. *Not me.* Jake suspected Mike was the last man standing at this little raiding party. *Good to know.*

"Give it up, Mike. Go home. Whatever you had planned is over!"

"Oh, hell no. I'm just getting started. You've got a lot of blood on your hands, Wheeler. First Ken. Now my guys. You won't get one drop of mine!"

Jake had to decide whether he wanted to become the aggressor. He had to assume Mike was at the top of the steps, waiting for any sudden movement to open fire. Jake had his back pressed against the port side of the hull, looking directly through a skylight above the bed. The skylight, which also acted as an escape hatch, led to the yacht's foredeck. If Jake could make his way through the hatch, he'd have the high ground on Mike, but he'd give up his line of defense as far as Ashby was concerned.

Jake squinted his eyes to focus on the hatch in the dark. He needed to keep Mike talking, distracted from the task at hand. He thought he could reach the hatch if he stood on the bed.

20

"Okay, Mike. Let's talk." Jake began the dialogue.

"The time for talking is over!" Mike shouted back. "I've got your guns, and you two are trapped. You come up with your hands high over your head. Or not—your choice. I'd rather just kill you and get it over with."

Jake eased up on the bed while holding his rifle so that it was pointed at the door. He reached for the two latches and turned them. The seal broke free and the hatch slowly rose on its hydraulic hinges. He immediately began talking to mask the hissing sound. "I'm not coming up unless I have some guarantees! It's me you want, not her. Promise to let her go!"

Jake knew that was a stupid request, but the idea was to keep Mike talking. Mike did not, however, respond.

Jake had to think quickly as he heard Mike's feet shuffling toward the back of the salon. *He heard the hatch open.*

Jake looked around the stateroom for something heavy. There was a piece of coral that adorned a nightstand next to the wall. He quickly retrieved it and threw it through the hatch opening until it landed on the deck with a thud.

Mike's heavy footsteps could be heard scrambling around the back of the boat to walk along the rails. This was Jake's chance to remove himself from the confines of the stateroom.

With his weapon leading the way, he gingerly stepped over the two dead men in the hallway to avoid slipping in their blood. As Jake reached the top of the steps entering the salon, he watched Mike's shadow move along the curtained windows on the port side of the yacht.

Jake swung to take the shot, but he was too late, as Mike had passed and began firing wildly into the stateroom. The sound of the gunfire was deafening inside the yacht as Mike angrily poured nearly twenty rounds through the hatch. The bullets tore throughout the stateroom into the bedding, finding the walls and penetrating the floor.

Jake moved to the aft side of the yacht and used the bridge as cover to get into position. He noticed the Cobia tied off to the teakwood planks of the transom and quickly assessed whether there were any other gunmen at the back of the yacht. Satisfied Mike was the last attacker left, he lowered his body and inched along the rail, ready to fire as soon as he rounded the salon windows.

Once on the foredeck, he discovered Mike, who'd dropped to both knees to look inside the stateroom. Mike began to stand, aimed his rifle at the foredeck, and fired again, this time through the fiberglass into the cabins below.

Jake quickly finished the fight, peppering Mike's body with four rounds to his upper chest, causing him to fall backwards over the rail until he splashed into the murky waters of the Pacific.

CHAPTER 6

The Pacific Ocean
Off the coast of Morro Bay, California

Jake hustled across the deck and looked over the rail into the darkness. Mike's body lay facedown in the water, remaining buoyant until the last air in his lungs escaped. He resisted the urge to call out to Ashby without one final sweep of the yacht and the Cobia, which was tied off to a rail.

He returned to the transom and glanced inside the open bow fishing boat. It was empty. Relieved that the battle was over, he called out, "Ashby! It's safe. You can come out now, but be careful not to slip."

Jake found the lighting panel and began turning on every light on the yacht. It would be several days before they would be comfortable sleeping in the dark again. Jake removed the bloody knife from his back pocket and set it on the instrument panel. A flashing light caught his eye, but he ignored it for now, as his priority became Ashby, who had not yet emerged from the head.

"Ashby! Come on out. It's over!"

When she didn't respond, Jake looked down the steps to the sleeping quarters and saw no movement. He immediately became concerned when he saw bullet holes in the wall next to the head.

"Oh no. God, no!" he shouted as he set aside his weapon and scrambled down the steps. He tripped over the dead men and crawled through their blood, which had begun to seep under the door to the bathroom.

With his outstretched bloody hand, he reached for the knob and tried to turn it, but the door had been locked from the inside. He began to pound on it, screaming her name.

"Ashby! Ashby!"

He ran his hands across the bullet holes in the walls created by Mike firing wildly through the hatch. Jake closed his eyes as he began to tear up.

He slammed his fist against the wall and continued to say her name in a softer tone of voice. "Ashby, please answer me. Please."

"Jake." He heard her voice through the wall. "I can't move. "I'm sorry."

Jake scrambled to his feet, thrilled that she was alive, but fearful of a possible gunshot injury. "Are you shot?"

"Almost."

Jake exhaled. Apparently Ashby was in shock, not physically injured. "Okay, don't move. I'll come for you." Jake hustled upstairs and retrieved his knife. Another red light was flashing on the instrument panel.

He arrived at the door to the head and pried it open with his knife, leaving the blade stuck in the doorjamb. He turned on the light and found Ashby curled up in a ball on the floor of the stand-up shower. Her hands were trembling as she gripped the handgun with white knuckles.

He dropped to his knees and crawled to her side. As he reached out to help her, he saw two bullet holes in the shower wall just above her head. He glanced to his right to see the corresponding holes in the other wall nearest the hallway. It didn't take Jake but a second to analyze the trajectory and reach an obvious conclusion—had Ashby been standing or sitting upright, she'd be dead.

"Come here," he said in a comforting tone. "It's over."

She didn't respond physically, but emotionally; she broke down in fits of sobs and tears. Jake wrapped his left arm around her back and helped her to sit upright. He held her tight, gently rocking her back and forth, allowing her to let out her fears and emotions. For several minutes, they held one another without speaking, allowing the strength of their love to bring her back into the present and away from the dangerous gun battle she'd tried to avoid.

She exhaled and was about to speak when an alarm began to sound from the salon. Ashby's body tensed and a look of horror overcame her face.

"Jake, are they back?" She broke their embrace and began searching for the pistol. Jake found it first and grabbed it before her nervous hands did.

"No, they're all dead. There were warning lights on the instrument panel. I need to see what they mean. Can you stand and go with me?"

"Yes." Ashby nodded and used Jake's shoulders to push off of as she rose. Jake joined her and held her hand as they eased their way into the hallway.

"Don't look, Ashby. Just stick with me."

Ashby followed Jake's footsteps to avoid the dead bodies and the ever-expanding pool of blood, but then paused when she saw the bullet holes in the wall. She lowered herself to look through them as if they were a peephole in someone's front door, and then she glanced into the stateroom at the open hatch.

She had to know.

She looked to Jake, who gave her a reassuring smile and squeeze of her hand. He said, "You're gonna be all right. *We* are always going to be strong together."

Ashby returned the smile and nodded to Jake before they continued up the stairs.

Jake released her hand and made his way into one of two bucket seats behind the ship's wheel. He looked at the many gauges and associated the flashing lights with the buttons just behind the wheel.

His chin dropped to his chest and he let out a noticeable sigh.

"Jake, what is it?"

"It's the bilge pumps. They're both working overtime, but if I read these gauges correctly, it's not enough. We're taking on water."

CHAPTER 7

The Pacific Ocean
Off the coast of Morro Bay, California

"What do you mean?" asked a nervous Ashby, who was beginning to recover from the trauma of lying on the shower floor, helpless and in the dark. Throughout the ordeal, her mind had regressed to when she was a little girl riding in the back of her parents' Dodge Ramcharger, curled up in the backseat as lava bombs from Mount Pinatubo crashed all around them. After the gunfire started, she considered helping Jake, but chose to remain hidden as he'd instructed. Eventually, a primal fear forced her to regress, and she dropped to the floor of the shower, an act that likely saved her life.

"We're taking on water from a breach in the hull," began Jake as he pointed to the flashing lights and the instruments. "My guess it's below the waterline based upon these numbers."

"What do we do?"

"Help me find some flashlights so we can look for the leak. We'll start with the boat that's tied off to the transom. They may have crashed into the fiberglass somehow."

Jake and Ashby began sliding open the doors of the teak cabinetry in search of flashlights. For such an expensive yacht, the cupboards were bare. There was very little food stored. Although there was an abundance of alcohol and mixers. *My Wet Dream* was more party boat than it was luxury yacht.

"I found them!" exclaimed Ashby as she pulled the bright yellow flashlights from two clamps holding them inside a cabinet door. She turned them on and tossed one to Jake, who was already heading toward the stern.

They entered the night air together and carefully stepped onto the wet transom. Neither of them wanted to enter the chilly waters of the Pacific, especially with a blood-soaked body floating nearby.

Holding the railing, Jake leaned around the side of the yacht and illuminated the hull with the flashlight. There were no marks on the hull and certainly no cracks that might have been created by the Cobia bouncing against the larger vessel.

"Hold this," said Jake as he handed Ashby the flashlight. He untied the ropes of the Cobia and walked around to the center of the transom, where he found two stainless steel boat cleats affixed to the stern. He allowed as much slack as the line would allow, and then he expertly tied a cleat hitch knot, one of many knots he'd practiced as a kid.

Ashby handed him back the flashlight. "Now what?"

"If water can find a way to get in, it will. We have to find how it's coming in and how fast. I need to go into the engine compartment and inspect the hull. Come on."

Jake raced up the steps into the salon and looked for the access hatch to the engine compartment. He expected to find a pull ring in the floor or under the area rug in the salon. There wasn't one.

He made his way to the stairs leading to the staterooms and turned in a circle, contemplating the design of the yacht.

"Jake, we're standing on top of it," offered Ashby.

"Yeah, and I think I know how to access it. We have to move the bodies. Are you up for it?"

Ashby let out a hearty laugh. "First things first. I want to remind you of something," she started as she made her way to the helm and grabbed the half-empty bottle of tequila. She removed the top and took a swig before handing it to Jake. Her face grimaced as she swallowed the harsh alcohol. With one eye closed, she continued. "We told ourselves we're not alcoholics. That said, sometimes a girl needs a drink to steady her nerves."

Jake laughed with her and took a swig, which resulted in the same *this tastes awful but I'm gonna drink it anyway* look on his face. "Same here."

Ashby took another quick shot and then corked the bottle. She was ready. Jake positioned the dead man on top so that his arms were dropped onto the short set of steps leading down into the sleeping quarters. He moved past the bodies and hoisted up the legs, allowing Ashby to take the lead by pulling the man by the arms. Together, they carried the first body through the salon, onto the transom, and rolled it off into the dark water.

For a moment, they stood and watched the body float off until it became entangled in the slack bow line of the Cobia.

"I'll take care of that in a minute," said Jake. "Let's go get the other scumbag."

Jake and Ashby quickly went back for the second body, observing the trail of blood left through the beautifully designed salon of the yacht. It would serve as a reminder of what they'd been through that night.

They hoisted the corpse up and toted it to the back of the yacht. This time, in order to avoid the bow line of the Cobia, they swung the body back and forth in order to toss it farther away from the transom. It landed with a splash in the water, sank slightly, and then bobbed to the surface, where it rolled over twice.

What happened next astonished them both. Initial fear turned to wonderment as they watched nature in action. With their mouths open in awed admiration and respect for the power of the beast that emerged from the depths of the Pacific, they watched a feeding frenzy reminiscent of one created in the digital studios of Hollywood.

A great white shark thrust itself out of the water, revealing itself as the king of the marine jungle. A great white's jaws were like a precision machine. They unhinge while attacking the shark's prey, allowing the teeth to extend their reach. This combination motion created a partial vacuum that served to suck in the prey before being clenched in the powerful jaws.

Despite the urgency Jake and Ashby had moments earlier from the yacht taking on water, they were now frozen in time by the spectacle. The first bite took half the dead man's body tangled in the bow line, easily ripping the torso in half and snapping the line, casting the Cobia adrift.

As the fishing boat floated off with the waves, the shark came around for seconds. This time, the bobbing body of the second man was the target. The shark was toying with its next meal, circling the body, mouth agape, before its jaws receded and bared its teeth.

With one large chomp, the head and shoulders of the dead man were removed. The shark whipped its head from side to side as it tore the body apart. Then it was gone, ostensibly carrying it meal to its lair in the depths of the Pacific Ocean.

"I've seen enough, how about you?" asked Jake, who'd remained remarkably calm throughout the feeding.

"That was amazing," muttered Ashby, her eyes transfixed on the remains that floated aimlessly behind the transom. "A little too close for comfort, however. Come on."

Ashby turned and was headed inside when a large splash caught her attention. The shark was back, and it had brought a friend. A smaller, younger great white appeared, calmly breaching the surface and whipping the water with its caudal fin.

The killing field was full of blood and bits of dead bodies serving as chum, ideal for the young shark to feed. While the larger great white swam around aimlessly, sometimes upside down as if intoxicated, the younger shark nipped at the dead, practicing its predatory feeding habits. Nature's fiercest predators were enjoying a rare feast, oblivious to their surroundings. Had it not been so gruesome, it would've been beautiful.

CHAPTER 8

The Pacific Ocean
Off the coast of Morro Bay, California

Ashby found several beach towels stowed in two drawers underneath the bed in the master stateroom. She laid them out on the blood-covered floor in the hallway leading to the short set of steps that also served as an entryway to the engine compartment. Jake lifted the steps upward on their hydraulic hinges until they locked into place. A toggle switch was just inside the entry, allowing the compartment to be illuminated.

Jake made his way into the engine compartment and wondered at the expert design. The twin Volvo diesel engines took up the majority of the space, with various other critical components interspersed throughout, such as generators, four bilge pumps, and the water tank. He leaned over to the bilge pumps and found three of the four were humming steadily.

He flashed his light under the equipment, looking for signs of water leakage. The floor was dry, indicating to Jake there wasn't a problem around the propeller shafts at the stern. All the hoses appeared to be intact, and there was no evidence of moisture anywhere in the compartment.

Jake looked around and discovered another hatch, which led to the front of the yacht. This access panel was secured by two slide bolts and removable hinges. He thought for a moment before he opened the hatches. He ran his fingers around the hatch, which had a rubber gasket sealing it tight.

He sat in a crouch, looked into the hallway, where Ashby stood in front of the master stateroom, and back toward the hatch. "Ashby, we have to clean up this blood so I can see the floor."

"I have extra towels already set out," she said before turning back toward the bed. She had three more colorful beach towels covered with the Tommy Bahama signature marlin across the front. "I can just drag the bloody ones into the shower stall and wipe up the excess with these."

Jake studied her demeanor. "Are you okay to do this?"

"Yeah, seriously, I'm fine. Between the shots of tequila and witnessing *shark week* back there, nothing can faze me for the rest of the night."

Without further discussion, Ashby swept the bloody towels into the guest head, then dropped another beach towel to the teakwood floor and monkey mopped it with her feet. Her efforts revealed what Jake had suspected; bullets had penetrated the teak floor and possibly breached the fiberglass.

"Okay, we may have discovered the source of our leak." Jake stood and looked around the engine compartment. He considered the ramifications of opening the sealed hatch and water flooding the space. He had to assume the yacht was designed to deal with excess water in the engine compartment too. The equipment was mounted off the fiberglass floor, and a six-inch dam was designed to prevent water from entering the sleeping-quarters hallway.

Ashby poked her head into the engine compartment and glanced at the hatch. "Are you going under the floor? I can't imagine that there's very much room under there."

Jake felt the door with the palm of his hand. He removed it and rubbed his fingers together. It was sweating. He handed his flashlight to Ashby and motioned for her to stay on the teak floor and away from the engine compartment floor.

He stood to the side of the sealed hatch and worked the handles until they were almost fully open. Then, in a simultaneous motion, he flicked both latches and stood to the side. A rush of water slammed the hatch door open and poured into the engine compartment, quickly spreading throughout the space until it reached a level of two inches.

Jake turned to ask for the flashlight, but Ashby, thinking like a trained surgical nurse anticipating a doctor's next request, tapped him on the shoulder with it.

He nodded and smiled as he took it from her. The marine flashlight was waterproof, so Jake had no concerns about getting it wet as he dropped to all fours in front of the hatch. As he did, the sound of the fourth bilge pump firing grabbed his attention, and the thought of being electrocuted immediately crossed his mind. Once again, he had to have faith in the boat design engineers that they had considered someone to be in this position, and therefore he should be safe from electrocution.

With newfound confidence, he crawled into the darkened space underneath the sleeping quarters and flashed his light around. Like the engine compartment, the completely fiberglass floor was designed to hold water in the event of a breach. The hull compartment was filled to its six-inch capacity, and as Jake moved deeper into the compartment, water sloshed over the hatch threshold into the engine compartment.

"Can you see okay?" Ashby asked from behind him. She flashed her light throughout the small space. "Look, you can see the bullet holes in the floor to the left of your head. Can you see the light shining through?"

Jake instinctively looked up and raised his head in the process, thumping it on a drain pipe from the shower where he'd found Ashby earlier. "Ouch."

"Watch your head," said Ashby with a chuckle.

The thump really did hurt, but her lighthearted remark eased the pain. Jake was glad she was coming around so quickly after her brush with death.

He tucked the flashlight between his jaw and bare shoulder. Then, with both palms pressed against the hull, he began to search the surface for bullet holes. He glanced up again to confirm there were two holes, and then he felt around some more, just to confirm.

"Got 'em!" he exclaimed as he continuously rubbed his fingers over the two holes. Water was coming in at a steady rate, but he found he could force his thumb into the holes and block most of the flow.

"Can we fix them?"

"Maybe. For now, I've got my thumbs stuck in the holes, which is slowing the rate of inflow."

Ashby flashed her light in his face. Jake was on his hands and knees and looking back at her. She smiled and chuckled. "Well, Captain, looks like you've got this under control. I'm going to have a few drinks and dinner. I'll come back and check on you later."

"What? Ashby, that's not funny!"

"Yes, it is."

"Why don't you come in here and take a turn?"

"My thumbs are too small," she quipped.

Jake was quiet for a moment as the water level began to recede thanks to the efforts of the bilge pumps. Then he mumbled in the dark, "I hate you."

Ashby laughed. "No, you don't. You love me."

"Maybe," was all he could manage as a comeback.

Ashby decided to stop teasing him and offered a solution. "Hold tight, pardon the pun. I have an idea."

CHAPTER 9

The Pacific Ocean
Off the coast of Morro Bay, California

Ashby left the engine compartment and closed the stairwell hatch behind her. She rushed back into the galley above the engine compartment. First, she rummaged under the sink to find a bucket she'd spotted earlier. Then she returned to the cabinet containing the flashlights and an orange toolbox. Also, pushed into the back recesses of the cabinet behind a flare gun, extra flares, and several air horns was an item she hadn't given a second thought to when she was exploring the yacht last night, but was glad her memory served her at this point in time.

She hauled all of her finds down the stairs then opened the hatch as they'd done before, until it locked in place.

"Jake, I found what I was looking for!" she shouted as she reentered the compartment.

"What's the plan?"

"Last night when I was rummaging through the cabinets in search of alcohol, I found this." Ashby used her flashlight to illuminate the front of a package labeled *West System Fiberglass Boat Repair Kit.*

"That's great, but will it adhere under water?" he asked skeptically.

"I haven't read the instructions, but I doubt it. We're gonna have to pump this water out of here and find a way to plug those holes, at least temporarily."

Jake added, "Stop the bleeding, or, in this case, the flooding."

"Right. Once we stop the flow of water, we can dry the area and work quickly to patch the fiberglass. It should at least enable us to get to shore and fix it properly at a marina."

"What do we plug the holes with? And, while I've been waiting, I've felt stress fractures around the holes in the fiberglass. I'm afraid the pressure could cause the breach to expand."

Ashby looked around and saw that the water levels in the engine compartment had fallen by half. "The bilge pumps are doing their job. I need to help eliminate water from the compartment where you are. Can you keep your thumbs in place?"

"Yeah, they're freezing cold, but they're still there."

Ashby grabbed the bucket and crawled into the cramped space just behind Jake's legs. She turned around so that their butts were touching one another.

"Hey, baby," said Jake in his best sexy baritone voice.

"Stow it, Captain. No hanky-panky until I know we're not gonna sink and become a great white's breakfast."

She began to scoop the plastic pail full of water and poured it over the threshold into the engine compartment. "Between the four bilge pumps, my hope is that we can empty the water faster than it's seeping in. I'm a little surprised the water levels in here haven't dropped more."

"It's possible there are more bullet holes we haven't discovered yet," added Jake.

"Marvelous," muttered Ashby as she continued bailing the water out. Soon the levels were dropping around them and the engine compartment was becoming fuller.

Jake was pleased with the progress. "We're getting close, but we still need something better than my thumbs to plug up these holes."

"Let me think." Ashby closed her eyes momentarily and focused on what she'd seen around the ship. She guessed that Jake's thumbs were about an inch wide. She needed something that was about that size.

Then she remembered lying sideways in the shower stall during the gunfight. She tried to put the sounds of the bullets flying through the sleeping quarters out of her mind and in turn focused on her surroundings.

"The toilet paper holder!" she exclaimed, which startled Jake.

"What?"

"I remember looking around the bathroom and how opulent it was considering this is just a boat. The spindle thing that you put the toilet paper on was made out of teak instead of plastic like everybody else's."

"That may work, but it will have to be a perfect fit. Is there anything else?"

"Yup. I'll be back."

Ashby set aside the bucket and climbed back out of the compartment. She made her way to the guest head and dismantled the toilet paper holder. She removed the bath towels from the towel rack and pulled down on the teak rod until it broke. The rod was slightly larger in circumference than the toilet paper holder.

She had started back when she heard Jake call out, "Grab my knife. It's stuck in the doorjamb." She abruptly stopped, almost slipping on the remnants of blood covering the teak floor, and pried the knife loose from the wood.

As she crawled back in with Jake, he gave her some bad news. "I think water is still coming in from another location. I've got my thumbs crammed in these holes, and a little water is seeping past, but it's still rising."

"Okay, we'll find the leak. Let's plug these first. What do you need the knife for?"

"Let me see the toilet paper spindle."

Ashby held it up in the light. "It's slightly larger than my thumb. I also have this." She showed Jake the broken towel rack's rod. It was larger than the toilet paper spindle.

"Okay, good." Jake began to explain his approach. "We're gonna trade places for a minute. While you plug the holes with your thumbs, or even the palms of your hands, I'm going to shave the teak rods into a tapered, cone-shaped plug. I'll gently hammer each piece into the two holes until the water stops seeping in."

Ashby pointed over her shoulder. "There's a tool kit in the hallway that has a hammer, razor blades, duct tape, and other things you might use."

Jake took a deep breath and said, "Okay, let's switch."

He removed both thumbs, and water immediately began to rush through the one-inch holes. Jake was unaware that nearly forty-seven gallons of sea water per minute could gush through a hole of that size located below the waterline. Two holes doubled the inflow. Combined, the four bilge pumps aboard the Grand Banks 60 model were capable of pumping out two thousand gallons an hour, not enough to keep up with the water intrusion.

Ashby slid past him and covered the holes with her palms. "Wow, the pressure is more than I thought it would be."

"The ocean will win this fight if we don't hurry," said Jake under his breath as he quickly carved away strips of teak, creating a pointed end that gradually tapered upward. He repeated the process on the other half of the broken rod until he had two tapered, rounded plugs to use to stop the inflow.

He entered the engine compartment, where the light was better, and compared the tapered rods to his thumbs. He identified the point on the rods where they were the approximate size of his thumbs. Jake quickly unpacked the toolbox and grabbed the hammer and the duct tape. He wrapped the duct tape around the rods with a single layer at the point where it was the width of his thumb. He hoped the flexible material would expand into the uneven bullet hole, stopping the flow of water completely.

"Here goes nothin'," said Jake to himself as he exhaled. He crawled back into the hull compartment next to Ashby.

"Will it work?" she asked.

"I hope so," Jake replied. "We'll do the right side first. Hold your hand over the other hole and open wide."

"Huh?"

"Your mouth. Open wide. I need you to hold the other plug while I tap this one in place."

He shined the light in her face and saw Ashby's scowl. She furrowed her brow and then opened her mouth as wide as she could, intentionally overexaggerating the act to make a point.

Jake stuck the pole sideways in her mouth like a dog who'd just fetched a stick, and he gently tapped under her chin.

She raised one side of her upper lip in a snarl in response, then clamped down hard on the wood.

Jake chuckled and gently moved her hand to the side as he forced the tapered rod into the hole. He used the hammer at first to tap it into place, and then he used his weight, together with a twisting motion, to firmly fill the void left by the bullet.

He smiled and nodded at what appeared a viable solution. He reached towards Ashby's mouth for the other rod and she playfully pulled away.

He reached again. She pulled farther away and growled at him.

"Ashby, I'm gonna put you in time-out!"

She smiled and allowed him to remove the rod, but not before taking a playful chomp at his hand.

She moved away from the second hole and gave Jake room to work. Using the same technique, he plugged the hole and then sat back on his heels to admire his work.

"The water is going down in the engine compartment again," said Ashby as she shoveled another bucketful of water over the threshold. "Take over and I'll find some more dry towels. Once we get the area around the holes completely dry, I think this fiberglass repair kit will finish the job."

Jake crawled next to her and gave her a peck on the cheek. She touched his face with her wet hand and crawled into the engine compartment.

After twenty minutes of bailing water and using the entire supply of dry towels on board, the hull compartment was dry. They worked together to create the right combination of epoxy, fiberglass fabric, and fillers to repair the cracks surrounding the bullet holes and fill in the miniscule gaps around the rods forced into the holes.

They sat there for a while in the cramped, dimly lit space, admiring the fruits of their labor.

"Do you think we would've sunk?" asked Ashby.

"It didn't look good, I'll put it that way. We were taking on water faster than the bilge pumps could expel it. Our next best option was to head for the coast or abandon ship."

"With the sharks? Not a chance."

Jake shrugged. "Well, one thing I forgot about was the Zodiac topside. We could've dropped it in the water and headed to shore. But in the heat of things, I didn't even think about it. We really need to learn everything there is to know about this boat."

"Yacht," Ashby corrected him.

"Yeah, yeah. Yacht."

"Well, that was my fault," she said apologetically. "Last night you wanted to be responsible and look through the manuals and check this thing out. I wanted to play. I won, and it almost got us killed by Mike and his goons, or by a sinking ship."

Jake pointed toward the engine compartment, which was nearly empty of water. They both crawled out, and he flashed his light inside the hull compartment one more time.

"There's one more thing that I'd like to do down here," he suggested. "Let's see if we can find some talcum powder, baby powder, you know. Anything like that. I want to dust the area around our repairs to monitor water intrusion. If the plugs begin to fail, we can see the water dripping through the talcum powder more readily than relying upon our eyes in this dim light."

Ashby stood and helped Jake to his feet. She wrapped her arms around him and gave him a passionate kiss. "You amaze me, Captain Wheeler."

"I'm proud of you, Ashby. Let's finish this up, and then I want to talk to you about a mistake I continue to make."

"What's that?"

"I shelter you too much."

"Yes, you do. Jake, honestly, I'd rather be fighting with you, side by side, than scared in the dark, lying on the floor like that seven-year-old girl I used to be in the Philippines."

"No, I get it, and I apologize. You've proven more than once that you can handle yourself. I need to stop treating you like a porcelain doll that will break just because the wind might blow too hard."

"That's right. We're a team."

"Okay. The first order of business after we decide whether we'll stay afloat on this thing is teaching you what I know about weapons and dealing with a live-shooter situation. Deal?"

"Deal," replied Ashby as she and Jake exchanged high fives and set about the task of cleaning up the blood.

CHAPTER 10

The Pacific Ocean
Off the coast of Morro Bay, California

The sun rose over the California coast at Point Buchon and reflected off the buildings of the Diablo Canyon Power Plant. Jake was shocked at how far their yacht had drifted during the night. It was a reminder to treat the ocean with respect and remember that no boat could withstand what the Pacific might have in store for them.

"It's still dry," announced Ashby as she pressed the stairwell hatch down until it locked in place. She twisted the latches so they dropped flush into the teak floor. "I would still feel better if we got it checked out. What do you think?"

Jake was looking through the front windows across the bow toward the Channel Islands National Park. The high-powered binoculars brought the islands, which were forty miles away, into focus. But it was something else that had caught Jake's attention.

He let out a sigh and lowered the binoculars before handing them to Ashby, who'd joined his side. "Take a look to the south. Do you think this is normal?"

Ashby took the binoculars and scanned the coast from Santa Barbara to the Channel Islands and beyond toward the Port of Los Angeles. "Whoa, how many are there?"

"Too many to count," Jake began to reply. "A thousand, maybe? It's hard to tell with so many small ones."

Scattered about the Pacific, sitting stoically on the water, were hundreds of boats of varying sizes. Large tankers and cargo ships were anchored amongst sailboats and pleasure boats. As far as the eye could see, the California coastline had become a parking lot, a nautical traffic jam, of vessels all trying to find their way to port.

Jake powered on the marine radio attached to the instrument panel near his knees. Attached to the teak was a hard-plastic chart of marine frequencies for California. He ran his fingers down it until he located the Port of Los Angeles. He adjusted the dial on his radio to VHF radio channel 73 and turned up the volume.

"Repeat. Recorded message. This is the Los Angeles Pilot Service. The Port of Los Angeles has been ordered closed by the mayor of Los Angeles. No vessels will be granted admission or safe harbor at this time. The Los Angeles Port Police is responding to your requests for assistance via its water patrols, but under no circumstances will you be allowed entry to the port."

"Repeat. Recorded message. This is the—"

Jake turned off the radio. "Well, that certainly rules out that option."

Ashby nodded in agreement as she set the binoculars above the instrument panel. "My guess is the docks are full because nobody is leaving. As the ash fallout begins to travel farther south, all business operations will shut down their machinery to avoid permanent damage. It's true, you know. It only takes a couple of millimeters of fallout, mixed with the fluids of these complex machines, to destroy their inner workings."

Jake pushed himself into the captain's chair and fiddled with the ship's wheel. "All the more reason for us to keep moving. I say we continue to monitor the hull, especially after we get under way. It'll have to become part of our routine. If something breaks underneath, then we'll make for shore and use the Zodiac to ride to safety."

"I don't think we have a choice," agreed Ashby. "We'll burn up our fuel looking for a marina. If the plugs hold, then we can refuel in a more desolate area than LA."

"Like Mexico," said Jake. "I'm sure there are marinas up and down Baja California to choose from. Let's take a look at the chartplotter. I found the manuals for every bit of the electronics, shoved up under a cushion on the sky bridge. I also checked out the antennas on the roof. In addition to a Doppler radar, there appears to be a HughesNet antenna. If we can find the passwords, you can access the internet."

Jake powered on the fifteen-inch display on the Furuno navigation computer.

Ashby ran her arm through Jake's and cozied up next to him for the demonstration. "Sweet. Tell me about this toy."

"The left side gives us a detailed map of our position relative to the coast, and all of these symbols indicate cities, ports, marinas, and other vessels."

Ashby pointed to a series of rings that looked like a bull's-eye. "Is that us?"

"Yes, and the sea of red and green symbols to our south are the boats we can see through the binoculars. We have to drive around them because plowing through might not be such a good idea."

Ashby pointed to the right side of the screen. "Is that a fish finder?"

"Yep. It shows their depth and also indicates the depth of the ocean floor where we sit." Jake pushed an X on the display's touchscreen and the fish-finder data disappeared. "This is what's the most important to us."

A series of gauges appeared showing their heading and positioning in relation to the shore, plus some information that had not yet been programmed. Jake continued. "We can plug in the coordinates of our destination, and the chartplotter will provide us the most efficient route, from a time, distance, and fuel-efficiency perspective. It will provide us warning signals when another boat is approaching our path. It even allows the autopilot to be controlled from this single access panel."

"Wow!" exclaimed Ashby. "Does this mean we can travel at night?"

"Yeah, it does, if I can overcome my need to see where I'm going. It's kinda like getting in one of those driverless cars. Am I really gonna trust that thing to take me from point A to point B? Not on your life!"

"What else does it do?"

"Weather updates are nice," said Jake. "We're in the middle of the

Pacific hurricane season. The storms usually cross the coast of Central America and head due east into the Pacific. Rarely do they trend north of Cabo San Lucas. It's not a problem for the next couple of days, but it will become something to keep our eye on after we turn eastward along the Central American peninsula."

Ashby leaned forward and looked toward the cloudless sky. "Looks like smooth sailing today. I say it's time to go."

CHAPTER 11

The Pacific Ocean
Off the coast of San Diego, California

Jake manually steered the motor yacht to the west of the large number of vessels congregated around the Port of Los Angeles. Once in the open ocean, and after repeated checks of their leak repair, Jake felt comfortable utilizing the autopilot. After some discussion, they chose to set their course for Cabo San Lucas, the southernmost point of Baja California, and a well-known tourist destination.

Jake and Ashby worked together to do some fuel calculations. Their fuel levels had dropped from its maximum capacity of fifteen hundred gallons to roughly twelve hundred gallons. Although the Grand Banks 60 was capable of a steady cruising speed of twenty-seven knots, they chose to move much slower to maximize their fuel efficiency.

With the aid of the chartplotter, they determined they could reach Managua, Nicaragua, if they maintained a steady speed of ten knots. However, they were both leery of the banana republics of Central America, especially those that controlled the Pacific shoreline in El Salvador, Nicaragua, and Panama.

Their ultimate destination was Peru. Of the countries in South America that they considered the safest, including Brazil and Argentina, which had treaties with the U.S., Peru was the most American-friendly on the Pacific Coast. Refueling the tanks in Cabo San Lucas would provide sufficient fuel to make it to the most stable Central American country of Costa Rica. A refuel there would give them an easy sail to Lima, Peru.

With their course set and the engines adjusted automatically to maintain their speed, they set about getting organized. Jake focused on taking inventory of their supplies—both in the form of weapons he'd brought on board and what was available to them on the yacht.

Ashby was giddy with excitement, as she'd found a small spiral notebook in the master stateroom that contained the log-in information to the HughesNet satellite network. She got settled on a sofa in the salon, centrally located to where Jake was shuffling through all of the storage compartments of the yacht. As he emptied the cabinets just to the side of the bloodstained carpet, Ashby reported the news of the day.

"They say more than half of Americans have left their homes and headed for Mexico and Central America. They're running out of fuel and making their way on foot. Jake, dead bodies are accumulating on the highways, and people are just driving around them or, in several instances, over them."

"Desperation and panic," mumbled Jake as he divided the yacht's supplies into several piles—food, medical, sanitary, and miscellaneous electronics and other devices.

Ashby continued. "Hospitals are overwhelmed, so much so that tent triage units are being established in parking lots around the facilities. Face masks have all been sold out or issued to first responders and law enforcement. People are starting to realize that breathing in the ash fallout is like ingesting particles of glass."

"You mentioned Toba once," said Jake. "That was a supervolcano, right? Based upon that eruption, are we gonna find a place that isn't impacted by the fallout?"

Ashby set her MacBook aside and talked as Jake continued to shuffle. "Toba, which is ironically on the opposite side of the planet from Yellowstone, erupted seventy-four thousand years ago. Much of the planet was covered with ash, for the most part, and a volcanic winter ensued. Now, I've argued that the ash fallout from Toba was not as great as scientists first deduced."

"Was it not that large of an eruption?"

"Oh no, it was a super eruption, one that may have taken place over a longer period of time than Yellowstone. I believe Toba erupted four times in relatively quick succession, but not all at once. And by quick, I mean a hundred years. As a result, the damage to the climate was from volcano-induced acid rain rather than ash fallout."

"Are you saying that could be the case here?"

"No," replied Ashby. "Yellowstone is a different animal from Toba. Its eruptive cycle will begin to die down soon. Rather than hitting us over a period of time with several smaller eruptions, Yellowstone's mega-eruption will blast us all at once."

"Is that good news or bad news?" asked Jake as he walked past Ashby and approached a tall cabinet door with a six-button numeric lock affixed to the outside. Jake studied the lock for a moment and then examined the cabinet door. Ultimately, he used his own method of opening a door. He pulled out his knife, pounded the tip of the blade into the wood near the lock mechanism, and broke it off. He then reached his fingers into the hole left in the door and found the location of the latch. Once again, using the steel blade of his knife, he pried the door all the way open, revealing the contents.

"I would say that it's good news for humanity, at least as far as the recovery process is concerned. For us, in terms of our destination, it certainly helps to be closer to the equator and in a southwesterly direction from Yellowstone. The Earth's atmosphere will have a better opportunity to help the ash fallout dissipate."

Jake stood to the side so Ashby could see inside the cabinet.

"Great, more guns," said Ashby sarcastically.

"Ammo too, which we need," said Jake. He'd loaded as much ammunition as possible into the Sikorsky when they left Yellowstone. Between the crash and the descent off the mountain to Challis, he'd abandoned much of the heavy ammunition as they carried Dusty to get medical attention.

Jake began to unload the contents of the weapons locker. Several marine shotguns and an ample number of shells were included. Also, a couple of Remington 1100 shotguns used for skeet shooting were in the cabinet. Two nine-millimeter sidearms rounded out the yacht's arsenal.

"The climactic impact has already begun," continued Ashby. "The ash fallout has extended as far south as Texas and into the southeastern states of Mississippi and Alabama. Trace amounts of fallout have forced airports to close around the country, except Florida and Maine. The continuous eruption spawned several gigantic umbrella clouds that have pushed ash in a thousand-mile radius, including upwind. I suspect Los Angeles was seeing the impact of the fallout, which led to shutting down their ports to activity."

Jake stopped for a moment to wipe the sweat off his brow. He retrieved a bottle of water from the galley and drank it down. "What about temperatures? Is it too early to take readings?"

"Not in North America," Ashby replied. "The super eruption spewed vast quantities of sulfur dioxide, which formed a sulfur aerosol in the atmosphere. The resulting cloud formation has already begun to block sunlight and reflect it back into space. Temperatures have dropped, and drought conditions are already being noticed."

Jake brought in the last of their weapons and meticulously lined them up, coupling them with the appropriate ammo. He stood with his hands on his hips and made an observation. "Well, the good news is we have enough firepower to fight a small war. The bad news is we can't eat bullets."

"We don't have much in the way of food, do we?"

Jake shrugged and sat next to Ashby on the couch. "My guess is Ken Kennedy didn't come to his yacht to sail around and enjoy a good meal. This was nothing more than a floating love shack for him."

"We have a bunch of snack food, and it's all edible," said Ashby with a hint of encouragement. "And a never-ending supply of liquor, it appears."

"Yeah, there's that. Listen, Cabo is only two days away at this pace. We'll travel at night, maybe taking shifts to keep watch."

Ashby kissed Jake on the cheek to reassure him. "No worries, Captain Wheeler. We'll be fine."

CHAPTER 12

The Pacific Ocean
Off the coast of Baja California, Mexico

The Grand Banks 60 held three hundred gallons of fresh water on board. Some vessels of her size came equipped with a marine seawater desalination system. Using reverse osmosis technology, the systems were capable of treating seawater into fresh water for any onboard use. Unfortunately, this yacht's desalination system had not been installed, and they didn't want to waste fresh water for anything other than drinking.

Ashby and Jake took the bloodied towels to the transom and scrubbed them with salt water on the teakwood. Jake located a larger bucket under the master head's sink, and they used liquid detergent to scrub out the blood the best they could. After another salt rinse, the towels were spread all over the foredeck to dry. They'd be hard and somewhat crusty, but useable in the future.

Afterwards, Jake wanted to start Ashby's weapons training. He started out by telling her which weapons she would use most often. He chuckled as he began.

"Never in my wildest dreams did I think I'd have to put my weapons training to use. You know, it was part of my job to go with the guys to Santa Rosa for two weeks. The Public Safety Training Center there was designed for law enforcement officers who were on the front line on California's streets, not glorified highway patrol officers driving the streets of Yellowstone National Park."

"Jake, don't sell yourself short. Even before Yellowstone erupted, the world had become more dangerous. People had become desensitized to the concept of killing. It was prevalent in our entertainment media, from big-screen movies to video games. Regardless of method, people were going to find a way to kill people. Frankly, it's in our DNA."

Jake sighed as he set several weapons on the dining table in the galley. He glanced over at the instrument panel and then through the front windows at the horizon to reaffirm they were on track.

"Well, I'm glad I did it. We've been put in a few different situations, all of which were tense. I hope we don't have to go through it again, but you never know. I need you as a partner in these scenarios, and like I said, it was unfair of me to stow you away. It didn't make you safer, but rather, almost got you hurt."

Ashby stepped up to him and looked in his eyes. "Yet here I stand, safe and sound. Teach me how I can help keep you safe."

"Okay," Jake said with a nod as he turned his attention to the table. "We have three primary weapons. This is the Mossberg 590 twelve-gauge shotgun. You've used a shotgun before, but this one is slightly different. You'll notice it has a pistol grip attached, like a handgun. It will provide you better stability."

Ashby picked it up and pressed it against her shoulder. She kept her finger off the trigger, as Jake had taught her, and he took notice.

"For today, all of these weapons are empty. Ordinarily, I'd advise you to check before you took a shooting position. We're gonna conduct some dry-fire training, and you'll be able to squeeze the trigger and rack another round as if you were in an actual gunfight."

Ashby put the shotgun down and pointed to her regular sidearm—a nine-millimeter pistol. "This is the gun I've been carrying since Idaho."

"Yes, and that practice will continue. We should have them holstered on us at all times, although on the open seas, while we're paying attention, it's not necessary." Jake added emphasis to his statement, as he was still angry with himself for letting his guard down the night before. Had he been on watch, he would have lit up the Cobia and its occupants before they got within a hundred yards of their yacht.

Ashby pointed at the AR-15 lying across the table. "Finally, I get my own machine gun."

"It's not—" Jake quickly interrupted, but Ashby laughed and held her hand up.

"I know, I know. I'm just kidding. It sure looks frightening."

Jake walked to the helm and retrieved his M16, which lay across the captain's chair. Once again, he scanned the horizon, a habit now incorporated into his situational awareness in this unusual environment. He set his weapon down next to hers. The M16 was much larger.

"Yours is a lot longer. Is mine less powerful?"

"They look similar, but they are different in several aspects. First, they're both manufactured by Colt, one of the oldest names in the firearms industry, along with Remington. Second, mine is a military-issue M16. It's fully automatic, which means I can squeeze the trigger and it will fire continuously until the magazine is emptied."

"Mine won't do that?" she asked.

"No, and I won't do that either when the time comes. Your AR-15 can be sold legally in stores; my M16 cannot. Your weapon is semiautomatic, which means you must squeeze the trigger to fire each round. Now, one thing your weapon has that most do not is what's known as a bump stock."

Ashby picked up the lightweight rifle and held the butt against her shoulder. "I remember those. Aren't they illegal?"

"They can't be manufactured, but the existing slide stocks already owned, or available for sale, were not."

"What's wrong with them?" asked Ashby.

"Well, setting the background and the politics aside, the slide stock enables you to hold the weapon firmly against your shoulder and hold the trigger down. As the rifle recoils, the bump stock recoils and forces the trigger back against your finger. This allows your semiautomatic AR-15 to almost mimic the firing speed of my full-auto M16."

Ashby set the rifle down and studied everything laid out on the table. "Good. Based on what we've been through so far, I'll take any edge I can get."

Jake raised his eyebrows and nodded. "One final thought on the fully automatic capability of my rifle and the simulated nature of yours. When we engage in that initial firefight, our attackers are going to hear my automatic weapon, and the bump stock will emulate the sound as well. Most people don't have this capability. I firmly believe it will have a deterrent effect on anyone who challenges us."

"Automatic fire will back them down?"

"I believe so, yes."

Jake took each weapon and showed Ashby the safety aspects of handling a gun. Then he talked about the day's training regimen, which would include skeet shooting to get Ashby accustomed to hitting a moving target, followed by close-quarters combat.

For the skeet shooting training, Jake used the Mossberg instead of the Remington 1100 shotguns that had been found in the yacht's gun cabinet. He wanted Ashby to train with the weapon she would be using in the future, even though it was not meant for skeet.

They took a quick break for a late lunch of crackers and canned deviled ham. They ate while Ashby practiced loading and unloading her weapons. Before starting the last aspect of their training, close-quarters combat, Jake discussed what had happened during last night's attack. With the events fresh in their minds, Jake was able to relate to Ashby the details of the attack and why he'd made the decisions he made.

Because their handgun would always be the most readily available weapon, Jake focused on its use. With her paddle holster firmly in place, Ashby repeatedly drew her pistol until the practice created muscle memory and conditioned her reflexes. If she had to challenge someone or draw to shoot, she could ready her weapon as if it was second nature.

Next, Jake showed her how to use the laser sights, which were built in to the trigger guard of her sidearm. During this process, she learned trigger control and aim. Using a small porthole window as a target, she drew the weapon and pointed it at the target. Jake taught her how to pull the trigger so the gun made a *click* with the sights still sitting on its point of aim. If the sights moved off their target before the *click*, she missed and would have to adjust her trigger pressure.

To finish the day, Jake and Ashby re-created the scene from last night. They took turns positioning themselves where Jake and their attackers had been located. They discussed what they would've done differently.

Finally, they went through the entire scenario again, assuming that Ashby was assisting as part of a team. The outcome would've been the same, Ashby had remarked, but less messy inside the yacht.

It had been a long day, and the two of them were ready to relax. They gathered up the dried towels from the foredeck and stored them away. Ashby fixed them both a cocktail, and the two of them convened on the sky bridge to watch another sunset just as they passed Ensenada, Mexico, to their east.

It was the first day they'd spent together that didn't involve interacting with another human being. It was nice, but short-lived.

CHAPTER 13

The Pacific Ocean
Off the coast of Baja California

Ashby volunteered to take the night shift, as Jake was typically an *early to bed, early to rise* kinda guy. He'd often lamented, however, that the practice had made him neither wealthy nor wise.

Ashby was selfishly glad to be alone with her thoughts. Since the moment their helicopter had lifted off from Grant Village at Yellowstone, they'd been on a whirlwind run for their life. Now they were no longer being chased by would-be killers, whether human or volcanic.

She began to run the scientific scenarios through her head and continued to reach the same conclusion—the lower latitudes, between the tropics, gave them a fighting chance to survive until the proverbial dust settled. Peru was certainly a good choice, but frankly anything near the equator would be ideal.

Her mind then began to focus on their next stop, Cabo San Lucas, a place with a reputation for tourism and partiers. Over the previous decade, the Mexican government had managed to control crime in the popular tourist destinations such as the Yucatan Peninsula and Baja California, which was located at the southernmost end of Baja California.

The northern part of the country along the U.S. border was where the cartel activity was heaviest. Led by the importation of illegal drugs into America, oftentimes coupled with human trafficking, the cartels had overwhelmed law enforcement along the Mexican side of the border.

All in all, Ashby considered Baja California a safe place for them to refuel and purchase some provisions. Traveling farther south into Central America provided them fewer options.

With Jake sound asleep below deck, Ashby settled into the bench seat on the sky bridge and wrapped herself in a blanket to stave off the chill of the open ocean. She turned on the yacht's radio and began to scan channels, hoping to catch some radio chatter from Mexico or Southern California.

She opened her laptop and accessed the internet via the HughesNet satellite. She researched the marina at Cabo San Lucas and was impressed. *Marina Cabo San Lucas* was much larger than the one at Monterey Bay, and the images of the mega yachts docked there put the sixty-foot *My Wet Dream* to shame.

In addition to having the usual boat services like fuel and repairs, there were several restaurants, including live entertainment, and a three-level mall alongside the marina, featuring duty-free shopping as well as basic sundries.

They had accumulated a lot of cash, allowing them to purchase supplies and clothing, even at tourist prices. Plus, Ashby would feel better if the hull was checked out by a professional and repaired correctly.

While she was scanning through the VHF frequencies with one hand, she turned her attention to the news with the other. A disturbing story crossed her MacBook's screen, and she took the time to read it.

Apparently, a fight had broken out at the border crossing in San Diego earlier that day, resulting in a temporary closure to American refugees traveling south. Frustrations were high because the Mexican government had increased the immigration fee twentyfold, while requiring the travelers to pay in Mexican pesos only, or precious metals like minted gold and silver. Now it would cost nearly $360 per person to enter Mexico by vehicle, regardless of your intended length of stay.

This sudden change in immigration rules created tension between the government in Mexico City and Washington. As the two sides looked for a diplomatic solution, a currency black market emerged on the U.S. side of the border. Black-market traders walked between the vehicles, offering their services. Rather than get out of line, Americans were willing to trade their U.S. dollars for Mexican pesos at an exorbitant rate of exchange.

Ordinarily, one dollar would be exchanged for approximately twenty pesos. This twenty-to-one exchange rate became even money under the circumstances. The American dollar had become increasingly devalued as the economy collapsed following the Yellowstone eruption.

If they didn't have sufficient dollars to trade for pesos, all manner of barter was arranged. Eventually, the heat of the moment, and the summer, caused tensions to boil over, resulting in the San Diego border checkpoints to be closed altogether. The reports indicated similar issues were being experienced at El Paso and Brownsville in Texas.

Ashby stopped the digital dial on a VHF channel with an American speaking. She set aside her laptop and listened in.

"… reports of violence against American tourists dominated our ham radio network today as the drug cartels have turned their attention from exporting drugs to the U.S., to feeding off the personal devastation resulting from Yellowstone.

"The Mexican government has devoted their resources to collecting revenues at the border and controlling the influx of refugees. Those who manage to get through are vulnerable to carjackings, murder, and more.

"If you are in the States, with plans on driving through Mexico toward the south, you need to find a way to hide a weapon in your belongings. I know, I know. The importation of guns into Mexico will land you in one of those cockroach-infested jails. That's the least of your worries. The criminal element in Mexico is having a field day, as they see easy pickings rolling down their highways.

"Make no mistake, they see you coming, and it's a long drive to Guatemala. Beware *is the word of the day."*

Static filled the air, so Ashby turned down the volume slightly. She hoped that Baja California was immune to the criminal violence since it was separated from the mainland by water. The static stopped as the man continued to relay his thoughts.

"*No part of Mexico has been spared from this lawlessness. Even Cabo San Lucas is under a curfew, as locals have taken advantage of the lack of police presence to better their lives at the expense of tourists.*

"*Luxury hotels have been raided by flash mobs. Stores have been looted by young people carrying knives and swords. Even the mega-yachts at the marina have been attacked, although the crews have effectively fought off the young people seeking to board them.*

"*Guns are truly mightier than the sword.*"

Ashby rolled her eyes and sighed. She turned off the radio, as she'd heard enough. She opened up her laptop again and began searching the internet for marinas along the Pacific coastline besides Cabo San Lucas. It was time to find a plan B.

CHAPTER 14

The Pacific Ocean
Off the coast of Baja California

"Where do you have in mind?" asked Jake.

Ashby walked him through the various options before settling on her first choice. She handed him the MacBook. Jake took it with his left hand and took another swig of coffee with his right. He considered the coffee grounds to be one of the best finds on the yacht, at least at that moment.

Ashby continued. "My suggestion is *Escalara Nautica* located at *Santa Rosalillita*."

Jake looked at her and smiled. "That's a mouthful."

"I've been practicing it, waiting for you to wake up."

"You came and woke me up, an hour early, I might add," said Jake with a chuckle as he turned his attention to the website.

"I was excited," said Ashby as she snuggled up next to him. "In reality, I missed you."

Jake read about the marina aloud. "The *Escalara Nautica*, which is Spanish for Nautical Ladder, was a megaproject started two years ago. It connects twenty-two ports spaced roughly one hundred nautical miles apart around the Baja California peninsula. The network includes marinas, docking, fueling, and basic shopping for boat provisions."

He set the MacBook on the top of the instrument panel and plugged the coordinates into the chartplotter. He studied the Doppler radar for weather and other boat traffic within a fifty-mile radius. Then he expanded it to encompass the one-hundred-mile radius that included the marina at Santa Rosalillita. There were remarkably few ships of any appreciable size within their range, and none within fifty nautical miles. If they continued to maintain their speed of ten knots, they'd reach the marina in just over eight hours.

"There, done. I've set our course for the Escalara Nautica."

"Sounds exotic, doesn't it?"

"Sexy, even." Jake turned to Ashby and reached around her waist.

She giggled and pushed him away. "No sirree, Captain. Hands on the wheel and off the merchandise."

Jake persisted. "Here's the way I look at it. You woke me up an hour early, and now you think you're going to bed an hour before your shift was supposed to end. As far as I'm concerned, there's an overlap of at least half an hour where we will be sharing the same bed."

Ashby laughed. "You're such a boy."

"That I am. And rule number one of this ship is the captain is always right. I am the captain, you've said so yourself. Therefore, I am right. Yes?"

"No, but it's your lucky day. Thirty minutes and that's it. Yes?"

"I'll take it," said Jake with a smile as he grabbed Ashby by the hand and led her below.

PART TWO

Bienvenido a Mexico

CHAPTER 15

Escalara Nautica
Santa Rosalillita, Baja California

The first harbor and marina planned for the Escalara Nautica project was located at Santa Rosalillita. The small fishing village located midway down the Pacific coastline of Baja California was an area revered by surfers. The exposed reef that juts out into the Pacific is known as *the wall*, a point break that provides surfers the added thrill of unexpected windswells from the north that could send them racing into the middle of a rip or pummel them against the rocks.

After Escalara Nautica was announced, the outrage was immediate. A harbor capable of holding large yachts was planned, which would change the face of the coastline and alter the surfers' paradise. The goal was to entice American yachts to sail the three hundred miles south from San Diego to Santa Rosalillita, load their vessels on large vehicular transports, and cross the narrow peninsula to get dropped in the water again at Bahia Los Angeles, the premier location for exploring the incredible Sea of Cortéz that separates Baja California from mainland Mexico.

Despite the typically chilly waters thanks to the cold California current hugging the shore at that part of the peninsula, surfers would travel south from Tijuana, stay in small three-wall shacks, and ride the waves. After the construction commenced, the protests and vandalism began. The outrage was so great that the American investor group got cold feet and pulled out of the project after dredging had commenced.

The result of the dredging, to the delight of surfers, was the harbor's unplanned sandbar, which created a newly formed wave to ride. Tourism grew, as did the town. The surfers, known for their partying ways, looked for ways to fuel their marijuana habits. The need for weed was just a gateway to all the illegal narcotics readily available in Mexico, which opened the door for the drug cartels to gain a foothold in the region.

Criminals fed off chaos. Government disarray created a vacuum, a void, that was quickly and easily filled by criminal enterprises ready to pounce. The same was true in the small fishing village of Santa Rosalillita.

After the tourist dollars began to pour into the region, the conservationists' efforts to preserve the pristine coastline adored by surfers withered under the weight of land speculation. The local ranchers and *ejidos*, community-owned and managed properties, salivated over the possible land deals as developers came to Santa Rosalillita, cash in hand.

Escalara Nautica was back on the table and quickly came to fruition several years prior to Jake's entry into the man-made harbor. The harbor was new, but the underlying criminal element of the small town was not. The drug trade flourished as wealthy Americans whet their appetite for illicit drugs they couldn't purchase in the States. With every vessel that entered the new harbor, dozens of sets of eyes scanned its decks to determine if this was a potential customer.

After the eruption of Yellowstone and the increase in lawlessness throughout Mexico, the eyes began to search with a different intent—prey upon the weak.

Ashby stood on the foredeck, the wind blowing her blond hair past her shoulders, whipping her blouse open from time to time. Jake cautiously guided the Grand Banks 60 alongside the longest dock, which jutted out into the harbor.

And a dozen onlookers bared toothless grins, salivating at the opportunity that had just presented itself.

CHAPTER 16

Escalara Nautica
Santa Rosalillita, Baja California

At this hour, the docks at Santa Rosalillita were abuzz with activity. The Mexican government, under the control of leftist President Andrés Manuel López Obrador, formally closed the border after tensions had boiled over with the president. He ordered the Mexican Navy to block all ports of call, and he enlisted the help of the drug cartels to assist in maintaining security at its border entry points.

Obrador had been elected in a platform that promised to change the dynamic between the government and the cartels. *You can't fight evil with evil*, he'd stated during the campaign, as he planned to focus on stopping the violence while opening the dialogue for legalization of certain drug-related activities.

He argued that the two hundred thousand dead Mexicans at the hands of Mexico's militarized assault was a direct result of Washington's pressure to control the drug cartels, which ostensibly stemmed the flow of drugs into America. His position was simple— *we will no longer kill fellow Mexicans because America cannot control its drug use.*

In the two hours prior to the arrival of the *My Wet Dream* at Santa Rosalillita, the orders were given and the Mexican military moved with remarkable speed to comply with the presidential directive.

So did the drug cartels.

With only a quarter of a million service members, the Mexican military forces were ill-equipped to control the entirety of its territory. The shared border with the United States and other Central American countries was twenty-five hundred miles. The coastlines measured nearly six thousand miles. With the Mexican Navy dedicated to operating its minimal naval fleet, the coastlines were of particular concern to the president. The naval personnel were ordered to patrol the coastal waters while agreements with the cartels were made to monitor the small towns and ports of call along the country's coastlines.

Over the years, Jake had docked the twenty-three-foot open bow powerboat assigned to the Yellowstone Law Enforcement Rangers after he'd pulled lake patrol duty. He'd once said that if you know how to dock a boat like an expert, you've probably embarrassed yourself many times along the way.

He continued closer to the pier at a slow rate of speed. He recalled rule number one of docking a boat—*never approach the pier any faster than you're willing to hit it.* The wind blowing into the harbor didn't help him with the arduous task. He'd throttled back completely as the stiff breeze forced him toward the dock. He kept his wheel centered, only using the power of the engines to move the yacht closer to the dock.

The chaos unfolding at the marina didn't help. The kids were running up and down, waving their arms. Some were shouting to Ashby in Spanish while others stretched to grab the dock lines she'd tossed to them.

Ashby positioned the yacht's fenders to provide protection as Jake got closer. He was certain that an expert captain could've whipped the yacht right into place in less than half the time, but Jake resisted the self-imposed pressure, to avoid looking like a novice. The yacht was their ticket to freedom and safety, and he didn't want to risk damaging it.

Jake left the engines running until he had an opportunity to inspect the dock lines. Once he was comfortable they were well secured, he shut off the engines and breathed a sigh of relief.

"*Buenos días señorita!*"

"*Eres muy hermosa!*"

"*Bienvenido a México!*"

Ashby and Jake walked along the rail, smiling and waving to the children. "They certainly are friendly," said Ashby.

"Oh yeah, and next, they'll have the paw out," said Jake somewhat sarcastically.

"Do you mean looking for a tip?"

"Oh yeah, it's the Mexican way," started Jake as he led Ashby into the salon. He changed his tee shirt to a longer one that covered his paddle holster, and Ashby did the same. He then stepped into the guest stateroom and pulled out the drawer that held their American currency. He used Ashby's Corona Beer messenger bag to stash several thousand dollars in hundreds together with several gold bars. Jake expected this shopping excursion to be expensive.

"Why do you say that?" asked Ashby.

"Oh, I really shouldn't talk this way. When I was a kid, my family took a trip to Monterey, Mexico, with my father while he was negotiating to buy a manufacturing plant that complimented his business. My mother and I toured the city, and every thirty feet was a shoeshine boy begging to shine my shoes for a few pesos."

"C'mon, that's cute," interjected Ashby.

"Sure. They'd call out *shoeshine, shoeshine,* trying in their best broken English to convince me they were the best *shoeshiners* in all the land."

"Did you let them do it?"

"Nah, I was wearing white Converse sneakers," Jake said with a laugh as he closed the access door to the sleeping quarters and locked the door. He then retrieved the keys to the yacht and stuffed them in his pocket. He joined Ashby at the rear of the salon and took a deep breath.

"Are you ready for this?" he asked as he handed her a stack of twenty-dollar bills.

"What's this for?"

"Tip money."

"A twenty? That's a little much."

"Not from what you heard on the radio," said Jake. "It's only worth a dollar now."

Ashby shrugged and took her stack of twenties. The two descended onto the transom and stepped up onto the dock, where several willing hands assisted them. Jake and Ashby immediately began to dole out the twenties as they pushed their way through the crowd and toward the gas pumps in front of the harbormaster's office.

Several small stores encircled the parking lot of the marina. The simple signs were hand-painted in Spanish—*Restaurante*, *Mercado*, and *Tienda de Surf*. Jake pointed toward the right, where several older men stood near a sign that read *Gasolina*.

"*Buenos días*," said Jake, which drew laughter from the men. Jake looked puzzled as he awaited their response.

"*Buenas tardes*," a heavyset man smoking a cigar responded with a huff as he pointed toward the setting sun.

Jake was unaware he'd wished the man good morning, when evening was more appropriate. Jake was, however, keenly aware of the disdain shown by the men for the two Americans. His guard was immediately raised as his level of situational awareness kicked into high gear.

He abandoned his attempts to endear himself to the locals and dropped the Spanish. "Diesel?"

"*Sí.*"

"How much?" asked Jake as he flashed a wad of twenty-dollar bills.

The men burst out into laughter. The heavyset Mexican pulled a twenty out of his pocket, took a deep draw on his cigar to expose a flaming red cherry, and stuck a corner of the bill into the hot ash. After a couple of puffs, the bill began to smolder and caught on fire. He held it out toward Jake and chuckled. "Here, you can have more of your American money. It burns, yes?"

The three men roared in laughter as Jake looked to Ashby. He had been afraid of this, but he had no choice but to persist.

"How much?" he asked again, never breaking eye contact with the men.

"Gold only. Do you have gold, *gringo*?" the man asked with a snarky tone.

"Yes. How much?"

The man spit onto the dock and then stomped the flaming image of Andrew Jackson. "This way."

As he walked past them, he intentionally brushed up against Ashby. Jake saw her cringe and slide her hand toward her pistol. He quickly reached for her hand to escort her up the ramp to the harbormaster's office.

"Let's go, dear," he whispered with a firm grip on her right hand. Now that Ashby had successfully trained with the sidearm, it was apparent she had no compunction in using it. "We'll pay for the fuel, pick up some supplies, and get the hell out of here before dark."

They continued to follow the man, but also noticed a crowd was starting to gather around the docks. Ashby leaned in to whisper, "Jake, I don't like this. Have you noticed something odd about all of this?"

"Besides the obvious hostility? What else?"

"Look at the boats docked here. They're all high-end yachts or speedboats."

"Yeah, like ours."

"Exactly. But where are their owners? Do you see a hotel anywhere? This looks like a village in an old Clint Eastwood western. Like a ghost town, except the ghosts are missing."

Jake glanced around and began to feel wary of their surroundings. "Let's play it out. Maybe paranoia is getting the better of us."

"Jake, if we see trouble, let's just go. We'll figure something out. Okay?"

"Absolutely."

CHAPTER 17

Escalara Nautica
Santa Rosalillita, Baja California

"Should I get started on picking up supplies while you handle the fuel?" asked Ashby as they approached the harbormaster's office.

Jake hesitated before he replied, "I don't like to be separated, but we can't watch them fuel us up, protect the boat, and make purchases at the same time."

He held the door open as he took one more glance around the marina. Ashby leaned into him and whispered, "It'll be all right. I'll gather what we need, set it on the checkout counter, and get a price. I'll come back and get the payment."

"Load up, because it's gonna cost us in gold, and these people won't be giving us change."

Ashby nodded, patted his shoulder, and darted off to the store. Jake stayed behind to negotiate with the locals for diesel fuel. As she approached the three businesses, she scanned the faces, looking for any Americans. There were none.

Ashby found it hard to believe that the boat owners were on their vessels, hiding away from the activity. Some of the speedboats didn't have sleeping quarters. It was a mystery she wasn't in the mood to solve, but also had no intention of becoming a part of.

As she made her way through the market, filling the basket with nonperishable canned goods and boxed snacks, her eyes continuously surveilled her surroundings. She was proud of her calm demeanor. She was not paranoid, but, rather, considered her heightened state of awareness something akin to managed paranoia.

With one basket full, she retrieved another one. As she did, an older woman behind the checkout counter spoke to her in English.

"No U.S. dollars, *comprende?*"

Ashby smiled at her and nodded. "Yes, gold only."

"Gold, *por favor.*"

"Okay. How much for two baskets?" asked Ashby.

"One ounce each. Two ounces pure gold, no jewelry."

Ashby nodded and continued her shopping. She considered purchasing some refrigerated meats and cheeses, but after studying the contents, she became queasy. The meat was old and probably close to spoiled. Despite the recent expiration dates of the packaged foods, she felt comfortable buying them because they were imported from the States.

Her last stop was the beer aisle. She picked up two six-packs of Corona and two quart bottles of Sol. She thought Jake would get a kick out of the man-sized bottles of beer. After this trip to the marina, he'd probably need one.

She addressed the woman at the checkout counter. "Two ounces, yes?"

"*Sí.*"

Ashby exited the market and shielded her eyes from the bright sun as it began to set over the horizon. She looked toward the harbormaster's office and saw a small crowd had gathered around the entrance. She strained to see their yacht and noticed there was no activity other than a few of the kids milling about.

Puzzled as to why they weren't getting fueled up, she quickened her pace and headed for the office. She found Jake pacing back and forth near the front door with his hands on his hips. He was clearly frustrated.

"Jake, what's going on?"

He grimaced and shook his head. "I don't know. For one thing, they speak to me in simple broken English. When they speak to one another, it's mile-a-minute Spanish. Even if I understood certain words, I couldn't make out what they're saying."

"Do they not have the diesel?" she asked.

"Oh, they have it, I think. The problem is the price and the quantity, I guess." Jake kicked at a rock, sending it tumbling toward the dock and into the harbor.

"What are they doing? Calling a town meeting or something?"

Jake smiled. "As a matter of fact, they are calling somebody, but I'll be darned if I can figure out who."

"I've got two shopping carts loaded with supplies. The lady wants one ounce of gold each."

Jake rolled his eyes and began to laugh. "Do they realize that's probably worth twenty thousand or more, for a couple of buggies of food?"

"Yeah, they do, and I suspect the price would go up if they knew how much gold we have. Should I go ahead and pay while we wait?"

"I guess—" Jake began to answer when the sounds of vehicles roaring in the distance caught their attention. The streets of Santa Rosalillita, which only see rainfall once a year, were kicking dust up into the air.

"What the—!" exclaimed Ashby as gunshots could be heard in the area of the oncoming vehicles. They rounded a curve and began to enter the parking area near the market.

"Run!" shouted Jake as he led Ashby by the hand toward the dock.

Suddenly, two of the burly men who assisted the gas man blocked their way down the ramp to the dock.

"Get out of the way," growled Jake as he came face-to-face with the men.

"*No comprende, gringo!*" one of the men hissed back as he pushed his rotund belly into Jake's chest.

Tires could be heard sliding to a stop on the hard-packed surface of the parking lot. Men's voices were shouting orders as they exited the cars.

"Jake, we don't have time for this."

"I know!"

The man, startled by Jake's sudden outburst, stepped backwards slightly, which was the opening Jake needed. He pushed the man in the chest with both hands to encourage his backward momentum.

The man tripped over the top step of the dock and toppled backward onto the wood planks.

The other man reached for Jake, but Ashby's draw was quicker. She was pointing the gun in the man's face in a flash.

"Stand back, *cabrón!*"

The man was surprised by Ashby's use of the Spanish obscenity. He held his hands up and stepped aside as Jake, followed by Ashby, ran down the stairs toward their boat.

Jake was screaming and waving his arms as he dodged the kids and onlookers who'd crowded onto the dock between them and where the yacht was tied off.

"*Pistola! Pistola!*" a teenage boy yelled when he caught a glimpse of Ashby's gun, which she was waving around to frighten people out of their path.

That was when the first round of bullets flew over their heads and embedded in a sailboat next to them. Jake and Ashby instinctively ducked, but several of the children jumped into the dark, oil-slicked water surrounding the docks.

Chaos ensued as more gunshots rang out.

"Here we go again!" shouted Ashby as she ducked below several more bullets whizzing overhead.

CHAPTER 18

Escalara Nautica
Santa Rosalillita, Baja California

The locals were diving for cover while others ran in the same direction as Jake and Ashby to avoid the men who were running toward the docks. Ashby immediately felt exposed and in danger. Jake reached for his sidearm, but his adrenaline carried him forward toward the boat rather than turning to fight.

"*¡Ándale, ándale!*" The men were running and firing their weapons, which threw their aim way off. Ashby glanced over her shoulder and counted eight pursuers, all of whom appeared to be armed. She took charge.

"I'll get the dock lines. You get us started."

Jake was twenty feet ahead of her now and was approaching the point where the dock formed a T. "You've got to hurry. They'll be on us before—"

"I've got this. Go!"

Jake hustled onto the yacht and scampered up the stairs to the sky bridge. Ashby scrambled around to quickly untie the dock lines and throw them onto the deck. Once the lines were loose, she took up a position behind one of the piers sticking out of the water where the right angle formed at the end of the dock.

She hid behind the large wooden pole that measured eighteen inches across, giving her some ballistic protection for what she had in mind.

Ashby took a deep breath and recalled what Jake had taught her. *Shoot short bursts. Take cover. Manage your ammo. Repeat.*

She leaned out from behind the pier and took aim. She fired three rounds into the men who were bunched together running toward her. The bullets found their mark, hitting two of their pursuers in the chest and knocking them to the decking.

The next two attackers tripped over the bodies, sending them sprawling. Ashby quickly fired upon the hapless gunmen. She hit one in the meat of the thigh and the other one in the top of his head.

This stopped the progress of the remaining four men momentarily as the sound of the big diesel engines came to life.

Jake shouted to her, "Come on! Now!"

"Not yet! Ease out, close to the dock!"

The men were coming again, but this time they were firing their weapons in a continuous barrage of bullets headed toward the boat. Several rounds embedded in the fiberglass and broke out windows in the salon. Others flew over Jake's head, causing him to duck.

The shooters were too close for Ashby to reveal herself, but she also needed to catch up with Jake. She was running out of precious seconds to make her move. She took a chance based upon videos of Taliban fighters she'd seen on the news. She always considered their method of fighting as cowardly, as they simply pointed their weapons around a corner or over a wall, firing wildly in the direction of their targets. Nonetheless, she considered it an effective way to slow her pursuers. She stuck her arm around the pole and fired in the direction of her assailants.

The gunfire stopped, and so did the sounds of their heavy feet pounding against the dock. Ashby stepped out from behind her cover, ready to fire. She surprised the men, who froze momentarily, allowing her to inflict flesh wounds on one of the frontrunners.

She'd bought all the time she needed to get away. She quickly turned and ran down the dock, turning right toward the yacht as it eased along the pier. She picked up her pace and timed her jump, pushing off the end of the dock and landing on the transom before crashing into the stern.

Ashby lost control of her gun and fell to her knees in an attempt to retrieve it before it slid between the teak planks. It turned sideways, and the barrel dipped into the water just as Ashby found the grip. As the boat accelerated, she turned her attention to remaining on board.

The forward momentum of the boat caused her to slip backwards toward the edge of the transom and nearly into the water. Her legs hit the surface with a splash, and Ashby struggled to find a grip on the transom.

More gunshots were fired in their direction and Jake gave the engines more throttle. Ashby was holding on with one hand, her legs trailing her body, which was now surfing on the water. Using the spaces between the planks as a ladder, she grabbed them with her fingertips until she could reach the cleats affixed to the stern. Then she yelled to Jake, "Hit it!"

The back of the boat sank into the water from the force of the twin diesel engines, causing the boat to lurch forward. Ashby held on as her entire body was soaked by the water covering the transom. Jake turned out of the harbor with the bow lifted high and the twin diesels roaring at full throttle. Eventually, he reduced his speed, causing the Grand Banks 60 to plane onto the surface. Ashby finally exhaled after her wild ride and crawled through the back half-door onto the aft deck.

The attackers, angry at being thwarted, fired several bullets toward the boat, pelting the roof of the sky bridge and ricocheting in all directions. Jake gave the engines full power again, easily navigating the boat around the man-made seawall and into the Pacific Ocean.

Ashby leaned against the stern wall with her arms draped over her knees and the gun hanging loosely in her hand. Her hair was wet and stringy, hanging in front of her face. She made a weak attempt at wiping the long, blond strands behind her ears, but her hair fell back in front of her eyes. She was still breathing heavily when Jake glanced down at her from the sky bridge.

"How're you doin' down there?" he asked, with a smile.

Ashby managed a laugh and looked up at him. "You know, I'm real tired of getting shot at!"

CHAPTER 19

The Pacific Ocean
Off the coast of Baja California

Jake continued to monitor the shoreline near the marina to determine if any boats were chasing after them. He didn't want a repeat of what had happened with Mike, who'd tracked their progress along the California coast before making his move.

"I think we're clear," Jake said to Ashby, who'd taken a moment to change clothes and take a shower. It was her first one in days. She approached Jake's side and gave him a hug. He immediately relaxed and enjoyed her touch. "Well, Dr. Donovan, you certainly clean up well."

Ashby was wearing a bikini top she'd found in the drawers of the guest stateroom, coupled with a pair of Daisy Dukes, cutoff jean shorts made famous in *The Dukes of Hazzard* television series.

"It's a new look for me. You like?" She playfully turned around to give Jake a long look at her figure.

"I do, ma'am. Why don't you come here and—"

"Not so fast, big guy," she said as she took a couple of steps backwards. While wagging her index finger at him, she smiled. "You, sir, are smelling a little, shall I say, *gamey*."

Jake lifted his arm and sniffed his pit. He sucked in his cheeks and wrinkled his nose. "I prefer manly, but I can take a hint. Why don't we take a shower?"

"Sorry, mister man. I've had my shower, and somebody needs to stand watch."

Jake pouted and then nodded. "You're right, rain check?"

"Maybe," she replied. She pointed to the chartplotter, which displayed a screen full of grayish static. "Do you have a course set in that thing? What's wrong with it?"

"I don't know. While you were down below, I powered it up to determine a route toward Cabo. I figured it couldn't be any worse than what we just went through. You know, more population, police presence, and maybe an American consulate annex or something like that."

Ashby noticed the ship's wheel moving ever so slightly as the boat continued forward. "Is it driving itself?"

"Autopilot, yes. I'm just not using the chartplotter to do it."

Ashby moved over to the instrument panel. Jake had set them on a south-southeasterly course. "How about the radar?"

"Same problem. Listen, we took fire during the melee. There are several things I need to check on, including our DIY plug in the hull. Let me start there, grab a shower, and meet you back up here. It'll be dark soon, and we need to make a decision about traveling at night."

Ashby gave him a peck on the cheek and pointed to the stairs. "Chop-chop. I'll try to identify where the bullets hit us and what damage it might have caused. I've already cleaned up the glass in the salon and checked the lower instruments and controls. No damage there that I could see."

Jake flashed a thumbs-up as he bounded down the steps to the engine room. Ashby retrieved her laptop and attempted to access the internet. She wanted a bigger picture of where they were located.

She began her search, but the MacBook indicated she didn't have an internet connection. She mumbled in frustration, "The radar, the chartplotter, and now the internet. Gimme a break."

She stowed away her computer and looked around the yacht, assessing the possible reasons for the electronics failing. She walked outside the covered area to the back of the sky lounge. On the port side of the open deck was a padded lounge seat, which covered a storage compartment they hadn't looked under yet. Exploration would have to wait. Ashby needed internet.

She climbed on top of the padded cover and stood on her toes to inspect the top of the sky bridge. The problem was immediately revealed.

Stray bullets had riddled the round Doppler radar antennas. Another round had shattered the central feed horn before embedding in the bowl-shaped, parabolic surface of the HughesNet satellite dish.

Ashby pounded the roof in disbelief. On the one hand, she was glad their attackers were such poor shots that neither of them was injured. On the other, *Did they have to hit our antennas?*

Ashby dropped to the cushion and sat with her legs crossed under her. "Now what?" she asked in disbelief as she looked toward the setting sun. She glanced back toward Baja California, which was completely dark, as there was little population along the coast until they reached Cabo San Lucas. The stars were beginning to show themselves on the eastern horizon, which gave Ashby an idea.

"Good as new," Jake proudly announced as he hustled up the stairs to the sky lounge. "Now, about that kiss."

"Forget it." Ashby threw cold water on his proposal. "We've lost our radar and internet thanks to those moronic banditos back there."

"Internet?" asked Jake.

"Yeah, look on the roof for yourself before it gets too dark. There are bullet holes in the radar box things, and the HughesNet is destroyed."

Jake leapt up on the cushion and then hoisted himself on the fiberglass roof. It sagged somewhat under his weight, but he moved carefully to inspect the electronic devices. He pounded his fist on the roof, just like Ashby, indicating his conclusion was the same. He lowered himself to the cushion and rubbed his hands through his hair.

"Well, that really sucks," he grumbled.

"No doubt," added Ashby. "It certainly prevents us from traveling at night. We have to be able to see where we're going."

Jake shrugged. "I'm kinda okay with that anyway. Seeing a blip on a radar is no substitute for seeing the boat and its passengers up close and personal. Radar blips don't reveal the sailor's intentions."

Ashby sat next to him and rubbed his shoulders, hoping to cheer him up. Jake had worked so hard to keep them safe, making tough decisions that skirted the edge of death in order to get them free of the destruction being wrought by Yellowstone.

"You know, back in the day, sailors didn't have all of this crap," she began, waving her arm around the sky lounge. Pacific Islanders, Columbus, and the Vikings navigated the oceans using the sky and the sea."

"Vikings?"

"Sure. You know there's an argument that Vikings landed in North America before Columbus and his pals."

Jake was still dejected. "Okay, but the problem is I know nothing about astronomy other than where the Big Dipper is. We can continue to travel with the coastline in view, but we run the risk of more encounters with other boats."

"I'd like to avoid that, too," agreed Ashby. Then she grew quiet. She jumped off the padded cushion. "Help me remove this thing."

Jake slid off the edge and lifted an end of the eight-foot-by-eight-foot cover and slid it toward the rear of the boat until it leaned against the rail. Underneath were four fiberglass hatch doors secured by simple finger latches. It was much darker now, so Ashby illuminated the flashlight to help them see. Each took a door and opened it, unsure of what they'd find.

Jake announced what he found. "Fishing gear. Deep-sea rods, reels, and accessories. This is sweet!"

Ashby smiled as Jake's mood lifted. However, what she found was just as important.

CHAPTER 20

The Pacific Ocean
Off the coast of Baja California

Jake and Ashby stayed up until midnight studying the laminated charts and maps she'd discovered under the lounging platform. In addition to the fishing equipment, they also found camping gear still in its original packaging—a large tent, sleeping bags, lanterns, backpacks, and a variety of camping tools. But it was the maps that garnered their attention.

"It's a shame Hawaii is out of reach," said Jake as he made notes of possible destinations for them. "It's due west of here, but three thousand miles is out of our fuel range. Here's the thing, if we can fuel up in Cabo, we have a lot of options as far south as we want to travel. If Cabo is out, then we have to stop in Guatemala—like the Port of San Jose."

Ashby summarized the plan. "Then it's settled. First light, we'll hug the coastline as safely as possible. Both of us will monitor the radio for information on conditions in Cabo during our shifts."

"Do you want first again?"

"Yessir," replied Ashby. "Let me ask you. What do you think about me using the marine radio to reach out to any expats I can find on the peninsula? You know, someone with firsthand knowledge of what's happening in Cabo. Why waste the time and fuel attempting to enter the marina there only to be turned away?"

"Go for it," replied Jake. "Try not to give our position away, or any details about the yacht."

"The position is no problem. I'm still not a hundred percent sure where we are. It's really weird, and a little scary, being adrift out in the Pacific like this. Mike's attack the other night is still fresh in my mind."

Jake hugged her and gave her a lasting kiss. He left Ashby alone in the salon and went to bed. She took a moment to wash their glasses in the galley, and then she straightened the laminated maps so they could refer to them quickly. She took another glance at the nautical chart, which included the ocean depths and certain points of interest.

Her geologist curiosity was piqued as she traced the shallow waters of Baja California to the point where the continental shelf began. The drop-off was dramatic. The shallow waters of the coastline, varying in depth up to sixty feet, suddenly dropped off to twenty-eight hundred and eventually to over four thousand feet deep on a consistent basis running along the west coast.

There was only a cluster of islands shown off the Mexican coast, most likely remnants of ancient volcanic activity. Ashby didn't profess to know the location of every dormant volcano on the planet, although she could reel off all of the active ones. Over time, she'd studied certain attributes of volcanic systems and even vowed to visit them all at some point, but her busy schedule didn't allow for sightseeing during her work.

Her mind began to drift to the long-lasting impact of Yellowstone's eruption and the volcanic winter that began to encircle the planet. She decided to go topside to enjoy the slight ocean breeze with its accompanying sea spray. She retrieved a Nautica jacket, which was hanging in the master stateroom closet. It was too large for her, but it would keep her warm from the temperatures that dipped into the low sixties.

She dimmed the lights within the sky lounge so she could sit in the dark, with the only light being the gauges, which let off a steady glow. It had become a rule on the boat to monitor the bilge pumps as a warning sign that their patch job on the hull had failed. Thus far, they'd been lucky and hoped for the best as they sailed south.

Ashby turned on the marine radio and began scanning the channels again. On a couple of occasions, she picked up an American speaking to nobody in particular—random thoughts on an ordinary night during the apocalypse. Ashby tried in vain to make contact with any of the English-speaking radio operators. She presumed her receiver had a longer range than her transmitter.

She did, however, learn about the conditions throughout Mexico. The borders were officially closed, and millions of Americans were stranded, from San Diego to Brownsville, demanding entry. Some reportedly undertook efforts to cross in obscure, desolate locations, only to be apprehended by the Mexican military or the drug cartels, who'd created an unholy alliance with the Mexican government to close the border.

Reports of violence against the refugees throughout the country were being repeated by the radio operators. The president of Mexico had joined other North American countries in declaring martial law. Curfews were established. Civil liberties were taken away. Citizens were put in fear of both the Yellowstone fallout and their government's heavy-handed approach to maintaining control.

Meanwhile, in Europe, the crisis had widened as Yellowstone's eruptive material crossed the Atlantic. European nations were shutting down their businesses and transportation. Food was in short supply, and societal unrest had escalated.

Toward the end of Ashby's shift, the radio chatter had subsided, and her eyelids began to grow heavy. She looked through the binoculars in a three-hundred-sixty-degree sweep of the ocean. There were no lights on the water, nor were any lights visible on land. She was contemplating lying down for a moment when she heard Jake's voice.

"Good morning, sunshine!"

Ashby snapped to attention, as she'd already taken a prone position on the lounging platform. "Yeah, yeah. I was just about to take a little nap."

"Busted!" he exclaimed as he helped Ashby to her feet. "Is there anything going on?"

"I was never able to speak with anyone, but I did learn the Mexican government has declared martial law and closed its borders."

"Completely?"

"Yes. Supposedly millions of refugees are stacked up on the American side with no hope of entry."

Jake shook his head. "What a mess. I feel a little better about our situation now."

"They've deployed the military to guard the borders, and they're using the drug cartels to help elsewhere," added Ashby.

"That explains yesterday," said Jake. "The delays. The phone calls. The whispering. That marina was nothing more than a glue trap for unsuspecting mice, like us."

Ashby kissed him on the cheek and made her way for the stairs. "Well, we're not gonna get trapped again. You know, the whole fool-me-once thing?"

"Agreed."

"Jake, I love you, but I'm going to bed. Wake me when you're ready to head out in the morning."

Jake followed her to the steps, planted a kiss on her head, and whispered, "I love you back."

CHAPTER 21

The Pacific Ocean
Off the coast of Baja California

Jake had just started a pot of coffee as the sun was rising. As the smell of the morning brew floated through the salon and galley, he descended the stairs into the sleeping quarters to wake Ashby. He gently slid in next to her, and they cuddled for a while until Jake heard the three simple beeps indicating the coffee was fully brewed.

Ashby recognized the familiar beeping sound and mumbled, "I. Need. Coffee." Three powerful, yet simple words. Some folks simply cannot start their day without it.

Jake hopped out of bed and fixed Ashby a Tervis Tumbler full of her favorite concoction. Despite the hot brew inside, the insulated tumbler prevented the heat from escaping to burn their hands.

"Enjoy. Take your time getting up. Everything's cool. I'm gonna fire up the engines and get us started on the course we discussed last night. Here's hopin' for a day of smooth sailing."

He kissed her again and bounded up the stairs and through the salon to the sky lounge. Both of them preferred to travel topside to enjoy the feel and smell of the Pacific. Despite the troubles they'd experienced, they continued to enjoy the adventure.

Jake got settled in and slowly pushed the chrome throttles forward, taking the boat up to ten knots. He was still proceeding with fuel economy in mind. They had enough to make the trip to Guatemala and perhaps the port at San Salvador, Nicaragua. Neither would've been his first choices, but Mexico was now ruled out.

Ashby arrived by his side about ten minutes later with a refill of coffee and a platter of various canned fruits. Pineapple, mandarin oranges, and English biscuits from Fortnum & Mason would have to fuel their bodies until lunchtime.

Jake relayed a story from his experience on *Survivor*. "When we were dropped off in Thailand, the two tribes were selected by the two oldest contestants on the show—schoolyard style. I knew my tribe was in trouble early on. The first sign occurred when two female members of our tribe paddled out into the sea to retrieve fresh water from a source designated on an island across a short span of ocean. It should've been easy, but they got lost. Back on shore, our people decided to play coconut golf instead of building a shelter. I didn't want to press the issue because I didn't want to take a leadership role or appear bossy.

"Anyway, that night it rained, was cold, and everyone was immediately suffering. We had no food, were already weakened by being exposed to the elements, and the result was consecutive losses at the immunity challenges."

"But you survived the tribal councils," interjected Ashby, who remembered Jake telling Dusty and Rita about his experiences on the show.

"You know, I adopted a survival mindset and prepared myself to live on that beach for thirty-nine days with absolutely no assistance from anyone, whether tribemates or television production. It's the only way I made it to the merge of the tribes before getting the boot."

"You mentioned they were afraid of your physicality," said Ashby.

"Yeah. In fact, it was the remnants of my own tribe that turned on me. I'd kept them fed for twenty-four days, and the first chance they got …" Jake's voice trailed off as he made a slicing motion across his throat with his thumb. The visual said it all.

"What's the moral of the story?" asked Ashby.

"Trust no one."

Ashby sat a little higher on her side of the bench seat. "No one?"

"Except," he stretched out the word as he began his reply, "the one you love."

Ashby curled her arm through his as they continued along the coast. The sun was fully awake and the seas were relatively calm. It appeared they were set for their first day on the ocean without drama.

Two hours later, Ashby went below to retrieve the charts. She laid them out on the sky lounge's padded cover and studied the shoreline through the binoculars. She'd hoped to identify a landmark on shore to identify their position relative to the end of Baja California, where Cabo San Lucas was located. Instead, she made an undesirable discovery.

"Jake, you'd better take a look at this."

She handed the binoculars to Jake, who had a concerned look on his face. Ashby pointed toward the southeast.

Jake sighed, lowered the glasses, and then raised them to take another look. Spread out in front of them, as far as the eye could see, were more than a dozen Mexican naval vessels. Led by several Sierra-class corvettes, the Mexican Navy was positioning itself to form a blockade around its Pacific coastal waters.

Jake recalled his days visiting the Hunter's Point Shipyard in California, the former naval base. Each year, the U.S. Navy would bring a variety of ships into San Francisco Bay for people to tour. The Sierra-class corvettes stood out in Jake's mind because of their name. Sierra was a childhood sweetheart of his who shared a love of the outdoors, and his father drove a Corvette. The two vehicles were completely dissimilar except in name.

The Mexican Navy used the corvettes for interception of drug smugglers and counterterrorism. It was the most versatile vessel in their fleet, and it was also the most cost-effective since the U.S. government gave them to Mexico at no cost as part of the war on drugs.

Jake checked their course and studied the direction of the oncoming naval fleet. They were destined to meet one another head-on in about an hour.

"They're forming a blockade, using their most versatile ships, where they anticipate activity to be the greatest—along Baja California."

Ashby took back the binoculars and studied the ships. "They look big from here."

"About four times bigger than we are, I think. They're a formidable show of force for anyone dumb enough to cross their line in the sand, or, in this case, the sea."

"What should we do?"

"Mind our business and keep on our heading, although I plan to veer a little westward to avoid any appearance of challenging them."

"Challenge?"

Jake started to laugh. "Poor choice of words. How about *invading their personal space?*"

Ashby gave him a playful slug, as his use of sarcasm under the circumstances was only marginally funny.

The two sat in silence for the next forty-five minutes as the ships continued their northwesterly course. Jake turned off the autopilot and adjusted his course to provide the ships a wide berth. There was no sense in garnering unwanted attention.

The first of the corvettes passed a mile to their east. The two-hundred-forty-foot-long vessels easily cut through the waves at about twenty knots. Jake studied the first ship in amazement, looking at their massive naval guns on the foredeck that were capable of engaging both air and surface targets.

"Jake, look!" exclaimed Ashby as she swung her body toward the south. "Do you see the smaller boats? They came out of nowhere."

He focused the binoculars on two smaller vessels speeding directly for them. "Maybe they are getting out of the wake of the larger ships or have been run out of Mexico's territorial waters."

Jake shrugged after he made the statement, not wholly believing that was the case. He handed the binoculars to Ashby, who inched toward the open window at the front of the sky lounge.

"I'm gonna adjust our course to a more south-southwest direction. Let's give these guys some room."

As Jake turned the wheel, he also provided more throttle to the engines. He was becoming nervous and wanted to get out of the way.

"They're turning with us. Jake, they look like they're trying to intercept us!"

"What for?" Jake responded in frustration, not expecting an answer. Instead he adjusted his course again, pointing almost due west.

Ashby yelled excitedly, "They turned toward us again! They're trying to chase us down!"

"Can you make out what kind of boats they are?" Jake asked.

"Fast ones."

CHAPTER 22

The Pacific Ocean
Off the coast of Baja California

The Mexican Navy was designed for one purpose—fight the drug trade. Its funding over the last several decades came through Washington and the United Nations, at the encouragement of the UN's biggest benefactor, the United States.

Designed to patrol its coastal waters, the Mexican Navy frequently encountered formidable, oceangoing powerboats capable of speeds nearing one hundred miles per hour. These vessels had advance electronics enabling them to travel at night without running lights to avoid visual detection.

The Mexican government's best weapon against the capabilities of these modern-day *rumrunners*, the historic term used for the ragtag fleet of fishing boats that used to bring illegal alcohol into the United States from the Caribbean during Prohibition in the 1920s, was the Defender B-class response boat.

Deployed by the Mexican Search and Rescue Unit, it was capable of reaching speeds approaching forty-six knots, or fifty-three miles an hour. They were slower than the powerboats that traveled up the Pacific coastline of Baja California, but they were equipped with a fifty-caliber Browning M2A1 machine gun on the bow and an M240B belt-fed machine gun at its stern.

Jake didn't take the time to identify the types of boats pursuing them as he gave the Grand Banks 60 full throttle and steered on a due west course. The large motor yacht began to vibrate somewhat as it approached its top speed of thirty-six knots.

The patrol boats that pursued them stayed directly behind them, riding parallel to one another as their bows broke through the gentle waves of the Pacific. Jake set the autopilot to maintain the westerly course and then asked Ashby for assistance.

"I'm not messing around again. I need you to watch the instruments and the compass. I need to get my gun."

"Jake, your rifle is on the bench seat," said Ashby, pointing to the M16.

"No, I need my hunting rifle. It has a better scope, too."

Jake bounded down the stairs into the salon and opened the upright cabinet where the guns were kept. He reached for his newest hunting rifle, the Browning X-bolt Hells Canyon model chambered in .300 Winchester Magnum. He'd used this rifle to take down an elk from one mountain ridge to another.

From the top shelf of the cabinet, he grabbed a bundle of cloth containing his new scope, a Vanguard Endeavor. It provided him consistently clear resolution and was ideal for weather resistance, which worked well today, as the boat was kicking up a lot of sea spray as it raced away from shore.

Jake quickly attached it to the rail and raced back to the sky lounge, where Ashby was watching their pursuers through the binoculars.

She glanced at his gun and then frowned. "They're getting closer, and I've got bad news for you. Their guns are bigger than your guns."

Jake spun around and dropped to a knee, which allowed him to rest the rifle on the half wall surrounding the sky lounge. He adjusted his rifle's optics and focused on the two identical boats pursuing them. They were starting to spread apart to avoid the wake produced by the yacht.

"Mexican Navy? Why are they chasing us like this?"

"Do you think it's because of what happened back at the marina? I mean, we left a pile of bodies behind."

"Maybe, but this seems like a lot of effort for the Mexican Navy to chase us down over a handful of thugs."

Jake looked through the scope again, and he saw a Mexican sailor standing on the bow of his response boat. He was studying Jake through his binoculars and then began to wave his arms to his companion boat. They immediately separated and picked up speed.

"They're gonna flank us!"

"Jake, what do we do? I get it now. Those are *real* machine guns. We can't fight them off."

Jake turned around and walked back to the instrument panel to study the gauges. So far, the Grand Banks was performing up to its full capabilities. Just as he was about to turn around, something glistened in the distance and caught his eye. He raised his rifle once again, but this time pointed it ahead of them, to the west.

"There's a freighter up ahead. I don't know what the Mexican Navy wants with us, but we have to be in international waters at this point, or at least close. If they plan on boarding us, or worse, then I want some witnesses on our side."

"A freighter?"

"Its captain and crew. After what we went through at the marina yesterday, I don't trust anything related to Mexico right now. Maybe the freighter will intervene somehow if these guys overstep their authority."

Ashby shrugged and took the rifle from Jake. "It's all we've got. You navigate, and I'll keep watch on their progress."

Jake glanced back and muttered, "It's gonna be close."

CHAPTER 23

The Pacific Ocean
Off the coast of Baja California

The Mexican SAR Defenders had closed the gap, but Jake was also getting closer to the enormous container ship, which ran on a southeasterly course in front of them. The massive Panamax, a term given to ships capable of travelling through the Panama Canal, was nearly one thousand feet long. The ship was ambling along, making its way to the canal, but its crew was enjoying the spectacle of the chase. They were lined up along the port-side railing, waving and slapping the top of the rail as if they were cheering on a horse in a race.

Jake turned off the autopilot and steered the Grand Banks slightly to the right in order to cross behind the massive ship. He didn't dare cross her bow, deciding instead to take his chances with the wake.

"I don't know for certain, but I'm gonna bet that ship is sailing in international waters." Jake explained his plan to Ashby. "Without our radar, it's impossible to tell where we are in relation to the shoreline."

"If I remember correctly, international waters are twenty-four miles from shore, or something like that. Territorial waters are right along the coastline, but we're so far out now, I can't even see the coast anymore."

Jake guided the Grand Banks to the right one more time. One of the Mexican response boats veered off to the left to cross the bow of the container ship, a move that was sure to anger the captain. The other kept pace with the Grand Banks as she slammed into the first of the container ship's ten-foot wakes.

"Hold on!" he yelled.

The hull crashed through the water, forcing the bow upward, but it quickly corrected and crashed down. Jake turned the wheel to the left as he prepared to ride the wake on the other side of the Panamax.

Ashby yelled excitedly, "Their boat was in the air! I saw its props!"

Jake glanced over his right shoulder and noticed the smaller chase vessel had lost control momentarily, forcing the crew to slow while they righted themselves. He continued forward toward the aft side of the container ship.

"Here we go again!" he shouted as the bow began to rise up the swale until the hull broke the crest of the wake and slammed down on the other side.

"Jake, the crew is cheering us on like it's some kind of game."

Jake leaned forward and saw a dozen or more men waving their arms, encouraging them forward. Jake slowed his speed to mimic that of the container ship. They were riding parallel to one another, barely a hundred feet apart, as the Grand Banks remained in the shadow of the massive vessel.

"They're behind us again!" yelled Ashby.

"In front, too!" Jake hollered in reply.

Ashby went to Jake's side and wrapped her arms around his waist as they waited to be intercepted, boarded, and then—

Suddenly, without warning, they were drenched in water.

The crew of the Panamax ship was using their water cannon anti-piracy system to send a barrage of water over their bow and behind their stern. The volume of water was so large that it caused the Grand Banks to shudder and veer off course slightly before Jake corrected her.

"What are they doing?"

"They're giving us cover! They're trying to help us!" he shouted his reply. Then he pointed to their rear. "Look!"

Another water cannon drenched the Mexican pursuers. Likewise, the cannon used to mask the motor yacht's presence was turned on the response boat. The same approach was being used against the oncoming vessel.

"It's working!" shouted Ashby, pointing to their rear. "They're falling back."

"The one in front just veered off and is turning around!"

The two of them jumped up and down in the sky lounge, fists pumping in the air, and exchanged high fives. They both ran to the back of the sky lounge and saw the response boat turn across the stern of the container ship and disappear. This elicited more joyous hugs.

Jake broke their embrace and said to Ashby, "Let's go thank our new friends." He set the autopilot to match the ship's pace and direction.

He took Ashby by the hand and carefully exited the sky lounge. They eased around the rail onto the foredeck. It was wet, but they were able to keep their footing. High above them, two dozen Asian men were hollering and applauding. Jake couldn't understand anything they said, but they were clearly pleased with their water-cannon assault on the Mexican Navy.

Jake waved to them. "We must be in international waters or they would've never helped us like that."

"They're heroes," said Ashby as she waved also. Then she turned serious. "Now what?"

"Well, I vote we ride alongside for a while to catch our breath and figure out what our options are. One thing is certain, we just burned up a lot of fuel."

CHAPTER 24

The Pacific Ocean
Off the coast of Baja California

The container ship traveled southwest at a slow rate of speed, and the afternoon winds kicked up, making it increasingly dangerous to run alongside the thousand-foot-long vessel. Jake steered away from the ship and slowed the Grand Banks so they could stop and regroup. After confirming there weren't any Mexican naval vessels lurking nearby, they sat down with a cocktail, the laminated charts, and a notepad.

"I can't believe how much diesel we wasted getting away from those idiots." Ashby continued to assist Jake in the calculations, but she couldn't help but complain about their predicament from time to time. "Other than slowing down, what are our options to conserve fuel?"

"There are so many factors to consider. Weight is one of them. We could toss stuff overboard, but other than furniture, we aren't carrying anything heavy that would make a difference."

"Maybe heading due south will help," added Ashby. "We're riding the current and the wind is behind us. If you throttle back slightly, we might maintain sufficient speed to take advantage of the conditions and conserve fuel."

"Yeah, makes sense." Jake sighed and leaned back. He glanced through the salon's windows that had been shot out.

Ashby walked behind him and rubbed his shoulders, trying her best to relieve the stress that had built up inside him. "It'll be all right, Jake. No worries."

Jake reached back to touch her hands and nodded. Jake was still dejected as he stated the obvious, "It's gonna be dark soon. Let me take another look."

He was desperately looking for a bright side to cheer her melancholy mood, and his. He studied the chart and created a makeshift ruler using the cardboard backing of their notepad. He stood over the table and moved the cardboard ruler around, using their approximate location as a point of reference.

"Look at this group of islands." He directed Ashby's attention to a small grouping due west of Puerto Vallarta, Mexico, and south of their present location.

"I can't imagine those tiny specks are inhabited islands."

"I didn't say it was Hawaii," he said jokingly. He pointed to the map. "There are four of them and they're directly in our path to Guatemala. We know we can't stop in Mexico, but I think there's a small marina on this island based upon this symbol. We don't need much fuel to get farther down the coast toward South America."

Ashby took the cardboard ruler and traced an imaginary line to Guatemala. "We have to sail right past them anyway. Can we make it there before dark?"

"No, we'll have another night on the open seas," replied Jake. "We'd be there midmorning tomorrow if we get an early start."

Ashby stood up and shrugged. "Works for me. Another drink?"

"Sure. It's all we've got to pack on calories. I'm losing weight."

Ashby pulled out the shorts she was wearing to reveal a two-inch gap from her waist. "These aren't mine, but I wouldn't have tried to get in them a week ago. Look, they're too big for me."

"We need fuel for our bodies, too," said Jake. He accepted the refreshed drink from Ashby and they toasted.

"To fair winds and a following sea!" Ashby cheerfully raised her glass.

Jake let out a laugh. "Outstanding! Where did you learn that?"

"I think it was in a shark movie or something like that."

"Great," Jake began. "You had to remind me of the sharks."

"Sorry, it's the only toast I know. Let's go topside and enjoy the sunset."

As the big orange ball began to settle over the western horizon, Jake and Ashby were once again reminded that not everything in the world was falling apart. The sea life of the Pacific Ocean continued to carry on their normal duties, to the delight of their onlookers.

Off the port side, hundreds of mobula rays congregated and swam along the yacht. Occasionally, one would launch itself six feet above the surface before plunging back into the water with a splash. Others quickly joined in the fun—jumping, twirling, and belly flopping as they moved southward through the ocean.

Their winglike fins extended to sixteen feet, which helped them rocket upward as they flew into the air.

"This is incredible," said Ashby in awe of the display. "Why do you think they're jumping out of the water like that? They don't appear to be going after smaller fish or birds."

Jake stuck his head over the backrest of the sky lounge. "They're showing off. It could be a mating thing."

"Look!" exclaimed Ashby, pointing to a very small mobula. "It's a baby ray. It's adorable!"

"They're faster than we are," observed Jake as the school began to take the lead. "Look at them go. Hey, they're turning!"

Jake ran to the front of the sky lounge and looked ahead of the boat. He was afraid they were about to run up on something. He was right.

A hundred yards in front of them, a gigantic humpback whale leapt out of the water and crashed downward, creating a huge splash. Jake grabbed for the throttles and slowly pulled them backward until the yacht was drifting on its wake.

"It's a pod!" yelled Ashby as she pointed to a smaller female whale with her calf by her side. "This is beautiful to watch. Listen."

Jake turned off the engines and they were surrounded in silence except for the waves lapping against the side of their boat. Another humpback emerged, his stocky black dorsal coloring blending in with the horizon.

"They're singing," whispered Jake as he pulled Ashby close to him.

"I've never heard anything like it." The male humpback emitted a series of long, higher-pitched whistles, followed by several short, baritone chatters.

"Another one, Jake. They're singing together."

Tears began to flow down Ashby's face as she became overcome with emotion. Then she made a profound statement, which was a reminder that everything in life happens for a reason.

"I hate what has happened to us because of Yellowstone. But without Yellowstone, you and I wouldn't be standing right here, right now, and witnessing this wonderful part of the world we live in."

"And," Jake added, "we might not have found each other."

PART THREE

Isla Socorro, a new adventure

CHAPTER 25

The Pacific Ocean
Revillagigedo Archipelago

Jake yawned as daylight greeted them for another day at sea. He checked on Ashby and then took a look at the makeshift plug in the hull, shaking his head in amazement at the resiliency of their repair. As he entered the salon and made his way to the helm, the sun was peeking over the horizon, its angle of ascent creating a bright glare off the port side of *My Wet Dream*. Jake fired the twin diesel engines. The roar and subsequent rumble shook the motor yacht to life.

"It's a beautiful day for an adventure," Jake said to himself with a renewed sense of purpose as he chose to make his way topside to the sky lounge. The vast Pacific Ocean spread out in all directions, with the water to their south and east sparkling with thousands of twinkles of light reflecting off the waves.

Thus far, the proverbial rocky seas had not been caused by the power of mother nature, but rather by their fellow man. Jake brought the throttles up to a steady ten knots and set the autopilot on a due south course. The twin diesels hummed along, pushing the yacht's bow through the water with a continuous swishing sound.

Jake was relaxed, yet excited about the prospects for their day. In the open water, away from shore, he felt safer and more at ease. Thus far, their troubles had been due to encounters with other people. *Not surprisingly*. His mind wandered to what the day would bring.

By their calculations, they'd be approaching the Revillagigedo Islands within just a couple of hours. The charts and maps indicated a boat launch, not a marina, was located on the largest of the four islands—Isla Socorro.

The small archipelago was made up of four islands in the Pacific approximately two hundred fifty miles southwest of Cabo San Lucas and six hundred miles west of the Mexican mainland. By their calculations, it was the closest land to where they'd encountered the Mexican Navy.

The largest of the four islands, Isla Socorro, pronounced so-KO-ro, took its title from the *Virgin María del Socorro*, which translated to Mary of Perpetual Succour, the Spanish word for help and relief.

Jake and Ashby had escaped the clutches of the Yellowstone supervolcano and searched for a safe haven ever since. Their hopes were dashed every step of the way, so their journey continued southward toward an unknown destination in South America, where the impact of the ash fallout would be less.

Jake looked through the binoculars and adjusted his vision to concentrate on the first land mass far off in the distance. Jake visibly shook his body to shake off the past and focus on the future. He allowed his mind to daydream for a moment. *Could a deserted island in the Pacific be a safe place to ride out the apocalypse?*

"Hey, Captain! Now that we've crossed the Tropic of Cancer, I come bearing gifts from the *coffee belt*," said a cheerful Ashby as she bounded up the stairs to join Jake. She stood on her toes to give him a kiss before handing him a tumbler of coffee. "I'm surprised you didn't make it already. You feelin' okay?"

"Yeah, I'm fine." Jake hesitated as he replied, "I guess, well, I was saving it."

"Saving it for what?" asked Ashby.

"Well, just in case we couldn't get any more," said Jake as he tapped the ship's wheel nervously.

"Listen, the last time I heard, South America was full of coffee beans. We may run out of food, but coffee will be everywhere to keep us jacked up!"

Jake laughed and took another sip. "Take a look. One of the islands is coming into view."

Ashby brought San Benedicto into focus. Her geology background identified its origin immediately—volcanic.

"Can you imagine what it was like for the early explorers who ventured out into the unknown? They would sail until they discovered land. They'd chart the islands, plant their flag, and maybe even establish settlements."

"My guess is these islands were discovered by Spaniards," added Jake. He was right. The Spanish expeditions of the early sixteenth century had sailed the uncharted waters of the Pacific for decades as they laid claim to Mexico and Central America.

"Wouldn't they be surprised to know this tiny island has more than doubled in size since they found it?"

"What?" asked Jake with a puzzled look.

Ashby handed the binoculars back to Jake, who was able to get a better look as they got closer. She explained what she meant. "Do you see in the foreground how the island is dark with a smooth surface?"

"Yes, and the taller parts of the island behind it have more vegetation, but not necessarily lush."

"Right." Ashby took a seat on the bench and folded her bare legs underneath her. She wrapped the oversized sweatshirt she was wearing around her kneecaps for warmth. "Wait a minute. This is starting to make sense to me now.

"What?" She had Jake's attention.

"I think I know where we are. You're looking at San Benedicto Island."

"How do you know?"

"It's a volcano. I know where all the volcanoes are. It's my job, remember?"

"Oh yeah," Jake said with a laugh. "What's unique about this one? I mean, you immediately recognized it."

"Of course, I've never been here which is why I didn't recognize it on the map," began Ashby, "but I recall from my studies that the island erupted in 1952 as a significant, magnitude three on the VEI. San Benedicto was covered in ten feet of ash and ultimately formed a cone a thousand feet high. What was interesting about this eruption was the lull."

"Lull?" asked Jake inquisitively.

Ashby continued. "After the vent opened and created the new cinder cone, the volcano rested for months. This was considered normal. Several teams of volcanologists traveled from the States and Europe to study the new formation at the north part of the island. Then, unexpectedly, magma broke through the island's southeastern base and started to flow into the sea. This continued for five months until the volcanic system became dormant again."

"Okay." Jake was interested but confused.

"It was San Benedicto, and other volcanic islands like it, that prompted my study of the volcanic system at Kilauea and Mauna Loa. This tiny island was a microcosm of what was happening on the Big Island of Hawaii. The magma chambers of the two volcanoes were interconnected, one feeding off the other, but not necessarily at the same time."

Jake looked at his heading and contemplated taking a hard turn to port to sail away from this volcano as quickly as possible. He was deep in thought as he did the fuel calculations in his mind when Ashby interrupted him.

"Jake?"

"Um, yeah. That's really interesting, Dr. Donovan. Listen, I was thinking, maybe we'd be better off closer to the mainland. I know people suck and they always try to kill us, but I can shoot back at them. I can't take on a volcano."

Ashby snorted out her coffee and began laughing. "Come on, you big baby. San Benedicto hasn't erupted in nearly seventy years. It'll be fine."

Jake turned to Ashby, tilted his head to the side, and raised his eyebrows. "When was the last time Yellowstone erupted?"

She quickly responded before catching herself, "Six hundred thirty thousand—okay, okay. I get your point."

"Exactly," said Jake with conviction. "So would you mind grabbing the charts and our cardboard ruler? I believe it's time to set a different course."

Ashby stood and forced Jake to scoot over on the bench to join him in front of the instrument panel. "No, we're not changing course. If this island, or any of the other four, were to show signs of an eruption, we'd have ample time to leave. I promise."

"We barely got away from the last one," mumbled Jake.

"That was Yellowstone. Big, big difference. Trust me, okay?"

Jake nodded, but he still subtly steered a little to port, giving the volcanic island a little wider berth.

CHAPTER 26

The Pacific Ocean
Isla Socorro

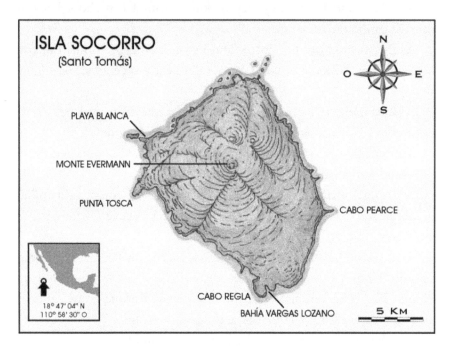

Isla Socorro, like its sister islands in the Revillagigedo Archipelago, rose abruptly out of the ocean as a result of submarine volcanic activity. Its coastline was a combination of steep, rocky cliffs and coves nestled into the fingers that jutted from the shore.

The island had been carved by years of strong winds, which blew from Baja California into the Pacific during the winter. *El Norte*, a combination of winds crossing Mexico from the Gulf, and natural Pacific Ocean wind currents collide midway down the peninsula before spreading toward the west.

In the winter, El Norte can develop rapidly, turning the ocean into a heaving mass of swells and strong winds. In the summer, the effect is minimal, but the sea breezes still manage to bring moisture to Isla Socorro, making the windward side of the island lush with vegetation.

Jake drove directly toward a gap between two rock outcroppings, where he could see a sandy beach. He assessed the natural harbor as a suitable spot to anchor and provide an easy means of going on shore.

Ashby explained the history behind the rock formations as Jake entered the calm bay. "These fingers are created by hardened lava, frozen in time, following an eruption of the volcano."

Jake throttled back and interrupted her. "This is a volcano, too?"

"Relax, they all are. This entire mid-ocean ridge, which runs parallel to Central America, is known as Mathematician's Ridge. Over many thousands of years, submarine eruptions pushed the seamounts from the ocean floor to the water's surface. Some continued to erupt, like Socorro, to form an actual island. Others, like San Benedicto, are strictly volcanic in nature and technically not considered an island."

"Which is more dangerous from a volcanic-eruption perspective?" asked Jake.

Ashby saw the concerned look on his face and she understood. It had taken her many years to get over the eruption of Mount Pinatubo. Oddly, she was taking Yellowstone in stride.

"Typically, the seamounts still have eruptive capabilities. The greater danger from seamounts are flank collapses. As dormant volcanoes get older, the combination of ocean currents and extrusions seeping in the—"

Jake interrupted her. "*No hablo ciencia, por favour.*"

"Sorry, but hey, that's pretty good," said Ashby with a chuckle before continuing. "Sometimes my brain causes me to speak too technical. Extrusive rock refers to the volcanic formations of an island, resulting from the hot magma flowing out onto the surface as lava. That's what you see resulting from the Hawaiian volcanoes. The main effect of the extrusion is that the magma cools quickly under the seawater, making it weaker than the rock formations cooled by the atmosphere above sea level."

"Thank you, Doc. I've got it." Jake slowed the yacht and allowed it to drift deeper into the cove, where a white sandy beach surrounded by palm trees awaited them.

Ashby continued. "Anyway, as the volcanoes get older, the extrusions can weaken, putting pressure on the sides of the volcano above sea level. Under these conditions, a future volcanic eruption would cause minimal damage to the atmosphere compared to the massive tsunamis generated by the landslides from the volcano's structure sliding into the sea."

"So I have to worry about the eruption and a tsunami? Good thing we have plenty of liquor on board."

Jake shut off the engines and checked the gauges on the instrument panel. They were in twenty feet of water. He dropped anchor two hundred feet from shore, knowing that once the anchor caught the ground, the winds would turn the yacht backwards, leaving the stern closest to the beach. Unless the weather turned for the worst, the yacht would float carefree in the middle of the volcano-made safe harbor.

Jake and Ashby immediately noticed the crystal clear, turquoise waters surrounding the yacht. Between the huge boulders and rock formations that created the lava fingers, hundreds of colorful fish swam in schools around them, occasionally darting out of the way of a slow-moving manta ray.

The giant Pacific manta rays, the largest of their type in the world, are slightly different from the mobula rays they'd witnessed earlier. These mantas can grow up to twenty-three feet across, although their average size was fifteen feet. They're not known to fly above the ocean's surface, spending most of their time milling about shallow coves like this one in search of food. Unlike many flat fish, the giant mantas cannot rest on the ocean floor, and they need to swim continuously to channel water over their gills to breathe.

The couple was mesmerized by the large triangular fins as they barely moved to push the ray through the water. The white tips of the rolled fins curled upward from time to time, propelling the ray toward a school of fish before flaring out to force water and prey into the animal's rectangular mouth.

Ashby looked around the cliffs surrounding the beach and into the water below. "Let's go swimming."

Jake smiled. "Seriously?"

"Yeah, these don't exactly look like shark-infested waters. Besides, the fish and the ray wouldn't be this calm. Come on, let's do it."

Jake seemed cautious. "I don't know."

Ashby left him and bounded down the stairs until she'd reached the stern. Jake stood and watched as she gave him a playful grin and took her clothes off before diving into the water. Her white skin and slender figure could easily be seen as she swam around the yacht.

"When in Rome," Jake began with a chuckle as he hustled down to join the love of his life. Within a minute, he too was skinny-dipping in the turquoise waters, surrounded by fish, the elegant ray, and under the careful watch of two pairs of eyes on the cliff above them.

CHAPTER 27

The Pacific Ocean
Isla Socorro

For the first time in many days, Jake and Ashby felt secure in their surroundings, as if the lava fingers had wrapped themselves around the couple for protection. They swam for nearly an hour and eventually made their way to the beach, where their childlike nature took over. Ashby ran into the lush vegetation and emerged with a large palm frond covering her naked body. She jokingly brought a very small one for Jake to use, claiming it had nothing to do with his *size*, and everything to do with her ability to enjoy looking at him.

Jake chased her around and the two adults playfully enjoyed one another before they agreed it was time to explore their newfound paradise. They swam back to the yacht, and Jake worked diligently to deploy the Zodiac while Ashby loaded their backpacks for a trek around the island.

The Grand Banks 60 came equipped with a Zodiac Yachtline inflatable boat, which was at the rear of the yacht, suspended on a hydraulic crane. The five-seat inflatable was powered by a Yamaha, forty-horsepower gasoline outboard engine.

Jake fired up the dedicated generator that powered the hydraulic crane and carefully maneuvered the inflatable boat over the water. The hydraulic lift slowly dropped the Zodiac just as Ashby emerged with their backpacks. She tossed them into the inflatable and towed it around to the stern, where she tied it off.

Jake began to reverse the winch, and Ashby shielded her eyes from the bright sun and looked up to him. "Which weapons do you wanna carry?"

"Our sidearms, your AR and my M16. Grab some extra magazines for each. You never know."

"I'm on it," Ashby responded as she reentered the yacht. Jake gave a final check of their position in relation to where he originally dropped anchor. They hadn't drifted at all.

Ashby reemerged with the magazines stowed in two fanny packs they'd found in a closet. "I've got the keys. Do you wanna change clothes, or are you good?"

Jake was wearing shorts and a tee shirt, together with sneakers. It wasn't exactly ideal attire for a hike, but most of his clothing had been left back at Fruitvale West. "I'm good. Let's go."

Twenty minutes later, they'd pulled the Zodiac onto the beach and tied its bow line to a palm tree's trunk. They fought their way through the thick foliage as they traversed the steep slope that led to the cliffs atop the northern coast of Isla Socorro. Once they arrived at the top, they paused to catch their breath and take in the view of San Benedicto.

Ashby was breathing heavily, bent over with her hands on her knees as she looked down to the yacht. "Well, that was a pain. It's a shame there isn't a trail."

"Actually, I'm glad there isn't one. It would mean we aren't alone."

"The maps showed a dock of some kind here. Someone must live on the island, right?"

"Maybe, or it was abandoned. One thing I learned on *Survivor*, not every island has a freshwater source. From the looks of the slopes coming off the mountain, all of the rainwater may run to the sea. No fresh water means no inhabitants."

"Perfect, just what we were looking for," interjected Ashby. "Deserted. Uninhabited. Lost. Whatever you wanna call it, I'll take it."

Jake reached for her hand and smiled. "I get it, but you can't drink seawater. Let's go look around, but before we do, let's make sure we can find our way back."

"That's easy," said Ashby. She walked away from Jake and stood sideways with her arms spread out, pointing in a north-south direction. "Check it out. The peak of our volcano is in perfect alignment with the two on San Benedicto."

"Wonderful, thanks for the reminder."

They began their hike, walking along the shoreline first as they searched for the dock indicated on the map. It was located on the south side of the island, but Jake was uncomfortable sailing their boat right up to it. He preferred to do a little exploring first, coupled with some surveillance if necessary.

As they traveled south along the east coast of the island, the ground became increasingly rocky with less vegetation. The lush, tropical foliage began to give way to scrubland consisting of cacti and a low-growing flowering plant from the croton genus.

"Look at the elevation difference," Ashby began to explain. "The northern side of the island and the areas at the base of the volcano are lush and tropical. I'm going to guess the peak rises to three thousand feet, maybe higher. The farther south we go, the more desertlike the soil becomes. I believe the winds coming from the north carry moisture that never finds its way to the lower elevations on the south side."

Jake glanced toward the cliffs overlooking the east coast of the island. "It may be flat, but it's not sea level. That's still a substantial drop-off."

"That's exactly what I was talking about when I mentioned seamounts earlier. Water currents and erosion caused the ocean to hack away at the island until it gradually dropped into the sea. Now, turn around and imagine what would happen if the side of the volcano suddenly collapsed into the Pacific as the volcano erupted. The land mass would crash into the surrounding water, creating an enormous displacement of the ocean. That would generate a massive tsunami."

"Like in Japan?" asked Jake.

"No, Japan, and India in '04, was caused by an earthquake along the ocean floor. Tsunamis caused by mountain landslides can be much more devastating. One of these days I'll tell you about Cumbre

Vieja in the Canary Islands. You have no idea—"

Jake immediately protested. "Stop it, Ashby. I'm in my happy place today."

Ashby laughed and gave Jake a playful shove. "Seriously, if Cumbre Vieja were to collapse, the wave of—"

"No!" yelled Jake jokingly as he quickly covered his ears.

They continued to walk, stopping occasionally to retrieve water bottles from their backpacks. The constant sea breeze kept the island cool, but dehydration can occur despite someone not feeling the effects of the warm climate.

"I've got an idea." Ashby changed the subject. "Let's play a game."

"Now?"

"Yeah, you know, as we walk. Or I'm gonna continue to tell you how cool this volcanic island is."

"Okay, okay. What game?"

Ashby laughed. "Let's play—Would you rather, island edition."

Jake caught up to Ashby and kissed her on the cheek. "I really love you, despite your silliness."

She blushed and leaned her head over for another smooch. "I love you, too. Now, play with me. I'll go first."

"Okay, go," said Jake.

"Would you rather be on an episode of *Lost* or *Survivor*?"

Jake grinned. "Easy, the answer is both."

"No, dope. You have to pick one."

"But I was on both. In '04, I was an extra on the fifth episode of season one, which was titled 'White Rabbit.' Matthew Fox, or, you know, Jack Shephard on the show, had a flashback to his past when he went looking for his father in Australia. I played an extra in a bar scene."

"You were in Australia?" asked Ashby.

"Yep, beautiful place," replied Jake. "Okay, my turn."

Ashby waited for her question. She reached behind her to retrieve the binoculars from her backpack.

Jake asked, "Would you rather be alone on a deserted island like

Tom Hanks in *Cast Away*, or with a bunch of misfits like *Gilligan's Island*?"

"Oh, that's an easy one. I'd go crazy being all alone. I don't know if I'd start talking to volleyballs, however. *Gilligan's Island* for sure. Plus, Gilligan was a real cutie."

Jake chuckled. "I think he was gay."

"He was still cute. The professor was all nerdy and boring. The Skipper was too … skippery."

"You drive me crazy," quipped Jake.

"Speaking of *Gilligan's Island*, back at ya. Would you rather— Ginger or Mary Ann?"

Jake laughed out loud. He knew the smart thing to do was tread lightly with his answer, shrugging it off as if wasn't something he'd ever thought about. But Ashby had been teasing him a lot today and had scored several punches in the process. He decided to throw it back at her.

"Ahh, the age-old question, one pondered by many a young man," he began, adopting a serious tone. "You know, sometimes there are choices in life that define you as a man. Do you prefer the sultry redhead with Marilyn Monroe sexiness worthy of a place on your ceiling next to Farrah Fawcett in a bathing suit? Or were you smitten with the girl-next-door charm of Mary Ann, who was cute in her own way, but certainly not the *yahoo, let's get crazy* option that Ginger put–"

"Okay, okay!" said Ashby, raising her voice. "I wasn't looking for a detailed analysis, and I sure didn't expect you to conjure up your teenage-boy fantasies of Ginger on a poster, on your ceiling, looking down—ugh, whatever!"

Jake had to stop as he roared in laughter. He'd gotten the best of Ashby this time. He just hoped he hadn't gone too far.

She stood several paces away from him with her arms folded in front of her. Jake instantly regretted that he might have hurt her feelings. He went to hug her, but she pulled away a little bit.

"Come on, Ashby, I'm sorry. I thought you were setting me up to mess with me, so I played it up too much. Seriously, I'm sorry."

A big smile came over her face. "Ha-ha, gotcha!" She spun away and started running ahead, causing Jake to chase after her.

"Really?" he shouted to her back. "You were acting? That's it. You're gonna pay this time!"

Jake was trotting behind her when Ashby suddenly stopped. He slowed his chase before he crashed into her.

"Shhh," she admonished him to stay quiet. Ashby immediately crouched on one knee and raised the binoculars to her eyes. Jake joined her side.

"Do you see something?" asked Jake.

"Take a look. It's a town or some kind of business. I can't really tell."

Jake took a turn studying the buildings a mile ahead of them. "Looks military," he deduced. "I see barracks, a central office structure, and a circle made of block containing a flagpole."

"Do you see any people?"

"No, and the flag is gone. It looks abandoned." Jake rose from his crouch and assisted Ashby to her feet. He scanned the landscape, looking for any other signs of modernization. Something toward the center of the island caught his attention. "I think I see a landing strip. There's one building there and a wind sock."

He handed Ashby the binoculars and she suggested they check it out first. It might hold some clues as to what the facility was used for. After taking in some more water, the two of them made their way toward the landing strip, intrigued, but with their rifles at the ready.

CHAPTER 28

The Pacific Ocean
Isla Socorro

Jake and Ashby waited fifteen minutes before approaching, taking turns surveilling the facility. There was an airplane hangar adjacent to a single runway, which sat atop a cliff overlooking the ocean. Across the runway was a simple block building with a concrete picnic table in front. There was no signage around the facility, so they assumed it was not a frequently used, public airport.

"Now's as good a time as any," said Jake as he rose out of his crouch and handed the binoculars back to Ashby. She quickly stowed them away and followed Jake through the scrub brush as he trotted toward the back of the hangar. Within minutes they were tucked behind the corrugated steel building, breathing heavily from the jog.

"Jake, can we leave the backpacks here while we look around?"

"Good idea. I'll take the far side and you take this one. Wait until you see me before you break cover. Look for an entry door to the hangar if the hangar isn't open air."

"Got it," said Ashby as she eased past him and slowly walked along the side of the building with her rifle ready. Jake moved quickly but quietly to get into position. At the corner of the building, he was in view of the block building, so he ducked into a crouch. He peered around the corner and saw that Ashby had done the same.

He held his fist out where she could see it. He counted down their approach to the front door, which was closest to Jake. Five fingers, then four, three, two, and one.

Ashby rushed in front of the building toward Jake, and he rolled around the corner with the rifle in his right hand, and using his left, he tried the knob. It was locked.

Jake retreated back to the side of the building, and Ashby ran to join him, tucking herself around the corner by his side.

"I really think the place is abandoned," said Ashby as her eyes darted around the runway and back to the block building. "Let's go check it out."

"I'm not comfortable with walking straight across the runway. We don't have any cover."

"I know, Jake, but look around. It's flat as a board and the plants barely reach our knees. I suppose we could get our backpacks and act like lost hikers."

"Or we just march across the concrete, rifles ready, and shoot anything that moves."

"Not a bad option." Ashby was cool and calm in her demeanor. As far as life in a post-apocalyptic world was concerned, she was more battle hardened than most.

Jake thought for a moment and agreed there wasn't a better option. Also, he was fairly certain the building was abandoned. He decided to go with Ashby's plan, with one caveat. He wanted to fire a round or two at the building to flush out any occupants. If there was no movement, then they'd proceed. If someone fired back, they'd grab their gear and run.

He aimed toward the building and fired over its roof. There was no reaction of any kind. This time, he aimed and plugged the wall to the right of the doorway with a round. Plaster splintered as the bullet embedded in the block.

Nothing.

Jake exhaled. "I think we're good."

"Leave the backpacks for now?"

"Yeah. Clear first; gather our gear later."

Still being cautious, they spread out and walked briskly toward the building. They covered the six hundred feet across the runway in a minute and arrived simultaneously. Pressed against the wall, Jake held his hand up, instructing Ashby to wait.

He pounded on the door and shouted, "Open up! *No problemo! Ola!*"

They waited for a moment and Jake shouldered his rifle. He waved for Ashby to join him. He turned and whispered, "I'm gonna bust the doorjamb open with my knife. Have your rifle ready and cover me."

Ashby nodded and raised her AR-15 and followed him to the door. Jake stuck the knife blade into the doorjamb near the lock and hit the end of the handle with his fist. Then, using his body weight, he pried the lock open and the door broke free.

Jake pulled his sidearm and kicked the door open. It swung violently into the room, with the door handle crashing into the cinder-block wall. With his weapon leading the way, Jake swung his arm from one side of the small single-room building to the other.

"Clear."

Ashby followed him in and looked around. "Well, this is exciting."

"Yeah, not a whole lot to it."

Jake tried the light switch. A bank of fluorescent lights flickered and then turned on fully. He walked around the desk and looked underneath. He reached down and found some CAT 5 cable, commonly used for internet connections.

"Hang on," he said as he slipped out the door and walked around to the back of the building.

"What were you looking for?" asked Ashby when he returned.

"Two things—power and internet."

"Well?"

"Bingo on both, I think. There are solar panels, which accounts for the electricity. I assumed they needed internet to monitor radar and incoming flights, and I was right. There's a dish on the back side of the roof."

Ashby looked under the desk and dropped to one knee. She fiddled with the wires and began to pull one of them out. She traced it behind the desk and followed it into a closet, which was locked.

"Jake, do you see any keys in the desk?"

Jake rummaged around and searched through the drawers. "Nope, but I've got this." He pulled his knife again and popped the door lock. The closet opened easily, revealing its contents.

Jake called out the contents. "A printer and here's the modem. We've got maps, some office supplies, and several DeWalt battery-operated tools. Good stuff."

Ashby reached into the closet and touched the modem like she was petting a kitten. "Are you kidding? Internet makes this one heck of an island paradise."

Jake walked outside to the front of the building. It was midafternoon. Ashby joined his side after pulling the door closed, although it wouldn't shut entirely.

"There's gotta be more to this place," Jake began. "If it's not part of a drug-smuggling operation, it may be private. I've seen no indication of anything military."

"I vote that we check out the hangar. What if there's an airplane in there? Think about the possibilities."

Jake looked at Ashby and beamed. "You are amazing, Dr. Donovan. I didn't know you could fly."

Ashby furrowed her brow and started walking across the runway. She pronounced with confidence, "I can't, but with the internet, I can learn how."

Jake shook his head, rubbed the sweat off his face, and jogged to catch up with *Amelia Earhart*.

They broke into the hangar, and unfortunately, *or fortunately*, depending upon how Jake wanted to look at it, there wasn't a plane inside. There was, however, an electric Cushman golf cart that was fully charged.

Jake rolled up the hangar door and pulled the golf cart out while Ashby retrieved their backpacks. Minutes later, the hangar door was closed and they were cruising down the runway toward the south side of the island. When they came upon a winding, paved road, the duo knew they were on the right track.

CHAPTER 29

The Pacific Ocean
Isla Socorro

After traveling four miles up and down gently sloping terrain, they crested a slight rise, where Jake pulled the Cushman to an abrupt halt. Below them, a compound consisting of a variety of buildings came into view. Jake quickly put the golf cart in reverse, and they found a hidden place from which they could observe the facility.

"What kind of place is this?" asked Ashby after she'd taken a turn with the binoculars. "Research facility? It sure isn't a resort hotel."

"It might be military," said Jake. "Toward the center of the complex is a circle drive and a flagpole. Governments like to plant flags. It's their way of pissing on something."

"That's colorful," said Ashby with a chuckle. "But I get it. Governments are territorial, and they like to let everyone know it. If I recall correctly, San Benedicto is part of Mexico. You have to assume this is, too."

"Yeah, maybe a naval outpost, or coast guard if they have one."

Jake nodded to Ashby and they retreated to the golf cart, which was out of the compound's view.

He continued. "Well, we have a couple of options. We can keep doing surveillance, maybe move around the perimeter to get different angles, but it's gonna be dark before we know it, which means getting back to the yacht will be difficult."

"Or," Ashby interrupted, "we can go in guns blazing like at the airfield."

Jake shook his head from side to side and frowned. "No. No guns blazing. That worked in a small location like—"

"Jake, relax. I'm just kidding. Listen, I think the whole place is abandoned. What if we ease into the place in the golf cart. Because it's electric, it's quiet. Sure, at some point we could proceed on foot, but I don't think anyone down there is just gonna shoot at us because we borrowed their golf cart."

"I would," Jake replied dryly.

"No, you wouldn't. Come on. Let's check the place out. Remember, if there are a few military guys around, we can buy an awful lot of diesel with our dollars and gold. It's not their diesel, and besides, they may not have received the memo that the American economy has collapsed."

Jake thought for a moment and then acquiesced. "Okay, but you drive. I wanna be ready to return fire if necessary."

They began the slow ride down the hill until they were a hundred yards away from the compound. Ashby pulled to a stop so they could take in the compound's layout.

The facility was carved into a hillside with simple block buildings constructed in the center and several residential-looking bungalows constructed up the hill. Down the hill from the center, simple block buildings with metal roofs stretched toward the south shore of the island. Every structure was made of block and stone that had been painted a bright white. On the hillside above the last of the buildings was a forty-panel solar array together with a ground-level water tower.

On the top of the main buildings in the center of the compound were a variety of antennas, all pointed in different directions. There was a large Doppler radar on the hillside between their position and the complex.

"Very interesting," said Jake. "I love seeing the solar power and the water tank. What I haven't seen as of yet is movement. There doesn't appear to—"

Ashby interrupted him by touching his arm. "Shhh, I heard someone."

Jake readied his rifle and tensed his muscles. "Was it a—?"

They heard a scream followed by a young girl shouting, "*No, señor! Déjame solo!*"

Another voice yelled, "*¡Basta! ¡Por favor.*"

Ashby gripped the wheel and started the golf cart down the road again.

Jake grabbed her leg and squeezed her thigh. "Stop. We can't just barrel in there like this."

"Jake, they're in trouble. That was a young girl's voice!"

"I know, but we have to be smart," began Jake. He pointed toward the Doppler radar structure. "Ease over there and we'll find out what's going on. Okay?"

Ashby nodded and turned off the road toward the small block building with the geodesic-dome-shaped structure on top. They parked behind the building and out of view.

"Nooo!" A girl was pleading for mercy.

"Jake!" Ashby was ready to go.

Jake pulled extra magazines out of the backpack and stuffed them into Ashby's pants pockets. "Sidearm in the front, AR-15 in the back. Remember?"

She nodded as Jake did the same with his extras. He checked his knife and adjusted his paddle holster. They were ready.

Jake led the way down the hard-packed surface to the back of the first block building. He could hear the sound of male voices, but he couldn't make out the language they were speaking. It wasn't English or Spanish.

He glanced around the corner and saw that they could make their way to the next building undetected. He waved his hand, and Ashby followed him quietly through the shadows of the taller structure until they reached a small courtyard between the two. A sidewalk connected them, with a covered awning. A sign on the door of the taller building read *la despensa*.

"*Vieni qui ragazza! No combattimento!*"

"He's Italian," whispered Ashby. "I recognize it from my trips to Mount Vesuvius."

Jake nodded and whispered back, "We need a better look. I think they're in the courtyard, maybe near the main building. Let me work my way around these buildings and I'll be back."

He took off as the game of tug-of-war continued on the other side of the buildings. Jake wasn't sure, but he thought he could make out three male voices in Italian and more than one Spanish-speaking child. He didn't understand Italian, but he could clearly sense *male predator* in their tone.

With a new sense of urgency, Jake darted from building to building until he could get a full assessment of what was happening.

CHAPTER 30

The Pacific Ocean
Isla Socorro

Jake returned to the side of an anxiously awaiting Ashby. "Okay, here's what we've got. There's a grassy courtyard just below the steps leading up to the compound. My guess is that it's used for receptions or even for athletic activities like playing soccer because there are several soccer balls scattered about."

"Are they attacking the girls?"

"No, not yet. I think that's the plan. They're toying with them right now."

Ashby stood out of her crouch and gritted her teeth. "Let's take care of this."

Jake reached for her arm and pulled her back beside him. "Hold on, we will. Let me finish."

"Okay." Ashby nodded sheepishly.

"The good news is that the compound appears to be abandoned. The only signs of life are three guys holding guns and a handful of Mexican kids. I counted two teenage girls and three much younger boys."

"Where are their parents? Where do they live? Why are there Italian men with guns?"

Jake looked into Ashby's eyes and gave her a knowing smile. "These are all questions that ran through my head. First things first. We need to get these kids away from these scumbags. While one holds a pistol on the young boys, the other two are harassing the teenage girls, pawing at their clothes in between taking swigs of alcohol out of a clear bottle."

"Sambuca," interrupted Ashby.

"What?"

"Sambuca was the favorite liqueur of Italian men," replied Ashby. "They drank it straight or in their coffee. Are they drunk?"

"I can't say for certain, but they are full of themselves. Here's what I want to do."

Jake laid out the plan and Ashby provided her own twist. When they agreed on the timing, Jake headed back to his prior observation point, and Ashby steadied her nerves. She made her way to the building closest to Jake's position, but in clear view of the attackers.

She took a deep breath, removed the hair clasp that held her ponytail together, and bent over at the waist to shake her long hair. Ashby was going to be the bait.

As instructed, she slid her paddle holster to the back side of her hip so that it would be out of view as she entered the clearing. She unbuttoned two more buttons on her blouse and allowed a little more skin to show. She was ready.

Ashby strolled out from between the two buildings and stood near the top of the block steps overlooking the courtyard. The young boys saw her first and appeared to snap their heads toward her in unison. By the slow reaction of their captors, Ashby presumed they were drunk.

"*Hola! Cómo estás?*" Everybody knew how to say hello, how are you, in Spanish. It was a universally understood phrase, even for drunken Italian men.

Ashby glanced to her right and saw that Jake had his rifle pointed toward the men who had been manhandling the young girls.

"*Ah, bellissimo!*" shouted one of the men as he drew his fingers close to his lips and then spread them toward the sky. He pushed the Mexican girl onto the ground next to the young boys. They immediately huddled together and began to cry. "*Vieni qui angelo!*"

The man tucked his revolver in his waistband and began climbing the steps toward Ashby, who remained stoic. The idea was to separate the three men and keep the children out of the line of fire.

Ashby tried to recall any Italian from her days studying Vesuvius.

It might not be grammatically correct, but the idea was to buy Jake time to take the shot.

She tossed her hair behind her head with her left hand and feigned a sly, seductive smile. *"Ah, bella signore."*

The man approached the first step and said, *"Sì, mio angelo."* Behind him, Ashby saw movement as the girl being held by the third man twisted her way free and started to run.

At that moment, the events occurred at the speed of sound in Ashby's mind. Jake's rifle erupted in a rapid-fire barrage of bullets, riddling the third man's body and spraying blood all over the screaming children and their captor.

Ashby's assailant didn't hesitate as he raised his gun toward her. She had drawn her weapon and was prepared to shoot when the man's head exploded from two more rounds fired by Jake.

The air was filled with screams and crying, creating enough chaos for the final attacker to begin his escape. He started running across the soccer field, dropping his bottle of liquor and firing wildly over his shoulder with a handgun.

Jake leapt over a half wall and jumped from the road to the grassy courtyard, skipping the three steps in between. The man was running faster now, and he'd run out of bullets, as his repeated pulls on the trigger only resulted in metallic clicks.

Fearing for his life, he ran faster and Jake chased after him. Then, unexpectedly, Jake stopped, fell to one knee, and trained his rifle on the man. He squeezed the trigger, firing four quick rounds in rapid succession.

All four found their mark, penetrating the man's back and blowing through his chest on the other side. As if suspended in animation, his arms flung out, and then he appeared to make a swan dive onto the paved road that encircled the courtyard.

Ashby turned her attention to the children, whose eyes and mouths were wide-open in shock. She walked toward them, but they were so frightened, they jumped out of their huddle and began to run up the stairs past her.

"Wait! Wait! We just want to help you!"

But they kept going. Ashby tried to jog after them; however, the combination of fear and youthfulness was no match for her. The children disappeared between the buildings as Ashby stopped and hung her head. Then, suddenly, one of the young boys returned to the corner and spoke two simple words to Ashby that brought tears to her eyes.

"Gracias, señorita."

CHAPTER 31

The Pacific Ocean
Isla Socorro

Ashby wiped the tears from her eyes. She'd taken a couple of steps toward the young boy, but he darted out of sight. By the time she reached the corner of the building, they had disappeared like ghosts. Ashby started toward the courtyard, and she saw that Jake was still kneeling in the grass. Concerned, she ran down the stairs and raced toward him.

"Jake, are you all right?" she yelled as she ran. Apprehension overcame her body. *Was he shot by the escaping gunman? Did one of the wild shots he took found Jake?*

He didn't respond.

Ashby approached him cautiously, scanning his body for evidence of blood and then studying the grass beneath him as well.

Nothing.

"Jake, honey, are you okay?" she asked again.

His body was shaking, so she put her arm around his shoulders. She gently removed his rifle from his hands and whispered in his ear, "It's over. We're both okay."

He nodded his head and then buried it in his hands. He began to sob.

Ashby wasn't sure what to do. Jake had killed a lot of people since their first encounter at Pressley Farm. Too many to count. She couldn't understand why these three bothered him so much. They deserved it. Ashby would've gladly done it herself.

No, this was something else.

She stood and looked around to make sure they were alone. It was an eerie feeling. Other than the three dead bodies lying around the courtyard, the entire complex was devoid of other human beings. She looked at the soccer balls and managed a chuckle despite the stressful situation. There they were—Jake and Ashby's *Wilsons*, the equivalent of Tom Hanks's volleyball.

But they weren't alone, were they. There were children, and probably adults to go with them. There was another settlement on the island.

She turned her attention back to Jake, who'd stopped crying. "Jake, please talk to me."

He finally responded, "I shot the guy in the back. I didn't even hesitate. I shot him in the back while he ran away."

"Hey, he was shooting at you, too, you know. You had every—"

"I heard the clicks. I knew he was out of ammo. I chased him down and executed him."

Ashby tried to console him. She'd never seen him this distraught except after Rita's death. He'd taken that hard and personal. This thug didn't deserve anyone's anguish.

Jake continued. "I couldn't let him live. He had to be eliminated. He couldn't live to fight another day."

Ashby placed her arms under Jake's and forced him to stand. For a minute, they held each other tight without saying a word. The rules of life, and the standards of morality, had been blurred after Yellowstone. As lawlessness spread, a simple rule trumped all others—*survival of the fittest*.

Jake recovered emotionally, at least enough to get his head together. He and Ashby worked together to move the bodies from the open courtyard and into a thicket near the road that descended toward the south shore of the island. They spoke very little, but Jake seemed to brighten his spirits when Ashby told him about the young boy returning to thank her.

"See, that's what it's all about now," began Ashby. "This may sound corny, but anytime we can protect *the innocents*, even if it means taking another person's life, good prevails over evil."

They walked back into the middle of the courtyard and looked around, taking in their surroundings for the first time.

"We need to take the time to clear the buildings," said Jake. He looked toward the sky and checked his watch. "It's gonna be too late for us to return to the yacht, even with the golf cart available to us. If the buildings are empty, which I suspect they are, we'll bunk in here for the night."

"Okay, but I've got two things. One, the children obviously aren't residents of this compound. They spoke Spanish. They came here to play because the courtyard is a perfect soccer field. And they ran off toward the north, running past me to get there. If they lived in the other direction, it would have been easier for them to go that way."

Jake nodded. He was back. "The bad guys ran toward where the dock was shown on the chart. Whadya wanna bet they have a boat down there?"

"Well, if they have a boat, there may be more of them, right?" asked Ashby.

"I see where you're coming from," replied Jake. "The dock's not that far from here. I have no doubt they would've heard my rifle. Yet the cavalry never came. Let's drive the golf cart down the hill and take a look. We don't have to get too close unless we want to finish the rest of these Italians off."

"You recognized the Italian dialect?" asked Ashby.

"Oh yeah, I watched the Godfather movies a million times as a kid. It was my mother's favorite."

"Okay, then, *Don Jacobi*. Let's go."

After confirming that the only boat parked by the dock was an inflatable similar to theirs, they drove all the way to the bottom of the hill and parked the golf cart. Jake and Ashby were still cautious in their approach just in case there was someone left behind to watch over their boat.

Fifteen minutes later, they were satisfied that no one else had accompanied the Italians onto the island. Ashby pulled out the binoculars to determine where the men had come from. Jake walked out onto the dock and pointed to the diesel fuel pumps on the dock. They were padlocked, which could present a problem, but he'd find a solution. He commented that the tanks most likely had diesel in them; otherwise there would be no reason to lock them up.

They reached the end of the dock, and Jake began to scan the ocean, looking for a larger boat. To the southwest of the island, he could barely see the bow of a large trawler or an older passenger ship. He handed the binoculars to Ashby, who took a look also.

"It's too small for a cruise ship and too crappy looking to be a yacht," she commented.

"These guys were pretty crappy," mumbled Jake. "The only way to get a good look is to walk to the west side of the island, but it's too late in the day for that."

"Do you think we're safe? At least for now?" asked Ashby.

"Here's what I think. These three clowns brought their booze on shore to party. They came upon the kids and young girls, which turned them into potential rapists until we came along. My guess is their buddies on that boat won't care if they come back tonight or not."

Ashby put her arm on Jake's shoulders. "They'll come looking at some point, don't you think?"

Jake nodded, looked around at the rocky bluffs surrounding the dock, and smiled. "Yeah, and when they do, they'll see what happens when people drink and drive on the water."

CHAPTER 32

The Pacific Ocean
Isla Socorro

Jake and Ashby were on edge as they returned to the compound. An eerie calm had replaced the screams of the children and the gunfire that ended three men's lives. Seabirds could be heard singing and chirping in the distance as night began to fall over the island named for the Virgin Mary, Our Lady of Perpetual Help in the Roman Catholic religion.

"Let's start with this main building in the center," said Jake as he led Ashby through the courtyard and up the short set of stairs that doubled as a retaining wall. "We need to clear all the buildings while keeping an eye out for others. Those kids may be back, with their parents. Then there's the boat people, whoever they are."

"You were right earlier," began Ashby. "It's too late to go back to our yacht. I don't wanna trudge through the jungle on the other side in the pitch dark."

"Yeah, I'm tired of surprises." Jake approached the double set of doors with his knife drawn. There were glass panes inserted into the upper half of each door, but he preferred not to break them out. He elected to jimmy the lock instead, which he did easily.

The smell of stale office air forced its way into their nostrils as they entered the dimly lit space. Jake ran his hands along the wall until he found a bank of light switches. He flicked them on in rapid succession with his left hand.

"Let there be light," he quipped as the reception area lit up. Four desks were lined up along the walls of the open space, each ostensibly guarding an office behind it. At the end of the rectangular space was a credenza with several framed photos and certificates standing at attention.

On the wall above the credenza was a large photograph of a man in naval dress whites in front of a battleship. Ashby walked closer to get a better look and pointed to a brass nameplate affixed to the walnut-colored frame.

"*Contralimrante Carlos Lanz, Comandante Isla Socorro.*"

"Obviously, Carlos is the boss man," said Jake with a chuckle. "He's got a lot of stars and quite a few ribbons on the shirt. My guess is he's an admiral, or something equivalent, in the Mexican Navy."

Ashby gave the photograph another look and turned around. "He's definitely the commander of Isla Socorro. That's a big ship, Jake. Way bigger than what could be parked at the dock we just left. Do you think there's another dock on the island? Maybe where the Mexican families live?"

"We're gonna find out tomorrow," he replied as he turned his attention to the offices. He moved through the hallway, reaching into the office doors and turning every light on in the building. "First order of business is to find the keys to the various buildings. The tall building behind us appeared to be a warehouse or storage facility of some type. Plus, our *comandante* probably has a nice bungalow for his quarters. We could stay there for the night."

"Okay, I'll start in here while you check out the offices," said Ashby.

The two of them set about searching for anything that might explain what the naval base was used for, and where its occupants went. The keys remained elusive as they focused their efforts on desk drawers and file cabinets. Ashby made the first meaningful discovery.

"Hey, I found a logbook, I think."

Jake joined her at the desk closest to the commander's office, which was designated by a brass plaque on the door. Ashby opened up the simplistic record book and pointed to dates.

"Look at the dates," said Jake. He pointed to the handwritten notes on a page that preceded a series of blank pages. "They ended their entries about a week ago. The handwriting isn't bad, but the words are just gibberish to me."

"Same here," began Ashby as she ran her index fingers down the page. "Maybe we can make something of it. Fortunately, both English and Spanish use the regular alphabet. Also, almost half of all words in English have a related word in Spanish. If we can make out a few words, it'll give us an idea of why they left."

"You're pretty smart for a doctor," said Jake as he bent over and kissed Ashby on the top of the head.

"Yeah, well, I've learned a lot of new stuff the last few weeks. Might as well try my hand at Spanish."

She found a highlighter in the desk drawer and began to use the fluorescent yellow pen to mark over certain words that appeared familiar in English.

Evacuación. Inmediatamente. Completar. Todos. Frontera, No entrada. Indefinido. Muchos años.

"Whadya make of that?" asked Jake.

Ashby muttered the words. "Evacuation. Immediate. Complete. Total. Indefinite."

"It sure seems they bugged out in a hurry," said Jake. "Whatever the reason, it wasn't important for them to take anything with them."

Ashby continued, "*Frontera, No entrada. No entrada* means no entrance or entry. But *frontera?*"

"Frontier, maybe?" Jake added his contribution to the mystery. "Frontier, boundaries, borders. They closed their borders, and the navy recalled everyone on the base to assist."

"*Muchos años,*" Ashby repeated. "*Muchos* means many. *Anno Domini*—Year of our Lord in Latin. *Años* refers to years. They expect to be gone many years."

Jake pulled over a chair from the other desk and sat down. "They've abandoned the place, at least for a while."

"Maybe even a long while," added Ashby. "Are you thinking what I'm thinking?"

"Yeah. I think we could take care of it for them until they return."

"Me too."

CHAPTER 33

The Pacific Ocean
Isla Socorro

Isla Socorro, located nearly three hundred miles southwest of Cabo San Lucas, was discovered by Spanish explorers in the early sixteenth century. The naval station was established as a small outpost in 1957 and eventually grew into a recently renovated base, which included housing for over two hundred naval personnel and their families.

The dock constructed at the southernmost part of the island, *Cabo Regla*, was used to bring in personnel and materials for the construction of the base. Over the years, the base had expanded to become a completely self-sufficient facility, with supply ships running weekly between the mainland and the base to provide food.

Electricity was generated by solar arrays spread throughout the compound. Fresh water was procured and stored with a massive rain catchment system stretching to the northern parts of the island. The elevation of the island was ideally suited for a gravity-fed water source down to the base.

Until the Mexican Navy established a foothold on the island, it was uninhabited except for a variety of birds and small mammals. The ocean surrounding Isla Socorro was teeming with a wide variety of fish. The sea-life-rich waters were the home to world-class yellowfin tuna and wahoo. In recent years, the Mexican government had closed the waters to commercial fishing operations, but limited licenses could still be obtained by charter boats.

Jake and Ashby finally located the keys to the facility in a simple metal wall safe that appeared to be an electrical panel. It took Jake longer to open the ten-by-thirteen-inch cabinet than a full-size door, but eventually it succumbed to the blade of his knife.

"There aren't very many, considering the number of buildings," Ashby remarked as she counted the eight keys on the ring.

Jake led Ashby to the front door and the two stuck their heads out into the night air. "My guess is some of these are master keys. Man, the sun disappeared quickly tonight. I wasn't paying attention."

Suddenly a crackling and hissing sound occurred, causing them both to instinctively duck. Jake raised his weapon and began pointing it from side to side, seeking out any threat.

The source of the odd noise eventually revealed itself as lights came on throughout the compound. Streetlights, together with ground lighting, illuminated the paths between the buildings and the courtyard.

"They must be attached to a light sensor," said Ashby. "Either that or a timer."

"Well, it makes our job easier. Let's check this place out, starting with the building behind us marked *la despensa*."

They made their way between the buildings and emerged at the point where they'd first entered the compound. Jake stood in front of the steel door and tried each of his keys. He was growing frustrated until he inserted the next-to-last key. It slid in smoothly, and with a grin, he hesitated before turning the lock to open the door.

It was dark inside the windowless building, but Jake easily located the light switches. The fluorescent lights flickered while their starters sent a jolt of electricity to the ionized gas inside the tubes. Eventually, all but one warmed to the task, brightening the open room and revealing its contents.

"Hello, Betty!" exclaimed Jake using a little-known phrase claimed by surfers to salute attractive girls on the beach. The saying dated back to the 1940s, but Jake was a throwback kinda guy.

"Who?" asked a curious Ashby.

"Nobody. Never mind. Check this out. We've hit the mother lode."

Ashby walked into the center of the room, in which a single desk stood with a ledger on top. Throughout the space were metal shelves stretching twelve feet high and spaced only wide enough to fit a rolling ladder between them. The shelves were stocked with canned goods, toiletries, and every supply one could want for a long time away from civilization.

Ashby became giddy with laughter. "Jake, if we don't go crazy, we could live here a long, long time with all of this stuff."

"Oh, yeah. We can catch fish for our main meals, supplemented by all of these supplies. Wow!" He paused and then he hugged Ashby, lifted her off the ground, and spun her around a few times.

Jake finally stopped and Ashby struggled to find her balance after the twirl. "We're lucky nobody else has discovered all of this."

"If the navy only bugged out a week ago, the locals, or those guys on the boats, haven't had the courage to look around. It could be those idiots today were supposed to, but they got distracted by their booze-infused attack on those kids."

Ashby nodded and patted Jake on the back. "Lucky for us. For them, not so much. They got what they deserved, Jake."

"Yeah, really, they did," he added before quickly changing the subject. "Let's check out the rest of the compound."

They went back to the administration building to retrieve their backpacks and made their way to the residential barracks. A single master key worked all the locks for the residential housing units.

On the lower level of the compound adjacent to the courtyard, the buildings were divided into six cubicle-style rooms, which shared a bath. The bungalows, which rose up the hill, varied in size and décor, with the first of the buildings belonging to Comandante Lanz, and the remaining bungalows set up for officers and families. Jake and Ashby chose the commander's quarters, which were only slightly better equipped than a Hampton Inn hotel room.

After they got settled in and cleaned up, they made their way to the buildings on the other side of the administration offices. There, they found a Catholic church and a mess hall adjacent to it. Because the solar array provided continuous power to the facility, the mess hall had large walk-in coolers not unlike any restaurant.

"Jake, they have fryers, cooktops, a griddle, and full refrigeration," summarized Ashby. "The walk-in freezer is stocked full of frozen meats and vegetables. The walk-in refrigerator has all kinds of vegetables, although they need to be eaten fairly quickly. They are most likely two weeks old."

Jake wandered around the picnic tables spread about the mess hall. The tables were covered with condiments like salt, pepper, and Cholula sauce. He shook his head and leaned against one of the tables. "I don't know what to say. I mean, part of me wants to jump up and down in excitement. But after what we've been through, I'm afraid to get my hopes up or put down roots. Each place we've found ended up in disaster."

"That's true, but you have to admit it looks good on paper," added Ashby.

"Okay, let's just say we decide to plant our flag here," began Jake, which drew a laugh from Ashby. "Claimed, as they said on *The Walking Dead*."

"Yeah, claimed!" parroted Ashby.

"We have some loose ends to tie up. Tomorrow, we need to get a handle on those ships anchored offshore, after I dispose of their dead buddies, of course. Then we need to bring the yacht around, fill up her diesel tanks, and stock it with provisions."

"You want to have it prepared for a quick getaway, right?"

"Yeah. We can't assume anything. With full tanks of diesel and enough nonperishable food for a couple of weeks, we can be real selective where we go in South America."

"I agree on all of this, and tomorrow it will be our number one priority. What about the Mexican children? Should we locate where they live?"

Jake nodded as he made his way past Ashby toward the walk-in refrigerator. He opened the door and a rush of cold air washed his body. He reached onto a shelf and grabbed a bunch of bananas. After handing one to Ashby, he continued. "That whole situation is odd. If the military pulled out, why wouldn't they take all of the dependents with them. Even if they weren't military, I can't imagine that they left them behind."

Ashby finished her banana and took another one from the bunch. As she peeled the overripe fruit, which was technically a berry, she couldn't help but remain upbeat. "I say we pig out tonight and figure it out tomorrow. I'm withering away."

Jake laughed and gave her a squeeze. "Let me take care of the cooking. You can stand watch out front, but remain in the shadows, okay? We don't know what to expect, and this compound is lit up like a Christmas tree. They'll be able to see us before we'll see them."

She exchanged high fives with Jake and grabbed her rifle together with a large bag of Planters trail mix, which was on a rack near the door. As she headed outside, she shouted over her shoulder, "Don't be shy in that kitchen. I'm ravenous!"

CHAPTER 34

The Pacific Ocean
Isla Socorro

"Ashby, where are you?" shouted Jake as he walked sleepily into the grassy area outside the commander's quarters. After they ate an enormous dinner, he'd taken the first watch because he was still hyped up from the gun battle with the men. After several hours of self-reflection, he justified his shooting of the escaping marauder. The naval compound was like finding a pot of gold at the end of the rainbow for him and Ashby. Isla Socorro had the potential to be their home for a long time, years in fact. In a post-apocalyptic world, if you can't defend it, it isn't yours. Shooting the man as he fled was just one of many acceptable practices necessary to protect what they had.

"I've made some new friends!" she replied from off in the distance.

Jake retreated into the bungalow, finished getting dressed, and grabbed his rifle, a constant companion now. He could hear Ashby speaking in soft tones, but he couldn't hear any responses. Jake thought maybe the children had returned, but when he turned the corner past the administration building and saw Ashby sitting on the benches in front of the mess hall, he managed a smile.

Ashby was surrounded by cats, at least half a dozen by Jake's count. She was hand-feeding them trail mix, careful to keep the raisins for herself. As they accepted the treat, in a show of appreciation, they rolled around on the short Bermuda grass in front of her, and then returned for more.

As Jake approached, the cats scattered, but not far away. They had to conduct their own form of threat assessment.

"Where did these guys come from?" Jake asked as he slid onto the bench next to her. They kissed and he set his rifle on the table before grabbing a seat on the other bench. He took a quick glance around the compound.

Ashby shook the bag, and one of the cats approached her cautiously. "At sunrise, I went into the mess hall to grab a few bananas. As I was leaving, I glanced under one of the stainless-steel tables near the serving stations and saw this bucket of cat treats." She showed Jake the clear plastic container of Little Friskies treats.

"You're feeding the cats?" asked Jake.

"Of course," replied Ashby. "Watch this." She shook the container and poured some into her hand. A beautiful gray and white cat cautiously approached her for a yummy treat. Ashby tossed them a few feet away from her feet. The cat glanced at Jake and then sat down to eat the treats.

"Wow, they're tame," said Jake dryly.

"Tame? They're not mountain lions. Have you never been around cats before?"

"Yeah, as a kid," replied Jake. "I'm allergic."

"Well, that's your loss," said Ashby as she shook the container again. "In the Philippines, there were feral cats everywhere. They're shy and skeptical at first, but eventually they'll warm up to you. Come here, Mama Kitty." Ashby poured some treats into her hand and tossed them in the direction of a particularly fat cat.

Jake laughed. "Mama Kitty? Really? You've named the stray cats. This is hilarious."

"They're not strays, they're feral. There's a difference."

Jake studied the group of felines as they moved a little closer to him. "They look alike to me."

"Stray cats have wandered away from their home and their human companions. They are much more receptive to touch than feral cats. It took me two hours to convince these guys to come anywhere near me. They even rejected the offer of treats. At first they hissed and appeared aggressive, but now they're used to me."

Jake shook his head in disbelief. "Can I feed them?"

Ashby shook the container again and poured some into Jake's left hand. "Don't make any sudden moves, or you'll scare them away. Also, they might scratch you."

"If one of these stray cats scratches me, I'll shoot it," growled Jake. His changed tone of voice brought a quick rebuke in the form of a hiss from one of the felines.

"You will not, or you'll answer to me," said Ashby. "Now, be sweet and give it a try. This is Miss Coon Kitty."

"Good grief," said Jake as he slowly allowed the treats to slip through his fingers onto the ground. The cat, whose markings lent the appearance of a raccoon, approached and began to enjoy the morsels.

"See, that wasn't so bad," said Ashby, sealing up the treat container. "I broke the ice for you. I still have one holdout. Do you see that big boy off to the side near the steps?"

"Yeah. What's his problem?"

"I'm not sure," replied Ashby. "He has yet to come forward."

"Have you named him, too?"

"Yep, that's Big Boy."

Jake leaned back and let out a hearty laugh. This caused the large tomcat to nervously walk back and forth along the top step leading to the courtyard.

"I see why you call him Big Boy, now. He's got quite a set on him."

Ashby slugged Jake, causing him to lose his balance slightly on the bench. "Shut up, Wheeler! He's named Big Boy because he's the biggest cat of them all."

Jake couldn't control himself. "He sure is. I'm thinking he's the baby daddy to most all of these cats. What a set!"

Ashby ignored Jake's laughter and finished feeding the feral cats. After he calmed down, she explained the names and pointed out the features that earned each of them their designations. In addition to the other three, she had Whitey, Button Nose, Happy-Tail / Squishy-Face, and Zero.

In all, seven cats had gathered around her for breakfast. After Jake got his typical manlike reaction and teasing out of the way, he took a moment to admire Ashby for her tenderness while interacting with the cats. It was a new side to Ashby, and just another reason he'd fallen in love with her.

The two of them stood and the cats scampered off. Ashby returned the cat treats to the mess hall and pulled the door closed.

"Don't you want to get some breakfast?" asked Jake.

"In a minute, but there's a building we missed yesterday that you need to see." Ashby pointed across the courtyard toward the barracks. She led the way past the bloodstained steps where Jake had shot the man in the head the day before. Neither of them paused to look at the evidence left behind.

Ashby moved between two of the residential buildings toward a stand of trees sitting atop a hill. "Can you see the door?"

"Yeah. It looks like the entrance to a fallout shelter or some type of underground storage space."

Ashby didn't respond but kept walking. She handed Jake her rifle and retrieved the keys to open up a series of heavy-duty padlocks attached to iron clasps. When the last one was opened, she turned to Jake and reached for the guns.

"We'll leave these out here, just in case," she said to a puzzled, but intrigued Jake. She handed him the flashlight. "There are no lights, so you'll need this."

Jake stuck his head into the dark, cool space and flashed the light along the crates stacked up around the block walls. He didn't have to know Spanish to understand what the words painted on the crates in stencil meant.

"*Precaución. Explosivos.*" Jake read the warnings aloud and entered the cramped space. He dropped to a knee and tucked the flashlight between his chin and shoulder. He carefully opened the top of the crate.

"Dynamite," he muttered to himself. He excitedly unpacked another crate. "C-4 and Semtex. What do they need with this stuff?"

Jake sat back on his heels and scanned the room. There were

several other containers labeled in Spanish that he couldn't understand. He planned on carefully removing everything and taking an inventory.

Jake emerged from the cramped space and wiped the sweat off his brow, not because he was hot, but because he was nervous.

"Jake, there are a lot of crates in there, which I assume are full of explosives."

"Well, some of them might be accessories like blasting caps, wires, timers, etcetera. Still, I'm shocked they left this behind when they left. This is seriously dangerous stuff."

"Why would they have it here in the first place?" asked Ashby before adding, "This base doesn't seem like it was geared up to do battle."

"Beats me, but I'll take it. They obviously had the presence of mind to remove all the firearms and ammunition. Somehow, in their hasty exit, they forgot about the big stuff."

Ashby closed the door and replaced the padlocks, giving each of them a firm shake to make sure they were secure. Jake wandered off toward the south shore and tried to catch a glimpse of the ships anchored to their southwest. The higher elevation brought them into view, but he couldn't make out any details from this distance.

He sighed and turned around. "This island is starting to generate more questions than answers. Let's deal with what we know first, and then worry about the unknown this afternoon. Breakfast, and then we're gonna have a burial at sea."

CHAPTER 35

The Pacific Ocean
Isla Socorro

Ashby led Jake to her second find from earlier that morning, an older Ford Explorer Sport Trac, assembled at the company's plant in Sonora, Mexico, many years ago. The keys were in the ignition, and the motor quickly turned over for Jake. He pulled down to the thicket of trees where they'd hidden the dead bodies from the day before. He made Ashby wait in the truck as he loaded them into the pickup truck's bed.

"I grabbed the Sambuca bottle for you," started Ashby. "What are you planning on doing?"

"Well, the bullet holes in their bodies will be a dead giveaway as to what really happened, pardon the pun. However, I'm counting on the local sea creatures to clean up that evidence for me. As for their boat, I need it to look like an accident caused by too much of that stuff."

Jake pointed to the Sambuca and then focused his attention on the steep decline to the dock. He stopped, made a three-point turn with the truck, and eased backwards onto the sturdy structure until he was alongside the dead men's inflatable. After taking anything of value from their boat, Jake tossed the bodies onto the back in a heap.

"What can I do to help?" asked Ashby.

"Take the binoculars and keep watch at the end of the dock. I don't know if their buddies will be able to hear me drive around, but if they do, we'll need to be ready."

Ashby retrieved the binoculars and began walking toward the end of the dock. "Wait, where are you going?"

Jake pointed over his shoulder. "Do you see those rocks jutting out into the ocean?"

"Yeah, lava fingers," corrected Ashby.

"Today, they belong to the grim reaper," said Jake with a smirk. "Just keep watch, and I'll be back in a bit."

"Jake, maybe we should talk about—" started Ashby before he interrupted her.

"No worries, it's like riding a bike," Jake said with a smile as he untied the lines and fired up the outboard engine. He expertly spun the boat around and headed out to sea. He gave her a thumbs-up and shouted back to her, "This won't take long. Enjoy the show!"

He sped off and glanced back at Ashby one last time before focusing on the task at hand. While he crashed through the waves, he took another look at the ships docked in the distance. There was no sign of any activity as far as he could tell.

Once he was several hundred yards offshore, he slowed to an idle. He hoisted the first of the dead men off the floor and dropped him overboard. A wave quickly swept over the body, causing it to roll under before bobbing back to the surface.

"Yeah, that's the ticket. Do that several more times and you'll look tasty to the fish with lots of teeth."

Jake let out a cackle, clearly recovering from his mental anguish over the kills from the day before. He'd convinced himself these men needed to die, and now he saw them in a different light, much the same attitude he'd taken with the killing of Ken Kennedy.

He allowed the waves to push him closer to shore before he tossed another body overboard. Jake was now covered in blood, but he put the slimy feeling out of his mind. He was preparing himself mentally for the final step in the ruse.

The remaining corpse was the man he'd shot through the head. The explosiveness of his M16's NATO round had obliterated the man's skull when it entered one temple and left through the other side. Jake's plan would cover the manner of death fairly well if he executed the stunt properly.

Drawing back on an experience he'd had while filming a stunt for a B movie, Jake positioned the corpse in the front seat next to the steering wheel. He wrapped the body's arms through the stainless-steel helm and pushed the corpse back against the seat.

Jake took a deep breath and exhaled to steady his nerves. He got his head right and focused. For this stunt, timing was everything, or there would be two bodies crushed in the grim reaper's bony grasp.

"Here we go, boys," yelled Jake, channeling his favorite rodeo cowboy, *Cooper Armstrong*. He forced the throttle down, and the inflatable boat lurched forward. Jake held the wheel to maintain his balance and keep the boat on course. It rode the waves directly toward the target he'd identified from the shore.

He was now a hundred yards away, speeding along at thirty-five miles an hour. The high-pitched outboard engine propelled the boat toward the lava fingers. Jake took another deep breath, but he held it this time.

At thirty yards away, he released the steering wheel and dove overboard, making sure to push as far away from the boat as possible to avoid the propeller. He would know within a second if he was safe, or chum.

He dove underwater, where the sound of the motor switched from a high-pitched squeal to a deep rumble. Jake swam as hard as he could to see the results of his effort. His head broke the surface just as the boat met its fate.

The inflatable crashed into a jagged hunk of hardened lava, crushing the bow and turning the boat upward. The sudden impact caused the man's body to lurch forward, headfirst toward the rocks. Jake couldn't hear the impact of body tissue colliding with the lava fingers at thirty-five miles an hour, but he was able to see the results. It was gruesome.

The boat flipped upward, the outboard engine whirring in midair before it came crashing onto the rocks. It splintered in multiple chunks of aluminum, plastic, and inflatable material as the boat bounced along the jagged rock until it slammed into the cliff.

And as fast as Jake's stunt started, it was over just as quickly. The seas were quiet as blood began to spread across the surface in all directions. Jake immediately recalled the great white sharks feasting on Mike and his buddies.

"It's time to go," he mumbled as he began to swim for the dock as quickly as his legs and arms could move him.

CHAPTER 36

The Pacific Ocean
Isla Socorro

Jake was exhausted after the long swim back to the dock, especially in his heightened state of anxiety. The rush he'd received from pulling off the dangerous stunt had worn off, and now he found himself exhausted as he climbed up the rusted steel ladder onto the dock. As soon as he saw Ashby's face, he knew he'd have a little more work to do.

She stood over him with her arms folded and tears streaming down her face. She wasn't relieved to see him, nor did she appear impressed at the feat. He wasn't sure what to say as he stood on the dock, dripping with water and still somewhat covered in blood.

"Ashby, are you okay? What's wrong?"

She shook her head and wiped her eyes with her arms. She tried to speak and then shook her head as if to tell herself to keep quiet. That was when Jake realized she was angry.

"I'm fine," she finally mumbled. "I'm glad you are, too."

Jake reached out for her and she picked up the pace to return to the pickup truck. Jake exhaled and allowed the last of the spike of adrenaline to subside. He trotted to catch up to her. He made his way in front of her and walked backwards as he spoke. She continued to look past him toward the pickup.

"Come on, Ashby. I'm fine. It wasn't that big of a deal."

Ashby stopped and looked him in the eye. "It was a big deal, Jake. You were flying toward those rocks. What if you had slipped on the wet deck or in some blood? Suppose your foot got caught on a rail and you didn't clear the boat? What if a shark found you before you got back to shore?"

Jake tried to defend himself. "There were no sharks yet. That's why—"

"No sharks? Really?" Ashby thrust the binoculars at him and swung her body around to point into the ocean. Jake took them from her and scanned the surface in the area where the first body had been dropped. The steel gray dorsal fins of several sharks were circling in the water near the first body, periodically nipping at what was left of the corpse floating on the surface.

She walked past him, leaving him to scan for the next body. He only saw a shoe floating there, with the man's lower leg attached to it. Now he understood.

He ran to catch up with her again. This time she stopped and allowed him to hold her. He whispered in her ear repeatedly, "I'm sorry."

After Ashby quit crying, she ran her fingers through Jake's hair and straightened it. She pulled a piece of seaweed out from behind his ear and flicked it on the dock. This drew a smile out of her and a slight laugh.

"I love you, Jake. I need you, too. I know you're capable of doing amazing things, I've seen that. But please don't take unnecessary risks. Something that might sound like a good idea in the moment might get you hurt, or worse. Okay?"

Jake nodded and a few tears rolled out of his eyes. He felt terrible for frightening the woman he loved. He'd never intended to hurt her by crashing the boat. There were certainly other ways to accomplish the goal of confusing any search parties. In that moment, he understood that his life was no longer just his own. It belonged to Ashby, too.

"Okay, I promise. I should've told you all the details before I did it. You could've talked me out of it."

"No, not necessarily," she quickly countered. "Sometimes another perspective is a good idea when you're planning something dangerous. Just don't discount my opinion."

Jake nodded again and they hugged.

Ashby continued. "Now that I've said my piece, let me say—that was amazing! It was like watching a movie. I mean, the body flying out, followed by the boat going airborne. I should've filmed it with my cell phone."

Jake wrapped his arm around her and led her to the passenger door of the Ford. He thought about talking about the rush he'd received during the stunt but decided to let it go while he was ahead. Besides, they had work to do.

He turned the pickup around and drove back toward the compound. At the top of the rise, he turned down a dirt road that ran along the top of the cliff along the southern tip of the island. After a little over a mile, the road narrowed and eventually ended where erosion had taken part of the cliff. Jake pulled off to the side and they exited the vehicle.

Anchored about six miles to their southwest were two large vessels. The first one resembled an older trawler with its pilothouse located close to the bow. There was a crow's nest coupled with a radar mast at the center of the ship. A large deck space with a covered awning contained several tables and chairs.

The hull was painted black, with the name of the ship emblazoned on both sides—*Quino el Guardian*. The ninety-foot-long former fishing boat had been converted to a liveaboard dive boat when the Mexican government halted commercial fishing in the Revillagigedo Archipelago.

Jake studied the ship, searching for any kind of movement that would indicate how many people were on board. The *Quino* rocked gently in the ocean but contained no visible activity. He turned his attention to the other vessel, which was anchored two hundred yards away from the *Quino*.

The other ship was similar in length but was originally designed as a research vessel. The decks were more spacious than the *Quino*, containing several seating areas covered with deck chairs, loungers, and dining tables. A teakwood bar sat under a covered awning. He even observed a hot tub on the end of the deck overlooking the stern.

The ship, named the *Nautilus Under Sea*, was occupied by several men that Jake could identify thus far. They were milling about the lower deck, constantly walking in and out of the main cabin. Jake had a better view of the stern of the *Nautilus*, and that was how he'd determined the two ship's primary functions.

"They're dive boats," he said to Ashby, who was watching debris from the wrecked inflatable crash up against the rocky shore. Jake lowered the binoculars and handed them to Ashby. "I suppose they could be part of some research project, but I saw ships like these in Thailand when we were being escorted out to the filming location."

"Liveaboards," added Ashby. "I've seen them in various parts of the world, too. They usually have five to eight guest cabins, a full galley, and a crew who operates the boat and leads the dives. Considering the sea life around here, it makes sense that this would be considered a hot spot for diving."

"I only saw one inflatable, how about you?" asked Jake.

Ashby looked again and nodded. "Same here. I think you took care of their other one. Those three Italians were either crew members or guests. It's hard to stereotype people, but the way they drank, coupled with the tattoo of an anchor I saw on one of their arms, leads me to believe they're crew."

"Plus," began Jake as he stood with his hands on his hips, surveying the two ships, "the *Quino* is missing its inflatable, and I saw no signs of movement on board. It could be these three guys ventured out on their own without coordinating it with the crew of the *Nautilus*. That's why nobody is looking for them."

Ashby walked a little closer to the cliff's edge. "No sign of life at all? Where are the passengers?"

"Good question," replied Jake. "They may have been moved to the larger ship. Or they were all taken back to the mainland by a third vessel and these guys decided to ride out the aftermath of Yellowstone on the water. It's anybody's guess."

Ashby looked down one more time and then returned to the truck. "It doesn't look like they're an immediate threat to us, so let's get goin'."

154

They made their way along the rocky trail and back onto the paved road leading to the compound. Ashby was searching through the glove box of the pickup, just out of curiosity, when Jake came to a sudden stop, forcing her forward in the seat and into the dashboard.

"Jake!" she protested.

Ignoring her, Jake spoke in a hushed tone. "We've got company."

CHAPTER 37

The Pacific Ocean
Isla Socorro

He inched forward, holding his foot on the brake and allowing the engine to pull the truck up the hill toward the courtyard. Then he hit the brakes and put it in park. Jake shut off the engine, allowing the ticking of the hot engine to be the only sound to be heard.

Standing along the steps leading to the administration building were a dozen people, both men and women. Jake glanced to his sides and saw that several men with rifles were walking slowly toward the truck. He instinctively reached for his handgun, and Ashby turned in her seat to retrieve their rifles from the back. As she did, the approaching men reacted, raising their aim directly at Jake and Ashby.

Jake slowly stuck an arm out the driver's window until it was held high in the air. He held his right palm against the windshield to show he didn't want any trouble. Ashby immediately mimicked his actions.

"How do you wanna play this?" she asked calmly.

"They're Mexicans. Locals, I suspect. We don't have any quarrel with these people. We just have to make sure they understand that."

"Jake, I don't know enough Spanish to negotiate for our lives."

"I know. We'll try a universal language."

"Which is?" Ashby asked.

"Smile. Make constant eye contact with the person in charge. No sudden moves or nervous fidgeting."

"That sounds simple enough," said Ashby. She glanced to her right and saw that the men were approaching the truck. "We're about to find out if it works."

"Let them open the doors for us and keep your hands up and eyes forward the entire time. It's our only shot at surviving this. Whatever *this* is."

The men opened their doors simultaneously and motioned for Jake and Ashby to get out. They complied, slowly, and then began walking toward the welcoming committee at the top of the compound. Jake heard the back doors of the truck open and shut, which indicated to him their rifles had been seized. Nothing about the situation they were in felt good, other than the fact they were still alive, for the moment.

As he got closer, he quickly assessed the situation. Using his peripheral vision, he counted eight men and five women lined up along the top step in front of the administration buildings. They were unarmed. Behind them and to their immediate side were another eight men, all armed with shotguns. All of the adults were Mexican and ranged in ages from teenagers to some nearing sixty.

One of the men, dressed in blue jeans and a white button-up shirt, stepped forward and descended the steps to greet them. He was wearing a worn straw hat with a wide brim, which shaded his wrinkled face from the sun. He held up both hands, indicating that Jake and Ashby should stop.

"Are you Americans?" he asked with a light Spanish accent.

"Yes. My name is Jake Wheeler, and this is my friend Dr. Ashby Donovan. We are from Wyoming in the United States."

"Yellowstone?" The man seemed skeptical.

"Yes, sir. Dr. Donovan is a volcanologist. She was studying Yellowstone before it erupted. I was a law enforcement ranger there. We escaped as the volcano exploded."

"That is your boat anchored offshore, yes?" The man gestured over his shoulder, but Jake was unsure of the direction he meant.

"No, we are not with the two dive boats. Um, the *Quino* and *Nautilus*. That's not us. Our boat is north, anchored in a—"

The man interrupted Jake. "Yes, we saw you arrive."

"You did?" asked Jake.

Suddenly, there was a commotion behind the people at the top of the stairs, and a young boy burst through the line of adults and ran down the steps toward Ashby. She dropped to a knee and held her arms out as the boy rushed to embrace her.

The armed men took a step closer and raised their rifles, but the leader instructed them to stand down. As he did, a younger woman ran down the steps after the young boy.

"*Luis, détente, ven aquí.*" Stop, come here.

The boy crashed into Ashby like a Labrador puppy, sending her backwards into the grass. He hugged her, and the two began laughing, much to the delight of the onlookers.

The leader smiled and waved to the men to lower their weapons, which they did as they stepped back. He then looked to Jake and extended his hand. "I am Miguel Cervantes. Welcome to Isla Socorro."

Jake shook his hand and smiled as he let out a sigh of relief. Ashby and young Luis recovered from the reunion and stood, but never let go of one another. This was the young boy who'd come back to thank Ashby after they'd saved their lives the day before.

The women gathered around Ashby and Luis while Miguel patted Jake on the arm. "My apologies, Señor Wheeler, for this greeting. After yesterday, we have been nervous. We know about the liveaboard dive ships, but the incident occurred after your arrival. We made a faulty assumption."

"Please, call me Jake. I'm glad this young man remembered us."

"All of the children described you. It is my job to be certain. Thank you for protecting them. I, and their families, will be eternally grateful."

The group gathered around and began to thank Jake and Ashby. Some spoke broken English; others used their native Spanish. But the warm smiles and generous hugs were unmistakable shows of gratitude.

With his arm around Jake's shoulders, Miguel led him back up the steps toward the picnic tables. Ashby was escorted by the women and children, who were smitten with her long blond hair.

"Let's talk, my friend," said Miguel as they arrived at the tables. "I will tell you some of the history of Isla Socorro."

Ashby reached into her pocket and pulled out the keys to the mess hall. "Who's hungry?" She looked around at the children, who seemed to have arrived from every nook and cranny of the compound. "Hot dogs? Mac and cheese?"

The kids jumped up and down, shouting in their thick Spanish dialect, "Easy peasy, mac and cheesy! Easy peasy, mac and cheesy!"

Jake reached for Ashby's hand and gave it a squeeze. With the kids dancing around her, she led the way to the mess hall followed by the women. Miguel gave instructions to his armed men, who fanned out around the compound and down toward the dock.

He smiled and pulled a hand-rolled cigarillo out of his shirt pocket. He offered one to Jake, who declined.

Miguel started the conversation with a profound statement. "We live in a different world now, my new friend."

Jake laughed and shook his head. "Miguel, you have no idea."

CHAPTER 38

The Pacific Ocean
Isla Socorro

While Ashby bonded with some of the families who resided on Isla Socorro, endearing herself to the kids in particular, Jake and Miguel sat in the warm sunshine and talked. Miguel first explained the history of Isla Socorro and how the Mexican Navy base was established. Then he recounted how the second settlement came to be built on the northwest side of the island at *Playa Blanca*.

"Socorro is part of Colima, a very small state on the central coast. Because of its rich Aztec heritage, the state was eligible for special recognition by the United Nations. *Islas Revillagigedo* are very unique. President Enrique Peña Nieto submitted the archipelago to be declared a marine reserve and a UNESCO World Heritage Site."

UNESCO, an acronym for United Nations Educational, Scientific, and Cultural Organization, created the World Heritage Committee to identify and protect landmarks or areas of unique significance. There were several criteria upon which a location was judged, including cultural, historical and scientific reasons. The Revillagigedo Islands, and Isla Socorro in particular, met all the criteria.

Miguel continued. "There was only one problem with the UNESCO application—there were no indigenous people on Isla Socorro. The president's advisors quickly came up with a solution. The military wished to expand its naval facility, which had been here for sixty years. They approached me, a building contractor by trade, to lead a group of Colima residents in a five-year project to inhabit the island and construct the improvements."

"You built all of this?" asked Jake.

"No, only the new bungalows behind us. It allowed the navy to make this base more attractive to its officers. Also, of course, we built our village at *Playa Blanca.*"

"Did UNESCO approve the islands?"

"Oh yes, to much celebration in Mexico City. You see, once the application was approved, the state of Colima became eligible for low-interest, long-term loans from the World Bank. Loans, quite frankly, that were never expected to be repaid. The government paid for the improvements here and new public works programs on the mainland. Because of this, Colima, which is the fourth smallest state in Mexico, has one of the highest standards of living and lowest unemployment in all the country. And it is crime-free."

"Well, you should be commended on what you have accomplished," said Jake. "Were you aware that the navy was leaving?"

Miguel nodded and furrowed his brow. "Yes, but not until the morning they left. I do not understand why they didn't give us advance notice. Perhaps they thought we would want to leave as well."

"Would you leave?"

Miguel, who could've played the part of Juan Valdez, the fictional character who appeared in Columbian coffee-grower commercials decades ago, removed his hat and wiped the sweat off his brow with a bandana. One of the women brought him a glass of water and offered Jake one as well. Both men took a long drink before Miguel replied.

"I will tell you, Jake, that we have come to love Isla Socorro as our home. While it is true that the amenities of Colima are not available to us, we enjoy the simple life. We fish. We grow our own food. We raise our children in the Roman Catholic religion and teach them as well."

Jake finished his water and added, "Sometimes, simpler is better."

"Yes, it is. However, we are dependent on the military to restock some necessities that we cannot make for ourselves. Basic hygiene items and medical needs are met by the base dispensary. It is restocked monthly. I believe that will stop."

"We found the keys to all of the buildings, including *la despensa*. It is full now."

"Yes, but the navy has abandoned us. I was told it might be years before they return."

Jake smiled and reached out to pat Miguel on the arm. The older man seemed distressed at the prospect of taking care of the people within his charge. Jake vowed to help.

"Miguel, we will find a way. Ashby and I will help if you will accept us as your neighbors."

"Of course, my new friend. You are part of my family now."

Two of the teenage girls delivered a plate of macaroni and cheese paired with two hot dogs for the men to enjoy. While they ate, they made more small talk about the island and what it had to offer them long term. As they finished, Jake felt compelled to bring up the elephant in the room, which was most likely on both of their minds.

"Miguel, what are we going to do about the dive boats?"

He grimaced and shook his head. "I do not know. They are a danger to us all. What happened yesterday was not the first incident."

CHAPTER 39

The Pacific Ocean
Isla Socorro

Miguel adjusted his seat on the concrete bench and let out a weary sigh. He and Jake were facing each other now. He told the story of two of his teenage nephews who were fishing off the southwest coast when they had an encounter with the liveaboard people. The event took place a week ago, the day after the naval personnel left.

"The men were in a small boat, circling the boys and creating large waves. Eventually, the boys' canoe overturned and they were knocked into the water. This meanness was not enough for the men, who continued to circle my nephews. As a final act, they took the boys' canoe and towed it deeper into the ocean. Fortunately, the boys are good swimmers and made it back to shore, but they lost their fishing gear, their canoe, and their catch."

Jake shook his head out of anger. He didn't know if the men were the same three Italians as yesterday, but clearly the occupants of the two ships had nothing but bad intentions.

"Anything else?" asked Jake.

Miguel furrowed his brow and exhaled. "Yes. Several days ago, two bodies floated onto the beach near our village. They were older white people. The bodies were badly beaten and stabbed."

"Murdered?"

"*Sí.*"

Ashby approached them, wiping her hands off on her pants before she sat down. "Why are you two so glum?"

"Glum?" asked Miguel.

Ashby smiled and replied, "Gloomy. Serious. Sad."

Jake answered her question. "Apparently, the people on the liveaboard ships are going to be a problem. A dangerous one, in fact. They harassed Miguel's nephews the other day and may be responsible for the murder of two tourists who were on board their ships."

"What should we do?" asked Ashby.

"I'm not sure, but we need to make a decision about security," said Jake. "It's a matter of time before they come looking for their dead friends."

Miguel leaned forward and lowered his voice. "We have to prepare to defend ourselves. My people do not understand the concept of battles and war. They came here to avoid the crime of the mainland and provide a place for their children to grow up with no drugs. The men are not trained. We were issued eight shotguns for our protection the day the navy left, but only eighty shotgun shells."

"Each?" asked Jake.

"Total. Only ten per gun. I am grateful for what they provided, but it is not enough against the evil that is out there." Miguel pointed toward the ocean in general, as if he was concerned about more than the occupants of the liveaboards.

Jake stood because he was ready to get to work. The women and children of the village started to huddle around their table, indicating to Miguel that he needed to lead his flock home.

As they were saying their goodbyes, Miguel made a suggestion. "You are a police officer, yes?"

"Sort of. But, yes."

Miguel waved to one young man who had remained close by the entire time. He was standing over Jake and Ashby's guns. The young man approached, carrying the rifles.

"The children told me of your capabilities, Jake. Can you make a plan to protect Isla Socorro from the evil that lurks beyond our shores?"

Jake didn't have an answer for that question. There were so many factors to consider.

Miguel saw that Jake was thinking, so he also asked, "Would you be willing to come to our village tonight? We will make a proper island feast for you both. I will introduce you to everyone, and then we can discuss a plan. Yes?"

"Of course, Miguel, but I am concerned about leaving the base unguarded. The supplies, the food, and the ..." Jake's voice trailed off, choosing to keep the matter of the explosives to himself.

"I understand. I will send my best men this evening. Three will guard the base while you are gone, and I will escort you across the island. The terrain is rugged, but we have a well-worn road to use."

Jake pointed to the Ford pickup. "Take the truck. The keys are in it. We'd be honored to have an island feast with you."

Miguel shook Jake's hand and gave Ashby a hug. Everyone waved goodbye as they gradually slipped through the buildings and out of sight. Two of the men, and as many women and children that could be stuffed into the backseat and truck bed, drove toward the airfield.

Jake sat on top of the picnic table and sighed. Ashby slid in next to him and wrapped her arm through his.

"Wonders never cease," she said dryly. "Why do I feel like we just became the caretakers for a whole village?"

Jake agreed. "I know, but we can help one another. It will be an odd coupling of two diverse groups of people, but it might just work."

"We have lots of decisions to make," said Ashby. "I know this, however. With their help, we can make this place a home for a long time until the world rights itself."

CHAPTER 40

The Pacific Ocean
Isla Socorro

Ashby stood with her hands on her hips and scanned the courtyard, slowly turning her body to take in the entire naval base. "Where do we start, Jake?"

Jake had just returned from the administrative building, where he'd noticed a topographical map of the island the day before. He unfurled it on top of the picnic table he'd shared with Miguel and motioned for Ashby to join him.

He pointed to the center of the island. "My expert analysis has determined that your beloved volcano is right here."

Ashby started laughing. "Oh, Jake, you're so smart. What gave it away? The fact that the elevation shows the peak at around three thousand feet?"

"Yup," he replied. "Seems high. Is that normal?"

"That's about right for these smaller volcanic islands."

Jake ran his finger toward the bottom tip of the map. "They have the naval base identified here, between Binner's Cove to our west and Braithwaite Bay on our eastern perimeter. The cove is where I crashed their inflatable."

"Don't remind me," Ashby said dryly. She changed the subject. "I see the airfield along the coast. I'm thinking the yacht is anchored to the north of the airfield."

"I agree. Also, over here on the west side of the island is Playa Blanca, where Miguel and the villagers live. The liveaboards are down here, on the southwest side of the island, where Grayson's Cove is identified."

"The island is bigger than I thought," started Ashby. "Based upon this scale, it's ten miles from one end to the other, in all directions."

"That's a lot of coastline to monitor and defend," said Jake with a sigh. "You and I will be challenged to protect the base alone, much less the whole island. We'll need to set up a rotation of scouts using Miguel's people."

"They need to be able to communicate with one another, too," added Ashby. "I know there's a whole lot to this base we haven't explored yet. We do have a pair of two-way radios. That's not enough, though."

"That's on my mental list, as well. I'll bring it up to Miguel. He might have some at his place."

Ashby pointed to a designation on the map that read *study sites*. "Do you see this black marking about two miles due north of the base? It designates a study site near a place marked *Grutas*."

"Do you have any idea what that means?"

"Oddly, I keep remembering my days in Italy at Mount Vesuvius. The word *grutas* appears similar to grotto, or *grotta* in Italian. Grottos are usually associated with caves, and where there are caves, there is potentially fresh water."

"Unless we're on top of a mountain in Idaho, right?" asked Jake with a chuckle. The bats had made an indelible impression on him.

"Very funny," said Ashby. "I'm curious what they mean by study site. Say, can we go by there when we bring the yacht around to refuel and stock?"

"Absolutely. If there is a spring, it might be another water source besides the gutter catchment system and whatever they have up the mountain."

Jake continued to study the map. "Their village is too far from us to help guard the base, and we're too far away to help them with our weapons and ammo. And I'm sure not gonna give up our arsenal to them. You never know when *attitudes* might change."

"Should we consider consolidating our two locations?"

Jake grimaced and looked at the sky. "I've thought about that several times since we let them know we have the keys to the kingdom around here. Miguel knew the navy personnel were pulling out, yet he didn't take it upon himself to break in like we did."

Ashby laughed. "They have more respect for other people's property than we do. *Exhibit A* is floating off the north shore of the island."

Jake managed a chuckle and then grew serious. "They haven't seen what we've seen. In any event, the cat's out of the bag, and we'll look like jerks by not sharing the supplies left behind by the navy."

"Do we consolidate our groups? Maybe bring them over here where we have access to the dock and can better watch for boats coming from the mainland?"

"Let's play it by ear tonight and talk privately about our options.

They have warm bodies, the ability to grow food, and a village full of fishermen. We have a variety of seeds, weapons, and experience. We'd mesh well."

Jake and Ashby rolled up the map and set about to search the base for things that could help them establish a perimeter security system around the base. As they searched through the buildings, Jake expressed his thoughts on their options.

"Normally, you protect your base camp from the outside in. With walls and fencing, the first thing you do is deter someone from entering your space. Add perimeter guards, and any intruder would walk away from the appearance of a robust security program.

"Absent fences, walls, and roving guards, the best thing you can do is get a heads-up that someone has breached your perimeter. The earlier you can detect an intrusion, the quicker you can react. That's the basis for every home alarm system."

Ashby relayed something from her childhood. "In the Philippines, some homeowners had dogs, which they tied to a tree or post outside their homes. It's no different than what you might see driving through rural parts of America. Whenever someone approached the home, the dog would bark, sending a clear warning signal to everyone. I didn't like that they were tied to a tree, but it was the best alarm system they could afford."

Jake laughed. "It's too bad your new feline friends can't bark."

They entered a nondescript white building with no windows. He flipped on the lights and found a dozen tall metal cabinets lining the room.

"I never bothered coming in here while I was wandering around this morning because it was so small," said Ashby. She opened a door and found basic first aid supplies stacked on the shelves.

Jake opened up a locker on the other side and discovered a variety of tools, including more battery-operated power tools. Another locker contained camping gear, while the fourth was full of fishing accessories.

"Here are some uniforms, too," Ashby announced.

"Bingo," said Jake after opening a locker stuck in the corner.

"We've got world band radios. Also, they have two-way units, both battery operated and rechargeable. Here are a couple of bullhorns, including one with a microphone."

Ashby pushed past him. "Sweet. A portable CD player. We've got music."

Jake pulled out a stack of CDs. He read the names of the artists. "Belanova. Julieta Venegas. Julio Iglesias. I've heard of him." Then he burst out laughing.

"What?" asked Ashby.

"Well, we also have Frank Sinatra and Guns N' Roses. That's an odd mix, don't you think?"

Ashby reached over and grabbed the Frank Sinatra CD out of his hands. "I'll take Ol' Blue Eyes, thanks."

Jake stood in front of the locker, staring for a moment. "I've got an idea. We need to create the appearance that the base is inhabited until we can come up with a plan."

He walked around the lockers and studied what they'd found. He continued. "Our biggest threat, at the moment, is located on those liveaboard boats. We're not in a position to take the battle to them yet. However, we can certainly make them think we're capable of defending ourselves by creating the illusion there are more of us than just you and me."

"Miguel's people?" asked Ashby.

"Maybe later on. For now, let's take a page out of the *Gilligan's Island* playbook."

"Ugh," moaned Ashby. "Jake, are you serious?"

"Yes. Hear me out. There was an episode in which natives came onto their island and threatened the castaways. They took their excess clothing, then dressed up coconuts and stick figures to make it look like their village was full of people. It worked."

"On a comedy show," said Ashby dismissively.

"Yeah, but the concept is still solid. Around the compound, we'll create scarecrows, for lack of a better term. Fully dressed naval personnel sitting just inside windows at various buildings. We'll play music through the CD player. We'll turn lights on to make the place appear occupied. In addition to running our own perimeter patrols, it might just help turn the bad guys away."

Ashby gave Jake a hug, perhaps to humor him, or out of gratitude. Either way, she quickly began to gather up everything to create the illusion he envisioned.

CHAPTER 41

The Pacific Ocean
Playa Blanca
Isla Socorro

Later that afternoon, Miguel and three of his men arrived in the Ford Sport Trac pickup. None of his men spoke English, but after Jake explained the security deterrents he'd put into place, the men understood their role and took up positions around the perimeter of the base. Their primary focus was going to be guarding the road leading to the dock, as the coastline on both sides of it was too steep and rocky for anyone to climb.

Their conversation on the trip to Playa Blanca focused on what was happening in the United States and the actions taken by the Mexican government to close its borders. Miguel was open-minded, but he used the word *karma* on several occasions, leaving Jake uneasy about his attitude toward Americans.

Jake and Ashby had discussed the evening's activities before Miguel arrived. They both looked at the potential relationship between the groups as two business entities merging with one another. The partnership had to be equal in scope and clearly defined—not unlike any new business relationship. If both parties brought something to the table, then the partnership could work for so long as one side couldn't overpower and drive out the other.

Overall, the initial conversation was cordial, ultimately turning to what Jake and Ashby had experienced. With only limited news received via a world band shortwave radio, Miguel was surprised at the levels of devastation being experienced in North America. He asked Ashby a logical question as they neared his village.

"This fallout of which you speak," Miguel began, "will it reach our island?"

"Yes, to an extent. The minute particles will fill the atmosphere around the globe. I don't expect it will impact the sea life in this area or your ability to grow food. The constant breeze coupled with the rainfall you receive on the northern side of the island will help. It will be important, however, to monitor the respiratory systems of your elderly and children."

Jake glanced back at Ashby as she made the statement. He immediately thought of the limited number of N-95 masks they had and whether they should share them. When they were gone, they were gone. If the fallout worsened and became a potential threat for years to come, the two of them would need all they had. He made a mental note to discuss it with her later.

"Do you have experience in the medical field, as well?" Miguel asked.

"No, but I'm familiar with the telltale signs of respiratory distress due to ash fallout. I'll be glad to help you."

Jake allowed himself a slight smile. Ashby was endearing herself to Miguel while also reminding him of their importance to this potential new partnership. Very smart.

Before they arrived, Jake tried to subtly remind Miguel of another weakness his group might have. "Miguel, have your men had any formal weapons training?"

"None at all. As you probably know, Mexico's gun laws are very strict, much like the United Kingdom and Australia. My people are block layers and carpenters, not police. The navy offered us the shotguns because they require less accuracy. With the limited number of shells provided, there is no opportunity to practice."

Jake had an opening to offer his expertise. "I can teach them with a dry-fire technique. They can learn basic gun-handling skills and shooting, but without the guns loaded. I taught Ashby this way and she is an excellent shot."

Ashby looked down and smiled. As she did, the bumpy trail opened up into a clearing overlooking the Pacific Ocean. The view of the lush landscape and over the top of the cliffs was incredible.

"Look at the fields!" exclaimed Ashby. "Every foot is covered with vegetables."

Miguel continued toward the village and described the hillside covered with crops for his visitors. Miguel smiled. "Oh, yes. In addition to being masons and carpenters, we are farmers. It is a part of our culture to plant, grow, harvest, and preserve our foods."

"What are you growing here?" asked Jake.

"We have all the staples that we grow on the mainland—corn, sugarcane, tomatoes, peppers, beans, avocados, and leafy vegetables. We have also included tropical fruits like bananas, mangos, kiwis, lemons, and limes. And, of course, coffee. There is room to grow more if seeds were available."

Jake raised his eyebrows and smiled as he thought of the wide variety of heirloom seeds he'd found on the winery raid that night. Miguel and the villagers might have to start small, but over time, with the heirloom seeds being reused, the agricultural aspect of Isla Socorro could expand.

The road wound its way toward the water's edge, and the homes began to appear. Nestled under tall palm trees were block and stone structures resembling the modest bungalows built for the naval base. These houses all contained metal roofs, open-air shutter windows, and were evenly spaced on the beach. Wooden boats painted in bright, vibrant colors were scattered about the beach in front of the houses.

Miguel stopped short of entering the village so Jake and Ashby could take in the view. "We built our village at Playa Blanca on the west side of the island for two reasons. The rainfall and gently sloped hills are ideal for growing. The cove we chose is shielded from the hurricanes and tropical weather that approach Isla Socorro from the mainland. We do not receive the fierce, brutal waves during the storms. The island shields us from the winds, and the water remains calm."

Miguel continued. "We have a traditional Mexican hierarchy here. The women tend to the children, take care of the home, and preserve the food. The men fish and work the fields. Our people are not immune to hard work, and the balance is a good one. You Americans have a saying, I'm told. Living on island time. Am I correct?"

Ashby was quick to answer. "Yes. My friend used to say *no rush, no worries.*" Ashby wiped a tear from her eye as she thought of Dusty.

"We agree with that. We move slowly here. Mainly because there is no place to go and there is no way to get there in a hurry."

The group laughed as Miguel continued down the slope to the beach. When he arrived in the middle of the village, he shut off the engine, allowing Jake and Ashby to soak it in. Everyone in the village had come out to greet them. Kids were playing on the beach. Women were carrying trays of food to wooden tables set up on bamboo sawhorses. The few remaining men stood in the middle, smiling and waving to the visitors.

It warmed their hearts and helped them make their decision. Despite their different cultures and backgrounds, both groups had something to offer one another. They needed to find a way to work together.

CHAPTER 42

The Pacific Ocean
Aboard the *Nautilus Under Sea*

In a post-apocalyptic world, opportunists are everywhere. They're drawn to one another like magnets, finding common ground and shared purposes. The situations and scenarios may vary, but the human trait of taking advantage of one man's travails often results in evil binding with evil. Such was the case on the liveaboard dive boats anchored off Isla Socorro.

Walter Sota was a drifter with several outstanding warrants for fraud and embezzlement pending against him in the United States. When he quit the employer who'd relied upon him to handle their internet technology issues for many years, taking over a hundred thousand dollars out of their bank accounts in the process, he went on the lam as his crime was discovered.

Initially, Sota fled for the raucous, hedonistic confines of Tijuana, Mexico, where he indulged in prostitutes and illegal drugs. One morning, hungover from a bottle of cheap mezcal and several injections of methamphetamine, Sota realized he'd burned through his ill-gotten gains. He was broke and an addict.

To feed his fix, he turned to petty crime, robbing young tourists who spilled into Tijuana to take advantage of the younger drinking age and lax law enforcement. The Mexican government had enough trouble battling the drug cartels. They couldn't act as the babysitter to American teenagers looking to grow up too fast.

During the next several months, Sota became an expert in running cons on his fellow Americans. Unsuspecting teens, looking to score drugs or cheap sex, would often follow Sota into darkened corners of

Tijuana—their hopes high, but their awareness low.

Using an inexpensive BB pistol, which, in the dark, looked very much like a 1911-style handgun, Sota stole cash and jewelry and occasionally raped inebriated young girls.

As time passed, Sota decided to up his game by traveling to Cabo San Lucas, located directly down the Baja California peninsula from Tijuana. In Cabo, the marks were not as easy, but they had more money.

However, frequently wasted from drugs and alcohol, he was unable to con the more sophisticated tourists in Cabo, who arrived by yachts and planes. The inability to continue his life as a petty criminal became a temporary blessing for Sota. He cleaned up his act, but not by choice. The cost of drugs was higher in Cabo San Lucas, and the law enforcement community was stricter on crooks like him.

So he took a job aboard the *Nautilus Under Sea*, a Cabo-based liveaboard dive boat. While living in Florida, Sota had taken up diving and became PADI-certified in several levels of experience.

One day, he met a divemaster who invited him to join the crew of the *Nautilus*. It was one of several liveaboards operated by the company, but as the smallest, it frequently traveled to the closest dive location—Isla Socorro.

By this time, Sota had kicked his drug habit, but his taste for tequila, marijuana, and young girls remained. All of the above were plentiful on the liveaboards. It was a close-knit community of nine ships that traveled the Revillagigedo Islands on regular, weekly dive trips, hauling tourists from all over the world. Because the *Nautilus* was an older ship, modified from a research vessel, and had a smaller capacity than the others, it was typically priced less per passenger. This made it popular with college kids who were looking to dive the islands at a bargain price.

There were three ships anchored off the southwestern coast of Isla Socorro the day Yellowstone erupted. The most elegant of the three, *My Cassiopeia*, returned to port immediately, taking some of the divers off the *Nautilus* and the *Quino* with them. Likewise, the younger, more adventurous divers from the Cassiopeia took up the generous offer to remain behind on the *Nautilus* and the *Quino.* You know, *to ride out the storm.*

Unfortunately, the storm was just beginning, and it wasn't due to Yellowstone. The crews of the *Quino* and *Nautilus* were friends outside of their workplace. The two groups frequented the same bars and after-hours clubs of Cabo. They shared the same women and purchased drugs from the same dealer.

After two weeks of partying and debauchery with their passengers, the unspoken dividing line between crew and passengers was obliterated. Soon, matters got out of control and violence took over the alcohol-infused parties.

Walter Sota was not the only criminal on board the two ships. In fact, most of the crews had criminal pasts, which included violence, gun crimes, and sexual assaults. Their old ways eventually rose to the surface and the passengers were ill-equipped to defend themselves.

The news from Cabo that the Mexican government was beginning to expel ex-pats concerned the crew members, the vast majority of whom were Americans and Europeans. They knew they couldn't return, only to be sent packing or jailed. They decided to take their chances on the ocean.

But the food began to run out, and the number of mouths to feed needed to be reduced. Quietly, one by one, passengers began to disappear. Some died at the hands of their divemasters, who continued to take them underwater for entertainment. Others ostensibly fell overboard during the drunken gatherings at night. Even elderly members of the crew were set adrift, with their throats slit, when they protested the activities of their younger counterparts.

The lawlessness of the mainland had reared its ugly head at sea, and Sota and his companions were ready to expand their territory by visiting Isla Socorro now that the Mexican Navy had left.

It had been two days since the three Italians on the crew had volunteered to go ashore and report back their findings. When Sota saw them passing around the Sambuca that morning before they left, he knew they would be gone for a while.

After the first night, he suspected the men had got drunk and slept it off. Now that the sun had set on another day, he assumed the Italians had found food, alcohol, and perhaps some of the young girls who lived in the village.

Sota became angry that he and his buddies were being cut out of the festivities by the Europeans. As they drank that night and passed around the young college girl from Iowa State, Sota vowed to lead an armed team onto Isla Socorro to find out what was going on.

He didn't care about the Italians. He might just kill them for taking advantage of the bounty on the island, if any. Sota was bored and he was in the mood for action. Tomorrow, he'd get it.

PART FOUR

Isla Socorro, a new life

CHAPTER 43

The Pacific Ocean
Isla Socorro

The next morning, Jake and Ashby awoke early, full of excitement. They'd thoroughly enjoyed their evening at the village. They were warmly welcomed, and both agreed that they were one hundred percent comfortable working with Miguel. This morning, their plan was to cross the island on foot to retrieve the yacht and bring it around to the naval dock. Miguel provided them a suggested route, one that would lend a surprise along the way for Ashby.

During their conversation with Miguel the night before, they agreed that the compound needed to be guarded twenty-four hours a day. Jake and Ashby agreed to take the night shift, which ran from dusk to dawn. Miguel would rotate his men back and forth during the day, using the pickup for transportation. Once his men arrived in the morning, Jake and Ashby were free to explore the island and take care of the yacht.

Jake led Ashby up the hill past the last of the newly constructed bungalows until he found the elevated pipeline stretching northward up the hill. "Miguel said to follow the pipeline until it ends. That's where we'll find our first point of interest. Then, he said go due north by following a well-worn path that runs parallel to the runway. That's where your surprise awaits."

"What do you think he's talking about?" asked Ashby as she lengthened her stride and moved past Jake. She'd taken the second shift and was still wide awake with the assistance of several cups of coffee.

"I don't know. He was kind of mysterious about it, but in a humorous way."

"He said the pipeline ends about two miles from here. Let's go."

Jake playfully cursed Ashby under his breath. She had always been more fit than he was. Her job took her around the world to high elevations that required a significant hike to reach. As a result, her legs were strong and her stamina was good. Once Ashby adapted to a new climate, she was raring to go.

After a forty-minute hike uphill, they reached the end of the pipeline and the source of their fresh water.

"Wow, Jake. This is incredible. Check them out!"

They stood in front of a series of grottos tucked into the face of the mountain. Covered with thick, tropical foliage, it would have been easy to walk past them had it not been for the pipe leading inside the largest of the grottos.

The unusual geologic formation consisted of cavernous tunnels created over many years of erosion. Over time, cracks had formed in the rock, which allowed rainwater flowing down the volcanic mountain to enter the caves. Kept cool and shielded from the algae-inducing sunlight, the water remained fresh enough to drink.

They pulled out their flashlights and made their way into the cave. The sound of dripping water could be heard, although the surface of the pond was perfectly still. Jake used his light to inspect the ceiling of the cave. He was pleased to find no evidence of bats.

Then he studied the drainpipe, which was used, along with gravity, to send water down to the compound. It consisted of two sections. The first was a screen designed to keep out larger debris. He stood on a ledge and knelt so he could flash his light inside the pipe. He saw a second screen, a fine mesh, which filtered out smaller particulates.

"Somewhere along this pipeline, or maybe in the water-storage container at the compound, there must be a filtration and purification system of some type."

"Charcoal filters?" asked Ashby.

"Most likely. That means they need to be changed periodically. We'll need to locate them and see if there's a logbook giving us a schedule."

The two backed out of the grotto and resumed their trek through the jungle. As they followed the trail, the foliage got thicker, so Jake took the lead. Using a machete he'd found in the storage lockers yesterday afternoon, he cut away at the low-lying plants and palm trees.

He also kept a vigilant eye out for snakes. They had already come across blue lizards, an iguana-looking lizard with a bright blue hue. They scampered across the trail as Jake plowed through the overgrowth.

Miguel had told them the feral cats had been introduced to help control the snake population. Although the night snake and the Island whip snake were nonvenomous, their bites had been known to cause infections. With antibiotics in short supply, Jake didn't want to take any chances.

"Hey, there's a clearing up ahead!" exclaimed Jake as he began to beat back the tropical leaves with vigor. Within a minute, they stepped into the bright sun and stared at the nondescript white block building with several antennas affixed to the top of its roof. Several smaller structures, resembling beehives with their white clapboard construction and flat black roofs, were scattered about the clearing.

"Is this supposed to be my surprise?" asked a dejected Ashby.

"I guess so. He must have a reason for saying that. Let's go see."

Ashby led the way to the front of the building and let out a, "Hell yeah," followed by, "Home sweet home!"

A plaque on the building read *Global Volcanism Program, HA06, Socorro Island.* Ashby tried the door handle, but it was locked. There was a numbered, mechanical keylock attached to the bolt lock, which required a code to be inserted.

She scratched her head and then turned to Jake. "Please break in for me."

"Do I look like a criminal? Some kind of burglar?"

Ashby pouted and then turned toward the door. She pulled the charging handle on her AR-15 and pointed the barrel at the door lock.

"Okay! Okay!" Jake shouted and moved to her side. "I was just kidding."

Ashby began to laugh. "So was I, sort of."

Jake had become an expert at popping locks with his knife, and within seconds, it was open. He turned on the lights, which were powered by a solar array on the metal roof.

"What is this place?" he asked as he wandered around the room, looking at whiteboards and several maps.

Ashby settled into a chair at a computer and explained, "Years ago, the Smithsonian National Museum of Natural History created this program to monitor volcanoes around the world that had erupted in the last ten thousand years. That may seem like a long time, but in relation to the age of our planet, it's a mere millisecond."

She paused for a moment as she turned on the computer monitor. After receiving a blank screen, she reached under the desk and found the Dell computer box and powered it on. While the Windows-based system took its sweet time to power up, she continued. "Anyway, they created these outposts around the world where the volcano's profile met the criteria they were looking for. Some outposts are more elaborate than others, and those are typically manned twenty-four seven."

The computer was almost finished booting, so Ashby rummaged impatiently through the drawers. She pulled out a logbook and thumbed through the pages with Jake looking over her shoulder.

"It appears this station was visited every ninety days, with the last trip just before Yellowstone's eruption. Ha, in fact, it was the same week I was in Hawaii studying Kilauea."

"What are all those notations?" asked Jake.

"The last volcanologist to visit here made notes of their findings, or at least a summary, for the next person. If there was anything of interest, they made a notation and pointed it out here."

Ashby read through the notes. The computer booted, and a screen requiring a password immediately appeared.

"Crap, I was afraid of that, but not surprised." She turned her attention back to the logbook and read aloud. "Logistical support from the Mexican Navy to measure seven fumarole and hot spring temps in the summit region of Evermann."

"Evermann?" asked Jake.

"Yes. Mont Evermann was the name given to the dome complex at the top of the volcano. Evermann was one of the first American scientists to study this region."

"Ashby, this volcano is dormant, right?" asked Jake.

She continued to flip the pages of the journal, studying the entries made every ninety days. "No, technically, it's still active. But remember, it's a shield volcano like Mauna Kea in Hawaii. Its lava flows are entirely fluid, with slow-moving eruptions. While we're here, we'll want to monitor the island for new fissure vents."

"Or we could find another island," interrupted Jake. "Hey, I could have the yacht tanked and loaded by sundown. We could move—"

"No, Jake. We're not leaving, especially over a tame volcano like this one. Think about it. I get it all to myself."

"Oh, joy," said Jake with a chuckle. "Are you locked out of their computer?"

"Yes, but they definitely have internet here as well. Between the military internet and this facility, I'll get back online as soon as I take the time to bring my MacBook."

"About that. We can come back here any time. We need to get the yacht and bring it to the dock. Let go of the keyboard, Dr. Donovan. Rubbing your fingers on the keys won't open it up."

"Yeah, yeah."

CHAPTER 44

The Pacific Ocean
Isla Socorro

"I kind of expected Miguel's men to come down and investigate our arrival," said Jake after he turned off the diesel pump at the dock. It had taken him twenty minutes to pull the large vessel into the dock, keeping it pressed against the black rubber tires that acted as bumpers. Ashby had moved quickly to secure two of the dock lines at the bow and stern so that Jake could tie off two more midship. They planned on securing the yacht under the assumption they'd be staying for many years.

"I can't wait to see them in the naval uniforms," added Ashby. Jake had asked Miguel to dress the men out in the extra service uniforms located in the storage building. The navy, white, and black digital camouflage uniforms would lend the impression that the navy still maintained a presence on the base. If the crew of the liveaboards came looking for their Italian friends, they'd find armed soldiers milling about the base during the day.

"Well, it would've been nice to get a lift up the hill, too," said Jake as he covered his eyes to assess the steep climb up to the base.

"One of the first things I want to do is get online if possible," said Ashby, ignoring Jake's comment. "Even if I'm locked out of their desktop computers, I can still get internet access. I hope." Her voice trailed off, as she wasn't absolutely positive of this.

Jake glanced back at the top of the yacht at the damaged HughesNet antenna and the destroyed Doppler radars. "I don't know much about electronics, but the hardware on top of the airstrip office looks similar to our damaged stuff. Maybe Miguel has an electrician who can help us scavenge parts from the military buildings to repair the antenna and radar on our roof."

They kept walking, gradually slowing as fatigue set in. They'd already hiked ten miles across the island, mostly uphill. This last stretch was brutal on them both. Ten minutes later, without any further discussion, they arrived at the circle drive surrounding the compound and stopped.

"Where is everybody?" asked Ashby.

"I don't see the truck either," replied Jake. He glanced at his watch. It was still hours until sundown. As he became more concerned, he pulled his rifle around in front of him and brought it to a low-ready position.

Ashby quickly mimicked him. "Jake, what do you want to do?"

He spoke in a hushed tone of voice. "Spread out. Stay on the road but walk at a low crouch. Keep your eyes open for any form of movement. Whistle once and point in the direction of the movement if you see anything."

"Got it."

Ashby quickly took the road to the right side of the compound, which connected to the airport road. Jake moved left toward the barracks. Keeping constant eye contact with one another, they moved up the hill until the compound leveled off. After five tense minutes, they met up in front of the administration building. Ashby slipped the strap of her messenger bag over her head and set it on a picnic table.

"I guess they decided to leave," she said as she rolled her head and neck around her shoulders. The tension wasn't going to release that easily, so she exaggerated the movement until a series of cracks and pops could be heard.

"Yeah, very disappointing. We counted on them to have our backs while we retrieved the yacht. Miguel even gave us some sightseeing to—" Jake cut his sentence short and then gave Ashby a concerned look.

"What?" she asked.

"I didn't see any evidence of foul play, did you?"

"No," she replied.

"We've been gone a long time," continued Jake. He started walking briskly toward the warehouse and the storage building at the back of the compound.

Ashby scurried alongside him. "Do you think they came and cleaned us out or something? Jake, they wouldn't do that."

Jake reached the door marked *la despensa* and tried the handle. He breathed a sigh of relief when he discovered the door was still locked.

Ashby reached past him and placed the key in the lock. She unlocked the door, and everything was still intact.

"That's a relief, but it still doesn't explain what happened to Miguel's men," said Jake. "I'm gonna get the golf cart and take a load of supplies down to the yacht. You know, just in case we have to leave. As I do, I'll bring some of the weapons back up here."

"Okay, do you want some help?"

"Nah, I can do it just as fast on my own. See what's happening in the world if you can. I'm getting cabin fever."

"Island fever?" asked Ashby.

"Yeah, same thing."

Jake pulled the door shut and Ashby locked it. In the distance, they could hear the pickup racing toward the compound. Nervous and unsure of what was happening, they ran to the front of the administration building and took up positions behind the block half wall that formed a semicircle around the flagpole.

The truck sped into the courtyard, leaving the road, and slid to a stop in the grass. Miguel and another man poured out of the front seat, waving their arms and yelling Jake's name.

CHAPTER 45

The Pacific Ocean
Isla Socorro

"*Rápido! Rápido!*" shouted Miguel to the man who was still dressed in the Mexican naval uniform. He pointed toward the dock, and the shorter, heavyset man, who was carrying the shotgun like he was cradling a baby, scurried across the courtyard toward the road.

Jake left Ashby and ran toward the pickup, taking the few steps onto the courtyard with a single leap. With his rifle ready, he shouted to Miguel, "What's happened? Why were the men pulled away?"

Miguel jogged around the pickup to greet Jake. He was sweating profusely and his chest was heaving, causing him to gasp for air. Jake shouldered his rifle and put his arm around the much older man. Miguel allowed Jake to guide him up the hill toward the picnic tables when he stopped and waved his arm back toward the truck.

"There is a note. In the front seat. Please hurry."

Jake glanced back at Ashby, who immediately turned to enter the mess hall. By the time Jake had retrieved the piece of paper containing a handwritten message, Ashby emerged with three bottles of water. They helped Miguel up the stairs and he quickly gulped down half a bottle before exhaling.

He nodded and wiped the sweat off once again. "Okay. I'm okay. *Gracias.*"

"Miguel, calm down and tell us what's wrong."

He took a deep breath and began. "While you were away, the men were patrolling the compound in the uniforms, as you suggested. One of the men stopped to relieve himself in the bushes and was hit on the back of the head with a rock. As he fell, he pulled the trigger on the gun, which alerted the others."

"They ran to assist him and saw three men running down the hill toward the dock. They stole Juan's gun."

"Did your people recognize the men, or how they arrived here?"

"Only by their boat," replied Miguel. "It is from the dive ship *Nautilus*."

"Did the men say anything?" asked Ashby.

"No," replied Miguel, shaking his head vigorously from side to side. "The note. Read it."

Jake had crumpled the page in his excitement to hear what had happened. He laid it flat on the picnic table and straightened it. It had moist bloodstains on it.

He glanced at the simple block script. It was written in English, so Jake read it aloud.

"Our friends are missing and their boat has been wrecked. We have your boys. You can have them back by returning our friends, giving up your guns, and providing us a new boat. If not, we will feed the boys to the sharks, one piece at a time. You have until tomorrow night at sundown. No excusas!"

"What is this all about?" asked Jake as he handed the handwritten note to Ashby. She shot him a concerned look and he nodded slightly.

"After the boat people left, they drove down the coastline toward the village. Um, my nephew and—"

Miguel couldn't continue as he broke down crying. In between sobs, he relayed the story as witnessed by some other kids who were standing on the cliff above the scene.

His nephew and his regular fishing buddy were trolling along the cliffs when the liveaboard's inflatable boat came speeding toward them. The boys paddled as fast as they could to escape the men, who were yelling and cursing at them, but they were quickly overtaken.

The boys jumped out of the boat and attempted to swim toward the cliff; however, the men positioned the boat between the rocks and the kids to block their progress. As they attempted to haul the boys out of the water and into the inflatable, the kids on the cliff started throwing large rocks at the inflatable, hoping to puncture it or sink it.

This angered the men, who fired two rounds of buckshot at the children. Although they weren't hit, they were frightened and ran back to the village, where they alerted Miguel. He sent two of his men racing across the island to retrieve the armed guards from the compound.

In the meantime, the inflatable, while towing the boys' fishing boat, drove along the shore of the village, taunting the women and children. One of the men was holding the boys at gunpoint while the others shouted at the villagers.

Finally, they fired the shotgun toward the houses twice, scaring everyone, before releasing the fishing boat and tearing off into the ocean. They found the note in the wooden boat, along with one of the boys' pinky fingers. Now Jake understood where the blood had come from.

Miguel continued to cry as Ashby joined his side to comfort him. Jake stood and wandered around the steps, kicking at stones and balling his fists. He was steeling himself for a fight, but he had to think it through.

Anger clouds judgment. Acting on clouded judgment will get you killed.

CHAPTER 46

The Pacific Ocean
Isla Socorro

"Jake, what are you thinkin'?" asked Ashby as Miguel began to regain his composure. "Are you considering giving them what they want? I mean, the Italians are dead. We can give them the Zodiac. I hate the idea of giving them any more—"

Jake spun around and calmly replied, in a deep, guttural tone, "We're gonna give them what they deserve. We're rescuing the boys and then they'll pay."

Miguel looked up and wiped the tears off his face. "Jake, my men are not fighters. We don't know how to shoot. They are willing to—"

"Miguel, this battle will not be won with bullets flying around. The boys are hostages and will be guarded. We have to take them by surprise, using a combination of distractions and quickness."

"You have a plan, yes?" asked Miguel.

"Maybe, but I can't do it alone," replied Jake. He stopped speaking and turned around to stare in the direction of the liveaboards. For a minute, he stood defiantly with his hands on his hips, considering his options.

Ashby stood to join him and rubbed his shoulders. "What do you want us to do? We have to help these boys. They are our family now."

Jake smiled and looked at the grassy courtyard. "He gave us until tomorrow at dusk, but we will make our move tonight."

"What is our move?" asked Miguel.

"Miguel, I need two of your best swimmers and two of your

strongest young men who can paddle the fishing boats quickly. I also need a man who knows how to fight with a knife. Five people, two boats. Do you have that?"

Miguel responded in part. "Our best swimmers are girls."

"They have to be fearless," insisted Jake. "All of them, Miguel. They must go with me without fear and full of determination."

"I will make sure of it, my friend."

"Good. Now return to the village, identify your people, and tell them to rest. Take the rest of your men and women and place them along the cliffs facing the dive ships. If these guys try to make a move early, I want to have some warning. Will your people help?"

"Yes. Absolutely. I had to stop them from going after the boys today in their fishing boats."

Jake was blunt and direct. "That won't work and would just get them all killed. We're settled, then. Meet me back here before midnight."

Miguel moved toward Jake and extended his arms to hug. Jake hugged Miguel and patted him on the back as the tears poured out of the eyes of the loving uncle.

"Please save these boys. They are good young men and don't deserve this."

"I will, Miguel," said Jake. "Now pick your people, and get some rest. I will see you tonight."

Miguel patted Jake on the shoulder and then made his way to the pickup truck. He left his guard behind and sped off toward the village. After the truck was out of sight, Jake took a deep breath and exhaled. He walked with Ashby to the picnic table and they sat next to one another on the bench.

"Do you really have a plan?"

Jake shrugged and responded, "Yeah, sort of. I mean, it's a plan that would work every single time in the movies."

"Does it involve a stunt like the one from yesterday?"

Jake sat quietly and stared off into the distance.

After he didn't answer for a minute, Ashby nudged him with her shoulder. "Jake?"

He deflected. "Um, do you think you can access the internet with your laptop?"

"Probably, yes. Why?"

"I need an interior layout of those ships. Hopefully, to attract tourists and to book dives, they have a website showing off their sleeping cabins, amenities, etcetera."

"But—" began Ashby before she was interrupted by Jake.

"There's another thing or two I'll need."

Ashby turned sideways on the bench and faced him. She scowled and reached for his face to force him to look into her eyes. "Not another word until you answer my question. Are you gonna do something dangerous like crashing that boat?"

Jake grimaced and shook his head. "Worse. Much worse."

CHAPTER 47

The Pacific Ocean
Isla Socorro

When Jake explained to Ashby that he planned to use the explosives she'd found as a diversionary tactic, she threw her arms up in frustration and stormed off. Jake had to run in order to stop her from going to the commander's bungalow. It took him twenty minutes to plead his case and provide reassurance after reassurance that he'd be careful. She finally acquiesced, under the proviso that his stunt days were over after tonight.

While Ashby used her MacBook to access the satellite internet system on the base, Jake gathered what he needed and took it to the administration building. One of the offices there also doubled as a small conference room with a large whiteboard affixed to one wall.

During one of his trips to the yacht to retrieve ammo and weapons, he took the road along the coast so he could take another look at the two liveaboards in the daylight. With the marine binoculars, he was able to gauge the distance between the two ships. Also, both the ocean currents and the winds turned them on their anchor lines.

Oddly, the *Quino* was anchored at both bow and stern. He'd never seen that before in open water. In tight coves, on a lake, for example, he'd seen houseboats anchored on both ends to limit the boat's swing.

Either way, it was a benefit to him, as the *Quino* continued to appear uninhabited, and it would act as cover and a perfect staging area for his raid upon the *Nautilus*. Jake completed his sketch on the legal pad and returned to the compound.

He reached for black spray paint to alter two of the brightly colored fishing skiffs at the village. Inside the storage lockers, he found several sticks of face paint in black and olive drab colors. He located several fixed-blade knives to choose from. Finally, he laid out the rifles for the oarsmen to use.

With the easier of the preliminary tasks completed, Jake joined Ashby in the commander's office to see how she was doing. When he entered, she quickly wiped a few tears away and continued to study her computer.

"Ashby, what's wrong?" he asked as he pulled her hair back behind her shoulders. He gently ran it through his fingers, allowing it to spread across her back.

"The devastation, and people's reactions. It's chaotic back home. The death toll from the blast itself is in the millions, but respiratory failure has taken the lives of tens of millions. But that was expected, this was not."

Ashby pointed at a video depicting people beating each other with pipes and aluminum baseball bats outside a FEMA trailer in Minneapolis. The newscast then switched to rioting in the Mall of America, where stores were broken into, looted, and then set on fire.

"They've lost their minds," said Jake as he watched society collapse. "Any word on the border situation?"

"Yeah, and the word is *stalemate*. Mexico continues to increase its demands of our government to let Americans pass to South America. We increase our requests for assurances the refugees will have safe passage. The Mexicans can't guarantee it, and they refuse to allow our military access to act as escorts."

"All flights are shut down?" asked Jake.

"Yes. Ship traffic off the east coast has halted as well. The ash fallout, as expected, is much worse to the east and southeast of Yellowstone. The debris density has risen considerably in Europe and the Middle East. Thus far, the amount of particles detected in the Far East and, more importantly for us, Hawaii, are miniscule in comparison."

"Good."

"Lucky, and that is subject to change. Remember, we're barely a month into this catastrophe and Yellowstone continues to emit noxious gas into the atmosphere. Eventually, the eruptive materials will subside, but it will take years for our atmosphere to absorb the impact. All of this stuff we see in these video clips show man's violent, irrational reaction to the eruption. The real trouble will come in the months and years to follow."

"They'll run out of food, and it doesn't appear anyone is prepared to step up and help. They're taking care of their own first."

Ashby nodded and leaned back in her chair. "I've printed out everything you'll need. Floor plans of the ships. Capacities, too, so you can get an idea of how many people might be on board. Also, I looked on the PADI website and studied the itineraries. At the time Yellowstone erupted, a third dive ship was slated to be anchored offshore. Unless it has moved to another island, it may have sailed back to Cabo, taking passengers from all three ships with it."

"That's good to know. What about, um, the other thing?"

"Your bombs?" Ashby said sarcastically. "That's in there too. Jake, I'm not gonna nag. You know I love you and I'm frightened about this whole thing. If you can think of another way, please consider it. Okay?"

"I will." He gave her a kiss and pulled the pages out of the printer. He thumbed through them, smiled and kissed her again.

He returned to the small conference room and read through the online information on the use of dynamite and C-4. Dynamite was the more volatile of the two explosives. He could actually detonate it with an accurately placed rifle round, as dynamite was shock sensitive. He recalled seeing blasting caps among the crates in the storage room.

C-4 was different, and it became a logical choice for this particular situation. C-4 was a composite material composed of explosives and plastic substances, which made it moldable. In addition, for Jake's purposes, it was safe to work with, as it could only be exploded through a shock wave from a detonator.

Jake retrieved the keys from Ashby and hustled off to the

explosives storage room. He grabbed three military-issue M112 blocks of C-4, which weighed a little over a pound each. According to the online information he read, one block of C-4 could destroy a truck. The ships were equal to three trucks in length.

Jake needed to create a diversion, and a single brick of the substance might sink a ship, but it wouldn't generate a significant enough blast to cause mass confusion.

He opened several crates until he located the C-4 remote detonators. He needed to match the frequencies to the charges so only one remote could be used per ship. He loaded several into a box to study his options. After one last glance around the explosives locker, Jake secured it and returned to the conference room.

Now he had to take a crash course in explosives, without blowing himself up.

CHAPTER 48

The Pacific Ocean
Off the coast of Isla Socorro

After the eruption of Yellowstone, Jake had become a leader. The helicopter crash atop that snow-covered mountain in Idaho had forced him into survival mode. From the moment he'd rescued Ashby from the chopper, through his efforts to save the Mexican children from the clutches of the liveaboard crew, Jake had become hardened. He still loved life and the outdoors. But he was no longer carefree. His fellow man had jaded his outlook on life.

"Some people suck," he began as he held Ashby one last time before embarking on his mission. "I could go on and on, but now's not the time. I'm just boiling mad that these idiots would kidnap children to get their way. They don't deserve to live."

"I don't disagree, Jake, but you've gotta keep your cool and not make a mistake. Remember what you said to me outside the YVO the day of the eruption. All that's important is what's right here in front of you. Me. I love you and I refuse to lose you. It simply can't happen."

"It won't, I promise you. I'll do my best with what I have to work with, but I won't lose my life over it. We'll get those boys back and eliminate a threat at the same time. Then we can breathe easier."

They hugged and kissed one last time; then Jake joined Miguel in the pickup with the rest of his team. Jake left Ashby standing alone at the top of the steps near the flagpole, suppressing the urge to rush back to her for one more hug.

He would never admit this to her, but he had his doubts about his ability to carry out this rescue. In a way, the loss of Rita, then Dusty had broken his confidence somewhat. The recovery of the boys offered the opportunity to redeem himself.

It took fifteen minutes for Miguel to navigate the rough landscape in the dark. He'd identified a cove that had a trail leading to it from the top of the cliffs. The boats and some of the villagers would be waiting for their arrival.

As they approached the edge of the cliffs, Miguel turned out the headlights and crept along in the pitch dark, thanks to a moonless night. Jake smiled as the night sky enveloped the pickup. *Darkness benefits the assassin.*

At the top of the trail, several villagers were ready to unload the gear Jake had gathered for their rescue mission. Everyone wanted to help and be a part of the rescue. Within minutes, a group of twenty villagers were standing on the beach of the hidden cove, spray-painting the boats and applying the camouflaged face paint to Jake and the five members of his team.

Using Miguel as an interpreter, Jake explained everyone's role. They nodded their understanding and their dark, steely eyes confirmed their resolve. Jake checked his watch and looked skyward. The conditions were perfect and the timing was right. It was just past midnight.

The oarsmen began rowing the boats gently toward the *Quino*, which they would be using for cover. As they went, Jake considered boarding the boat that appeared to be abandoned. He assumed the crew of the *Nautilus* had stripped the *Quino* of supplies and consolidated them on board their ship.

Considering what he had in store for the *Quino*, he considered it necessary to make sure no one was being held hostage on board. Also, it would be an opportunity to work with the young man who would be boarding the *Nautilus* with him.

Pedro was slender, with somewhat darker skin than others in the village. He was lanky, but muscular. And quiet. During all of the hushed chatter on the beach in preparation for their launch, Pedro was the only person who didn't speak to the others. He had a mystery about him that Jake would have to ask Miguel about afterwards.

Pedro had drawn one of his knives from a sheath tied around his right thigh. He had a matching leather sheath on the other. He handled the knife with care, but periodically twirled it through his fingers without fear of cutting himself. Jake admired the young man's focus.

Jake also smiled as his confidence grew in his most important member of the team. Pedro and Jake would be entering the unknown when they boarded the *Nautilus*. He needed someone who'd have his back as he used his own weapons skills to eliminate threats. Pedro was the perfect guy for the job.

They had crossed the mile of Pacific Ocean in less than thirty minutes, taking care not to create any splashing sounds as they paddled through the water. The *Quino* remained dark, while the *Nautilus* had a couple of lower cabin lights illuminated and a strand of string lights that encircled the canvas-covered dive deck.

Jake took a moment to study the *Nautilus* through his binoculars. He'd memorized the floor plan downloaded and printed by Ashby. The illuminated windows were guest rooms except for one toward the front of the ship. The main cabin and galley had all of its lights on, and the only movement of the crew occurred in there.

Topside, Jake couldn't make out how many people were sitting in chairs under the canopy, but smoke floated over the sides of the boat, indicating they were smoking.

He also identified the two entrances to the main cabin. One was via the stairs above, near the crow's nest. The other was on the port side. The two entrances would enable Jake and Pedro to attack the crew from both sides, effectively trapping them in the middle.

The rowboat drifted up to the transom of the *Quino*. Jake and Pedro carefully crawled onto the ship without rocking it. Anchored at both ends, and at ninety feet long, it was doubtful their body weight would make a difference, but Jake didn't want to derail their mission before it started.

Jake led the way, using his recollection of the ship's layout from Ashby's research. He entered the salon through a rear door. When he opened the door, the smell of rotting meat mixed with cheap perfume hit his nose. He and Pedro immediately covered their nose and mouth as the stench of death crossed over their bodies.

He quietly closed the door, and the latch made a slight click when it engaged. Jake looked at Pedro, who shook his head. Nobody was alive inside the *Quino*, a ship destined for a burial at sea.

It was on to part two of the mission. The two female members of the team were ready to perform their function. Jake had prepared the C-4 to accomplish two things. One was to blast the hull of the *Quino* so that it created a spectacular explosion to confuse the crew of the *Nautilus*. Two, apply a third charge near the propellers and engine compartment of the *Nautilus*. If Jake needed a second diversion, or simply wanted to sink the larger ship, he'd be able to detonate the C-4 and disable the ship without necessarily killing the hostages.

The better of the two swimmers made her way into the water and swam through the darkness to the stern of the *Nautilus*. The other swimmer slipped below the surface to attach the C-4 to both the bow and then the stern of the *Quino*.

At that point, Jake and Pedro, along with the oarsmen, had to break cover. They left the swimmers behind, who would now make their way back to shore. These young women knew the risks of swimming a mile in the Pacific Ocean, which was full of sharks. Their loyalty and love for the people of their village gave them the strength they needed.

The newly painted, jet-black fishing boats had moved past the *Nautilus*, farther out to sea, to a point where the men on the upper deck couldn't see them. Now it was time for Jake and Pedro to make their move. Jake protected his handgun and the detonators in plastic Ziploc baggies tucked into a fanny pack around his waist.

Using hand signals, he gave the oarsmen their final instructions, and they nodded their understanding. At their present location, they were protected from the debris and could easily close on the *Nautilus* when Jake found the kidnapped boys. They also understood they were to make the boys their priority. Jake and Pedro would find their own way back if necessary.

With a deep breath and a nod of understanding with his partner, Jake slipped into the water first. It was time.

CHAPTER 49

The Pacific Ocean
The *Nautilus Under Sea*
Off the coast of Isla Socorro

Jake and Pedro eased themselves around the inflatable tied off to the port side of the *Nautilus* and held onto the mesh transom used to load divers and their equipment out of the water. Using a steel stepladder, which extended beneath the surface while anchored, Jake and Pedro climbed onto the ship's transom.

Jake peered over the stern's half wall to look for anyone on the dive deck. It was dark and empty. He could hear muffled voices coming from above them where he'd seen cigarette smoke earlier.

The attack would occur at lightning-fast speeds once he detonated the explosions underneath the *Quino*. He and Pedro would have to split up to be effective. Because Jake had a gun, he opted to take on the crewmembers inside the salon while Pedro used a shock and awe approach to neutralize the men topside.

Jake held off for a moment to allow their bodies to drip dry. He removed the fanny pack and took out the Ziploc baggies. He slid the extra magazines to his .45-caliber handgun into the pockets of his shorts and tucked the weapon in his waistband. Then he removed the two detonators, being careful to keep the one dedicated to the *Nautilus* separate from the one needed to destroy the *Quino*.

He took a deep breath and exhaled. Pedro did the same and managed to smile at Jake. They were ready. Jake motioned for Pedro to begin climbing the stairs to the top deck. The young man removed the knives from their sheaths. He held one in his left hand with a fighting grip and carried the other one by the blade. Jake surmised one would fly at its target as soon as the opportunity presented itself.

With full confidence in his partner's abilities, Jake drew his handgun and stood next to the salon door. He glanced in the window and saw two men playing cards and drinking liquor. They were laughing and oblivious as to what was about to happen to them.

Jake's eyes darted around the salon and then toward the galley in order to identify any other readily available targets. He was puzzled by this. He felt certain there were more than four men aboard the ship. He clenched his jaw. It didn't matter. The explosion would flush them out.

He held the detonator high over his head and pointed it in the direction of the *Quino*. He slid his thumb under the protective shield over the button and pressed it. The resulting explosion was not what he expected at first.

Upon detonation, there was a whooshing sound as water was displaced and the ship's hull was breached, but that was immediately followed within milliseconds by a massive explosion as the energy displaced by the initial blast moved in all directions around the *Quino*'s hull.

Jake didn't hesitate to observe the destruction. He slammed open the door to the salon and immediately shot the two shocked men who sat at the dining table. They both slumped on top of their card game, blood spilling out of their heads across the shiny teakwood top.

Above him, Jake heard a man moan followed by the shuffling feet of a brief struggle. He knew it was over when the loud thump of a body dropping to the fiberglass upper deck could be heard.

Jake didn't hesitate as he rushed down the stairs to the lower deck where the staterooms and the crew's quarters were located. His first instinct was to eliminate any members of the crew. Logic would've sent him to the crew's quarters, but the tables had been turned on the passengers, if any, located aboard the *Nautilus*. Most likely, the crew members were in the staterooms, so he started there.

He forced open the first door to his right and found a nude young woman tied to a bed. She shrieked and squirmed in an attempt to cover herself, but Jake was looking for her attacker. As he entered, the door of the stateroom slammed into Jake, causing him to lose his balance and stumble backwards.

Jake didn't hesitate and quickly fired three rounds through the door and into the nude body of a man behind it.

"Help me! Please! They're animals!" the girl plead for help, but he didn't have time.

"How many are there?"

She hesitated for a brief moment and then replied, "Six, I think. Plus others like me. Please!"

But Jake had already exited the stateroom. Then he heard a shotgun blast from above deck, followed by a splash in the water.

"Dammit," he muttered as he kicked open the door to the stateroom across from him. It was empty. He moved down the short hallway and opened another door.

"Of course," he said to himself. The leader was in the premium suite on the top of the ship.

Jake quickly approached each stateroom and found them empty. Then he turned his attention back to the crew's quarters while carefully listening for the gun-wielding man above him. He had to assume Pedro was dead or had fallen overboard. Jake got the sense he was on his own.

A steel door appeared at the end of the hallway, blocking access to the crew's quarters. A chain was wrapped through the wheel, which turned to open the door. It was padlocked. Jake paused to listen and then retrieved a fire axe off its hooks in the center of the hallway.

He swung at the lock in an attempt to break it, but he was unsuccessful. He tried wrapping the handle of the axe through the chain and twisting it, hoping the steel links would give way, but that didn't work either.

Muffled voices could be heard through the doorway, convincing Jake he'd come across the boys and possibly more hostages.

Then he took notice of the pipe the chain was wrapped around. It was loose. Jake began to pound away at it with the axe. With each successive swing, the pipe buckled, but began to hiss. It contained some type of high-pressure gas or fluid inside, but he couldn't smell anything.

He swung one final time and the pipe broke loose, hissing hot steam into the air and immediately forming condensation on the ceiling. Being careful not to slip on the moisture-soaked floor, he pulled the chain away from the pipe and cranked open the wheel that sealed the door shut.

With a clank, the door opened and people poured out of the darkened space. Two girls and a young man pushed past Jake as they ran for the stairwell. The man was halfway up the flight of steps when a shotgun blast echoed through the opening. The man's chest had been torn apart, and his bloody corpse fell backwards on top of the women who were right behind him.

"Hide!" screamed Jake before he stuck his head into the darkened crew's quarters. He searched for a light switch and then thought better of it. Instead, he whispered into the room, using Spanish words that would've ordinarily made no sense, "Um, *bambinos*. *Amigos*. I am Miguel's *amigo*. Shhh. *Comprende?*"

A quiet voice responded from the dimly lit recesses of the crew's quarters. "*Sí, señor.*"

Jake swung around and thought of his options. He had found the boys and three female hostages. Unfortunately, they were trapped.

CHAPTER 50

The Pacific Ocean
Aboard the *Nautilus Under Sea*
Off the coast of Isla Socorro

The other female hostages had entered the first stateroom and untied the third woman. As Jake was contemplating his options, one of them stuck her head out to sneak a peek. Jake put his finger to his lips and motioned for them to come out and go to the stateroom at the end of the hall. He knew his .45-caliber bullets would penetrate the thin walls that separated the cabins, and he wanted them out of the line of fire.

The three women immediately responded and followed one another to the last stateroom near the stern of the ship. Jake glanced back to where the boys were hiding. He stuck his head into the room and whispered, "It's okay. *Bueno. Sí?*"

"*Sí,*" the boys responded in unison.

Jake pushed the steel door closed but not all the way, allowing light to filter in the room and not further frighten the kids. Now that everyone was protected as much as possible, he'd deal with the man wielding a shotgun.

He'd already fired three times. Unless he had the presence of mind to reload, which for an untrained gunman in the heat of battle wasn't likely, he only had four or five shots left. Jake decided to test his nerves as well as reduce the man's ammunition levels.

He slipped his tee shirt off and draped it over the axe so it looked like a broad-shouldered man. Extending the axe handle outward from his body, he quietly moved along the wall until he was in a position to thrust the tee shirt into the shooter's view.

Slowly, Jake inched toward the opening and the position where the dead young man bled out on the floor. When he was ready, he shoved the axe handle into the opening, revealing the tee shirt to the shooter. The response was immediate.

The man fired one blast into the shirt, quickly racked another round, and fired again.

Jake smiled. "Nice shot, captain!" he yelled in a deliberate attempt to taunt the man.

"Shut up!" the man shouted back and then fired another round down the steps.

Good. Anger. That was six rounds spent.

"Give it up, captain! Your crew is dead. Your play toys are taken away. And now it's you and me. Trust me, you don't wanna tangle with me. I've killed a lot of people lately. You'll just be another notch on the belt."

The man started cackling in laughter. "You're trapped down there. You aren't going anywhere."

Jake slid his hand down to his pocket and considered his secret weapon as an option. There were eight steps from the lower level, up the ladder, and to the salon. If he blew the C-4, he'd only have a few seconds to make his move.

The bigger problem he had was the position of the three women. He'd moved them to the back of the ship to get them out of harm's way. But they were now sitting on top of the engine compartment and the propellers. The C-4 blast would come through the floor.

He closed his eyes to focus when he felt a slight sway of the ship. It wasn't much, just an imperceptible wiggle. He trained his senses on the stern and the dive deck. Heel, toe. Heel, toe. Bare feet walking along the deck.

"Arrrgghh!" a voice screamed before crashing into the man at the top of the stairs. His itchy trigger fingers fired off another round, but it shot into the ceiling above the steps, indicating the man had been attacked.

Jake raced up the steps, crawling on all fours to maintain his balance and keeping his body low. When he arrived in the salon, he saw Pedro, his shoulder covered in blood, but well enough to pummel the gunman with one punch to the face after another.

Jake yelled to him as he slid on his knees to Pedro's side, "Pedro, *no más. No más!*"

Pedro took one more massive swing with his right fist, breaking the man's nose and hurling blood mixed with mucus across the floor. The man was unconscious, but not dead.

"Come here," said Jake as he comforted the brave young man. Jake gently wiped the blood away and looked at Pedro's shoulder, which had at least three rounds of buckshot embedded in it.

Jake helped him off the floor and set him on a bench in the salon. Then he retrieved the man's shotgun and handed it to Pedro with instructions to shoot him if he tried to get up. Pedro managed an evil smile and a nod. Without saying a word, he expressed his hearty *no problemo.*

Jake made his way into the lower deck and dragged the dead man into one of the staterooms and closed the door. He then called for the girls to come on out.

"It's over, everyone. Come on out." Jake moved to the crew's quarters and called for the boys to come out as well. They quickly followed his orders and ran to Jake, crying and thanking him in Spanish.

When the girls saw the blood, they shrieked, but quickly recovered as they confirmed their ordeal was over. They ran up the stairs and onto the dive deck, where they broke down and cried. The young boys, tired from their captivity, made their way into the salon and immediately rushed to Pedro's side. A familiar face lifted their spirits considerably.

Jake gathered up everyone and removed them to the dive deck. He located a dock line and cut it into a smaller piece with his knife. While the others waited, Jake tied up the still passed-out gunman so he couldn't get away.

He then helped everyone to the stern, where he loaded them into the inflatable. He waved the other boats over, and the two oarsmen drove them back to the island, towing one of the fishing boats behind the inflatable. This left Jake his own fishing boat and the *Nautilus*, with some unfinished business to attend to.

With the man still unconscious, Jake explored the ship, looking for things of value. Useful items of electronics, weapons, and food were loaded into the fishing boat. He added some dive equipment and tanks, as well as two wetsuits he found in a closet. There were also a couple of harpoons.

The eighteen-foot-long fishing boat was getting full, and therefore heavy, which would make it difficult for Jake to row back to shore. But he was full of adrenaline and thankful for a successful rescue. He also knew Ashby would welcome him with open arms.

Jake determined the man's name was Walter Sota by rummaging through his gear in the premium stateroom. He was not, however, the captain of the *Nautilus*. The picture Jake found was of an older man, dressed in proper dress whites, and his smiling wife next to him. He suspected Sota and his thug buddies had killed the couple and overtaken the boat.

"Karma's a bitch, Walter," said Jake as he grabbed the man by the ankles and dragged his unconscious body along the aft side of the ship toward the bow. Using the excess dock line he'd used to tie Walter up, Jake wrapped the man's ankles and tied off a series of knots that would only become more difficult to release if he squirmed. Then Jake tied the other end of the line to the cleats located at the bow of the *Nautilus* and gave the line a firm tug to set the knot.

"Okay, Walter, here ya go," snarled Jake as he hoisted the man's badly beaten body up and over the rail. Had the rope been tied around the man's neck, it would've snapped like a good old-fashioned hanging. Instead, Jake wanted the man to awaken with his face mere inches from the ocean surface with no way to escape.

After one final look around, Jake was ready to leave. The sun was rising as Jake untied the wooden fishing boat and prepared for his return to the island. He thought of what the passengers and other crew members had been through at the hands of these thugs.

He'd only rowed a hundred yards when he stopped. He'd planned on keeping the vessel for its limited remaining supplies and another means of leaving the island when the time came. Jake mumbled to himself as he decided to do something impetuous.

"Ah, screw it. A boat's just something you sink your money into anyway. Why would anyone want two of them?"

He pressed the detonator and the stern exploded, throwing dive equipment in all directions and creating a gaping hole in the back that immediately flooded the lower deck.

The explosion must have awakened Walter Sota from his beating. He could be heard screaming as he wiggled like a worm on the end of a fishing line.

"Hey! Cut me loose! You can't leave me like this! I'll drown!"

He continued to yell and Jake sat rocking in the small fishing boat as he watched the *Nautilus* slowly sink into the Pacific. The stern was completely submerged and the ship tilted upward so that the bow was sticking nearly straight out of the water. Walter was being hoisted higher into the air before he would be dragged to the bottom of the Pacific.

Then it happened. It was so sudden that Jake almost missed it.

As the boat reached its final moments above water, Sota continued to swing wildly on the rope in an attempt to work himself free. In his frenzy to gain safety, he never saw the jaws emerge from the depth of the dark ocean, opening wide before clamping down on his torso, leaving nothing behind but his tied-up legs and what was left of his intestines.

CHAPTER 51

The Pacific Ocean
Off the coast of Isla Socorro

After sitting in the boat for several more minutes, fatigue swept over Jake's body. He turned sideways on the bench and tried to determine where the cove was located. Like good soldiers, Miguel and his men were practicing proper light discipline, leaving a pitch-black shoreline and no discernible target for Jake to row towards.

Jake could make out the silhouette of the cliffs against the midnight blue sky. The island seemed almost as dark as the ocean. All that separated the Pacific from the rocky cliffs formed by volcanic eruptions of the past was a short stretch of beach tucked away in a cove that Jake couldn't see.

He thought of Ashby waiting for him back at the compound, and then he laughed out loud. He knew her well and loved her headstrong nature. He thought to himself that most likely she'd waited at the compound for maybe fifteen minutes before taking the golf cart and following the pickup to the edge of the cliff. In fact, he'd be shocked if she wasn't standing barefoot in the cold sand of the cove, waiting for him to return.

He grabbed the oars, gripped them firmly, and dipped them into the water. The gentle, rhythmic splashing that followed put him into a trance. Stroke after stroke, the oars propelled him a little closer to the shore that was a mile away.

The great white shark, one of several that devoured the remains of Walter Sota, swam away from the sinking dive ship and sought out the rhythmic sound. The combination of the splash and the motion piqued the eighteen-foot killer's attention.

It moved quietly through the darkness of the ocean, propelled by short, but powerful thrusts of its crescent-shaped tail fin. Its mouth was open slightly, allowing a rush of water over its gills, and the bloody remains of Sota to ooze out.

The great white was a freak of nature. A finely tuned machine that could ease through the water at a high speed if it wanted to. Otherwise, its motion was imperceptible, aimlessly moving forward with an occasional course correction by slightly raising its dark gray pectoral fin, which broke the surface of the Pacific.

Like a bird adjusting its wings in flight by dipping one wing and lifting another, the great white eased through the water effortlessly, seeking out its prey. In the darkness of the ocean that night, the great white was blind to an extent, although his other senses transmitted information to the creature's simplistic brain. A brain that didn't need to retain information or knowledge. A brain that was only required to act upon instinct dictated by millions of years of evolution.

From a hundred yards away, the shark sensed a change in its surroundings. The rhythmic sounds of the oars hitting the ocean's surface continued. Running throughout the great white, from nose to crescent fin, were a series of tiny crevices, filled with mucus and replete with nerve endings. The nerve endings detected the vibrations caused by the oars and signaled the brain of the menacing killer—food was nearby.

Jake continued to row, taking his time to conserve energy. *No rush, no worries*, he thought to himself, a phrase used often by Dusty and repeated by Ashby recently. His mind wandered to think about their future. They had finally found a home, although it might be temporary, as in just a few years.

Miguel and the other villagers had welcomed them with open arms. Jake had learned never to underestimate the depravity of man. Walter Sota and his crew being prime examples of that concept. That said, Miguel and the others didn't have that evil within them, which was important for Jake and Ashby's future safety. Living a life on a deserted island with other people might just work. But doing so while constantly looking over your shoulder or sleeping with one eye open at night would not.

Jake picked up the pace as the excitement of his new life with Ashby on Isla Socorro raised his spirits. He rowed a little faster, and a little deeper, fighting against the low tide. His efforts of digging deeper into the ocean paid off, as his speed quickened.

The vibrations were stronger now and the great white sensed that its prey was near. The sweep of its tail hastened as the creature's excitement rose. Its giant body thrust forward with a speed that caused the tiny fish just below the surface to scatter. The miniscule fluorescent sea life became agitated, causing them to glow like sparks around the great white as it swam through them toward the splashing.

The King of the Ocean was in the house.

Closer. Closer. Assessing.

The great white closed on the fishing skiff and rushed past, giving its prey twenty feet of space. Now six feet below the surface, the killer stalked its prey, giving it a casual glance as it sped by.

Jake felt the fishing boat list slightly—a wave of pressure that seemed to lift one side of the skiff and ease it down again. He stopped paddling and immediately lifted the oars out of the water like a toe recoiling from a cold swimming pool.

His head swiveled in all directions, looking for the cause of the motion. *Was it a wave? Did a porpoise swim by? Maybe a piece of driftwood?*

Jake held his breath and then exhaled, hoping to calm his nerves. Then he chuckled.

"Come on, Wheeler. You shouldn't be afraid of things that go bump in the night."

Jake dropped the oars back into the water, hesitated, and then slowly restarted the process. Despite his internal pep talk, his senses were on high alert. His strokes were no longer smooth. They were short, choppy slaps at the water. Then he'd stop to listen. His anxiety rose as he continued this odd rowing pattern.

The great white smiled, but not as we would envision a happy shark in a cartoon. The smile had nothing to do with emotion and had everything to do with preparation.

Preparation to eat.

The great white broke the surface for the first time, allowing more of its sensory perceptions to assist in the hunt. It could smell Jake now. The smell of sweat and adrenaline. The previously rhythmic motions of the oars stroking the water had been replaced by erratic, sharp movements. To the great white, that was a signal of distress.

It began to circle the source of food from a greater distance of forty feet, but not so far away that the great white couldn't close quickly. With its dorsal fin breaking the water and its tail thrashing back and forth, the smooth plane of the surface became violent. The great white's body began to shake as tremors shot through it. Food was near and the beast had worked itself into a frenzy.

For the first time, Jake was frightened. He couldn't see the great white, but Jake concluded that the disturbance in the water could be only one thing—it was close. Jolts of energy shot through Jake's body, generating a warmth that caused his face to flush and his hands to shake.

He glanced back toward the island, which still remained half a mile away. Jake turned back around and looked in all directions; then the bow of the boat lifted a few feet into the air and crashed back down onto the ocean's surface.

Jake resisted the innate reaction of screaming for help. Or simply screaming out of fear. He had to keep calm, or he would die. He searched the water again, looking for the telltale sign of the great white—its dorsal fin appearing above the water.

Thirty feet to Jake's left, the great white circled around, dropped below the surface once again, and turned directly toward the boat. With three quick shakes of its tail, the great white was racing directly for Jake.

Jake saw it coming and braced for impact. He knew he had to stay out of the water, and if the shark collided with the skiff, it was over.

In the face of certain death, Jake Wheeler summoned all of his courage. He pulled his handgun out of his waistband and turned to straddle the bench, facing down the ocean's most efficient killer.

The great white rose to the surface as it sped toward him, allowing its massive jaws to open and bare its sharp teeth. Jake had one opportunity to live, and he wasn't even sure it would work.

He took aim at the great white, allowing it to move closer so he didn't miss, but not so close that the collision was inevitable.

The jaws opened wider and Jake fired. Round after round after round, penetrating the roof of the great white shark's mouth and exploding through the top of its body. The shark continued forward, but slower, and it was dropping below the water.

Not enough, however, to avoid an impact with the boat.

The center of the boat lifted out of the water, throwing Jake backwards on top of the supplies he'd removed from the *Nautilus*. He lost control of his weapon, which fell to the wooden floor. The skiff crashed back to the surface but shook violently from side to side as the wake created by the great white's attack disturbed the water.

Jake crawled back to his seat and looked around the skiff, hoping to see the carcass of the great white floating nearby. There was nothing. It wasn't over.

He frantically searched the bottom of the boat, looking for his gun. He pushed aside boxes taken from the *Nautilus*. *Did it fall overboard? Where is it?*

Jake was beginning to panic when he sensed the great white's return. The powerful beast brought with it a presence, a dominant force that was now unmistakable to Jake. With one eye on the approaching dorsal fin, he scrambled about, looking for the .45-caliber handgun that was no match for the great white.

The creature broke the surface again just as Jake found his gun. He'd lost track of how many rounds he'd fired, so he dropped the magazine and quickly inserted a new one into the grip of the pistol in a fluid, efficient motion, much like his adversary's motions.

This time, Jake took aim for the top of the great white's head in an attempt to pierce the outer skin, cartilage and skull. Before the great white bared its teeth, Jake fired at its snout and between its eyes. Three, four, five rounds were spent, blasting away at the massive fish in an attempt to stop its advance.

Then Jake heard it. A hissing sound emanating from the mouth and nostrils of the great white. It was familiar to him. Ken Kennedy had made a similar sound at the moment of his death when Jake killed him.

Jake knew the battle was over.

CHAPTER 52

The Pacific Ocean
Isla Socorro

Jake sat on the bench with his hands shaking uncontrollably. He felt certain he'd killed the great white, but fear caused him to continue searching the surface for the creature's carcass. Sharks lack the floatation bladder common to other fish. Once it stopped its continuous forward movement, which pushed oxygen-rich water through its gills, it sank to the bottom of the Pacific to die from the gunshot wounds or anoxia, whichever came first.

Jake was brought out of his daze by the sound of a boat motor approaching from the island. Within seconds, the inflatable driven by Miguel and containing two of his men armed with their shotguns had pulled alongside the fishing boat.

"Jake, *que pasa?*"

Jake managed a shrug and then began to laugh as relief swept over his body. Somehow, he mustered up a bland, coherent response. "Hi, Miguel. I'm really glad to see you guys. Have you got room for me in there?"

Miguel gave Jake a puzzled look. As his men held the two boats together while the inflatable's wake subsided, Jake quickly disembarked the skiff.

After giving Jake a bottle of water and tying the bow line of the fishing boat to the back of the inflatable, they made their way back to shore. Jake glanced backwards several times to make sure they weren't being trailed by the great white.

"Jake, we heard gunshots. What happened?"

Jake decided to lie. Retelling his encounter with the great white would not serve to make the villagers feel better about the evening's successful return of the boys and the rescue of the three women. It certainly wouldn't make Ashby feel warm and fuzzy. Some things a man just needed to take to his grave.

Jake feigned a laugh. "You know how it is when you're on the water at night. Something goes bump and you panic. After the rescue, I was still hyped up and got a little nervous for no reason. That's all."

Inwardly, Jake patted himself on the back. He was glad it was dark so Miguel couldn't see his face. He hoped he'd be able to convince Ashby with his lame explanation, but somehow, he doubted it. She had an innate way of knowing when he was fibbing.

The inflatable eased up to the shore, and several villagers rushed into the water to grab the bow line to pull it onto the sand. Jake would've ordinarily jumped out of the inflatable to help, but he was a little hesitant to set foot in the water. In fact, he was most likely never going swimming again, or at least for a long time.

As his feet hit the sand, he struggled to maintain his composure. He was immediately surrounded by the villagers, who were crying and thanking him for saving the young boys. One woman tried to put a necklace holding her gold crucifix around his neck, but Jake wouldn't accept it. He placed it back in her hand and squeezed it tight before kissing her tear-covered cheeks.

Jake stood and looked over the heads of the shorter villagers, thinking that his visualization of Ashby waiting on the beach for him might become reality, but he didn't see her anywhere.

More people came up to thank him, including the young boys he saved, who hugged him continuously throughout the emotional reunion. Jake formally met the young girls, all of whom attended college in the States. They were wrapped in brightly colored serapes, handmade shawls and blankets worn as a cloak in Mexico.

Jake accepted various gifts, ranging from bananas to Mexican rag dolls. It was truly a hero's welcome. The sun was beginning to rise, casting an orangish glow across the water. With a final look out into the ocean, which was now free of dive ships and pirates, Jake accepted his final accolades from the villagers. After several minutes, the excitement subsided and he made his way through the crowd to the path that led to the top of the cliffs.

That was when he saw her perched on a rock, sitting alone. Ashby was beaming as tears streamed down her face. She covered up with her hands, trying to hide her emotions, but she couldn't contain herself any longer. She stood, but her feet were stuck in place.

Jake ran to her, closing the thirty-foot gap in seconds. He wrapped his arms around her, squeezed her tight, and lifted her off the beach.

"God, I love you, Ashby. I love you so much."

"I love you, Jake. You have no idea what you've done for these people. You are a true hero to them. And me too."

Jake kissed the moisture off her cheeks, and then he burst into tears, as well, as the reality that they were safe, and together, overwhelmed him. He whispered in her ear, "There is nothing on the planet more important than this right here. You and me. Holding each other. Just the two of us."

Ashby looked past his shoulder and said, "But you have a fan club, Jake. Look."

He let her down and turned back toward the beach. The entire group was smiling, holding each other, and crying as they watched Jake and Ashby's tearful reunion.

"I think they're happy for us both. Come on, let's go feel the love."

Jake led her by the hand and into the group, where the thank-yous and praise started all over again. For several minutes, until the entourage began to make their way up the path to the top of the cliffs, Jake and Ashby enjoyed the moment with their new extended family.

CHAPTER 53

The Pacific Ocean
Isla Socorro

At Miguel's insistence, Jake and Ashby retired to the commander's bungalow, closed the blinds, and blocked out the rest of the world. For the first time since they'd arrived on the island, they were able to sleep together without fear of outside threats sneaking up on them. The liveaboard boats and their motley crews were gone, and the villagers took up round-the-clock security around the naval compound.

Jake slept until two o'clock that afternoon before slipping out of bed and slipped on his pants. He peered through the blinds and noticed a lot of activity in the courtyard. At first, he thought it was children playing, and then he realized it was a steady stream of villagers walking from the pickup truck, up the stairs, and toward the mess hall.

"Jake, is everything okay?" asked a sleepy Ashby as she stirred in bed.

"Yeah, I think so, but something's going on. A lot of the villagers are here, and they seem to be unloading things from the truck. Maybe we should check it out?"

"In a minute," she purred. "Come back to bed for a little while."

Jake chuckled and sat beside her on the bed. She reached for his arm in attempt to pull him down next to her, but he evaded her clutches.

"Relax, missy. There's plenty of time for that later. Miguel has promised a round-the-clock security detail for us. We don't have to sleep apart anymore."

"Good, come back to bed, then."

He swatted at her hands as she continued to grab for him. She countered with a pillow throw, and Jake returned the favor. Within seconds, the two were heaving pillows at one another and wrestling in the tangled mess of sheets.

Eventually, Ashby succumbed to Jake's suggestion, and the two of them emerged from the bungalow. They were first seen by the kids, who ran from the courtyard to greet them. The young boys grabbed Jake by the hands and the girls hugged Ashby as they led them past the administration building and toward the mess hall.

Outside the entrance, half a dozen villagers were bustling about, laying out platters of fresh fruits, vegetables, and smoked fish on the picnic tables. Several looked up from their work to smile and wave to the happy couple before fussing over the spread of food.

The kids pointed Jake and Ashby toward the mess hall door, which they slowly entered. The villagers were decorating the interior with colorful tapestries, tropical foliage, and even a handmade piñata made of papier-mâché, pottery, and brightly woven cloth.

"Is this for us?" asked Ashby. "Miguel asked to borrow the keys to the mess hall while we slept. I had no idea this is what they had in mind."

"Looks like a heckuva party to me," replied Jake. He squeezed Ashby's hand as Miguel approached them.

"My friends, welcome to your surprise party! The children were supposed to keep you occupied while we finished setting up, but since you are here, let us enjoy this joyous day!"

Miguel was exuberant as he led Jake and Ashby toward the food. It was a duplicate of the spread outside on the picnic table.

"This is incredible, Miguel. You've gone through so much trouble—"

Miguel stopped and turned to Ashby as he interrupted. "Now, listen to me, my friends. You saved the life of my nephew and another boy dear to our hearts. Do you see those young ladies over there?" Miguel pointed toward the college girls, who were learning how to fill the piñata.

"They seem to have recovered," said Jake.

"They have been through a terrible ordeal, and I am sure they will continue to need the love and support of us all," said Miguel. "For now, they can rejoice in the celebration with us, and when the time comes, we will all lend them counsel and prayer."

Jack and Ashby smiled at one another. Two of the women came up to them, provided cloth napkins, and kissed them on the cheeks. Then they turned to Miguel and spoke in Spanish.

"You are our honored guests and shall be served first. Please, let's sit at the center table here."

The women of the village had created a fabulous tropical display, including the native croton plants, birds of paradise, heliconia, and palm leaves. Jake and Ashby got settled in, and soon plates were being placed in front of them, which included all of the island delicacies created by the women of the village.

For the next hour, the kids sang Mexican folk songs while one of the men played a Mexican *guitarrón* and another played the maracas. The festivities began to wind down by four that afternoon, which allowed Jake and Miguel to walk around the compound alone. The conversation turned serious as Miguel spoke.

"Jake, I am a private man, as I know you might be as well. I am concerned about something."

"What's that?" asked Jake.

"Our people have grown attached to you and Ashby. You are our family now, and as family, we become dependent on one another. I am sure when you arrived at Isla Socorro, you did not plan on staying here. I hope that you will consider staying."

Jake stopped and smiled. He placed his right hand on Miguel's shoulder and said, "I'm honored that you'd take us in. Ashby and I have talked about it and would love to stay. There is a logistical problem, however."

"Yes, I have thought of this too. I have talked with the elders in the village about building a home for you both. They have agreed to do so."

Jake was flattered by the statement, but he wanted to make another suggestion. "Miguel, have you considered moving your people here, to the base? Our ability to translate the Spanish in a logbook we found was not the best, but it appears they will be gone for years while they protect their borders."

"I was told this as well when they left. However, my people don't want to leave their homes. They would be uncomfortable here. For me, this base is a resource we must protect from any other wandering boaters who might come upon Isla Socorro. For that reason, both the village and the compound must be protected. You may live with us and assist in protecting the compound."

"That is a very nice offer, Miguel. I don't want to insult you by saying no, so I hope you understand my reasoning. Any future intruders will likely come from our east and northeast—Central America and the United States. We must maintain a full-time presence here to guard against that likelihood. Also, there are electronic resources here that Ashby can utilize to keep all of us informed about the coming ash fallout from Yellowstone."

Miguel nodded and put his arm around Jake as they walked back to the mess hall. "I cannot disagree with you, my friend. We will work out a security plan using your expertise and my people that is good for all of Isla Socorro. Perhaps we can use the barracks to relocate some of the young men who will be assigned here."

"Yes, absolutely," said Jake. "We also have the three college girls. Ashby is a professor and knows how to interact with girls their age. They can pick a bungalow to move into and will become integrated into our new community."

Miguel stopped and extended his hand to Jake. Jake reached out and shook it.

"It is settled, then," pronounced Miguel.

Jake looked past Miguel, and his eyes moved up the side of the mountain behind the compound. He hesitated and then said, "Yes, I think so. However, Miguel, we all have our demons that haunt us from the past."

"Oh yes, this I know."

"Ashby has one she needs to address, and now is as good a time as any."

CHAPTER 54

The Pacific Ocean
Isla Socorro

"Are you kidding me? Now?" asked Ashby excitedly. "I mean, I expected we'd get around to it at some point but not so quickly."

Jake took the rolled-up copy of the topography map and playfully swatted Ashby's butt. "Hurry up and get in the golf cart before I change my mind. Miguel has shown me a trail that will take us up to the top."

Ashby didn't waste any time in scurrying to the front seat of the Cushman. Jake had already loaded a backpack with food, water, and camping supplies in the event they wanted to stay overnight. With Miguel's men guarding the base, he and Ashby had the freedom to explore that they'd hoped for early on. Now was as good a time as any.

As Jake followed the overgrown trail up the side of the Evermann volcano, Ashby chatted away about how islands were formed through volcanic activity. She told Jake everything she knew about Mathematicians Ridge, a mid-ocean ridge that had been formed by tectonic activity three and a half million years ago. As the underwater volcanic activity became inactive, the few islands that were formed, like Isla Socorro, remained relatively dormant.

She continued to relay her knowledge to Jake as he made his way to the crater. "Did you know that Isla Socorro is the only silicic peralkaline volcano in the entire Pacific Ocean?"

Jake glanced at her and smiled. He decided to play with her, before he realized she wasn't listening to him. "Actually, I did know that and—"

She ignored his response and continued. "Peralkaline rocks are aluminum deficient. What we are driving on is likely the last volcano to have been formed along these plates in the history of our planet."

"That's exciting, Ashby," said Jake dryly. "My question is whether it will happen again."

"Jake, it's like I said. It requires monitoring and further study. I'm so excited. Mont Evermann is all mine!"

Jake chuckled and pressed forward, periodically stopping to remove fallen debris or to cut down foliage. It wasn't time wasted, as he saw it. It appeared Ashby would be making this trip to the top often.

They reached the base of the steep cone, which rose into the sky. Jake put on the backpack and motioned for Ashby to take his hand.

"Are you ready for this? Miguel says it's a short hike, but it is steep. We have to watch our footing and—"

Ashby let go of Jake's hand and ran in front of him, pushing through the thinner plant material as she wound her way around the cone toward the west side of the volcano. She didn't slow until she reached the peak and approached the cone. Then she froze.

Jake hesitated and rested his hand on his pistol, thinking Ashby had come across some type of animal or a snake. He approached her and saw that the path was clear.

"Jake, I can't believe I'm about to do this. For all these years of studying volcanoes, I've never stepped into the crater. It was something like this that killed my family and has haunted me ever since. I thought watching Yellowstone erupt would wipe out those memories, but it only made me want to learn more about how these things work."

"We can turn back," said Jake as he reached for her hand.

She tugged at him instead. "No. I can do this. Come with me."

The beauty of a dormant volcano's crater mostly consists of unique colorations of rock, silica, and plant life that found its way inside. Plus, in some cases, the enormous power the crater holds underneath it.

They stood at the rim for several minutes, taking it all in. The rocky edge created an almost perfect circle that allowed them to walk around it. Jake adjusted the backpack and joined Ashby as she traversed the rocky walls leading into the inverted bowl below them. On the far western side of the crater was a clearing and a trail, which appeared to lead inside the cone.

The vegetation inside the crater resembled the low-lying crotons on the south side of the island. Erosion from wind and rain caused the inner walls of the cone to collapse from time to time, creating rockslides that buried the plant life until it could regenerate.

"Are you okay?" asked Jake as Ashby continued toward the western rim.

"Yeah, actually I am. Now I'm totally intrigued about what it's like in there."

Jake grimaced. He wasn't intrigued enough to walk inside a volcano.

"This reminds me of Haleakala on Maui, except this crater is much smaller. Haleakala is dormant and big enough that you could place the whole island of Manhattan inside its outer rim."

"So you've been in a dormant crater before?" asked Jake.

"Yes, Haleakala, but it's not the same. For Pete's sake, Jake, we stood in the middle of the Yellowstone caldera a month ago, and look what happened there."

"Okay. I just thought you might be hesitant—"

"—to come up here?" Ashby finished his sentence. "I am, or, um. I was. I'm over it now." She stopped as they reached the western rim of the crater. It was just after six and the sun was making its way into the ocean. She pointed to a couple of square boulders, which gave them a view of the sunset and the volcanic crater behind them.

Ashby climbed up on them. She sat with her legs crossed under her hips and her hands tucked around her ankles. Jake dropped the backpack and joined her.

"Meet me where the sky touches the sea," she mumbled as she stared out toward the ocean. "My mom used to say that to my dad. They really loved the Philippines, as did I. It was a beautiful place full of loving people. It was our home, and not just a temporary one. My parents would've lived there forever in that simple house at the base of Mount Pinatubo."

Jake draped his arm around Ashby and pulled her close to him. "Your parents would have been very proud of you and what you've accomplished. You have to believe they're watching over you right now."

Ashby smiled and looked up at the sky before she closed her eyes. When she opened them, the sun had slipped a little further into the ocean.

"Jake, I want to believe that we've finally found our home together. We've faced so much adversity."

"I know, but—"

Ashby interrupted and continued. "Is it over? Are we safe? Will trouble start to pass us by rather than beat on our door and force its way in?"

Jake leaned over and kissed Ashby on the cheek.

"You know what they say. This too shall pass. It may pass like a kidney stone, but it'll pass. For now, we wait and focus on our survival."

THANK YOU FOR READING
YELLOWSTONE: SURVIVAL,

the final installment in the Yellowstone series.

If you enjoyed it, I'd be grateful if you'd take a moment to write a short review (just a few words are needed) and post it on Amazon. Amazon uses complicated algorithms to determine what books are recommended to readers. Sales are, of course, a factor, but so are the quantities of reviews my books get. By taking a few seconds to leave a review, you help me out and also help new readers learn about my work.

And before you go …

SIGN UP for Bobby Akart's mailing list to receive special offers, bonus content, and you'll be the first to receive news about new releases in the Doomsday series.

VISIT Amazon.com/BobbyAkart for more information on the Doomsday series, the Yellowstone series, the Lone Star series, the Pandemic series, the Blackout series, the Boston Brahmin series and the Prepping for Tomorrow series totaling thirty-plus novels including over twenty Amazon #1 Bestsellers in forty-plus fiction and nonfiction genres. Visit Bobby Akart's website for informative blog entries on preparedness, writing, and a behind-the-scenes look into his novels.

www.BobbyAkart.com

CPSIA information can be obtained
at www.ICGtesting.com
Printed in the USA
LVHW091922271118
598388LV00008B/201/P